Armistead Maupin was born in Washington D.C. in 1944 but was brought up in Raleigh, North Carolina. A graduate of the University of North Carolina, he served as a naval officer in Vietnam before moving to California in 1971. Maupin is the author of *Tales of the City*, *More Tales of the City*, *Further Tales of the City*, *Babycakes*, *Significant Others*, and *Sure of You*, which are all available in Black Swan paperback and Corgi Audio. A major TV series of *Tales of the City* was recently shown on Channel 4 and more series are planned using the later novels in the sequence. *Maybe the Moon* – Maupin's first novel since ending his *Tales of the City* sequence – was a number one hardback bestseller and is now available in Black Swan paperback and Corgi Audio. He lives in California with his lover, Terry Anderson.

MORE TALES OF THE CITY

Armistead Maupin

BLACK SWAN

MORE TALES OF THE CITY
A BLACK SWAN BOOK : 0 552 99086 8

First publication in Great Britain

PRINTING HISTORY
Corgi edition published 1984
Corgi edition reprinted 1985
Corgi edition reprinted 1987
Corgi edition reprinted 1988
Black Swan edition published 1989
Black Swan edition reprinted 1990 (three times)
Black Swan edition reprinted 1991
Black Swan edition reprinted 1992
Black Swan edition reprinted 1993 (three times)
Black Swan edition reprinted 1994
Black Swan edition reprinted 1995
Black Swan edition reprinted 1996
Black Swan edition reprinted 1997

Set in 11 pt Linotype Melior by
County Typesetters, Margate, Kent

Black Swan Books are published by Transworld Publishers Ltd,
61–63 Uxbridge Road, London W5 5SA,
in Australia by Transworld Publishers (Australia) Pty Ltd,
15–25 Helles Avenue, Moorebank, NSW 2170,
and in New Zealand by Transworld Publishers (NZ) Ltd,
3 William Pickering Drive, Albany, Auckland.

Printed and bound in Great Britain by
Cox & Wyman Ltd, Reading, Berkshire.

For Ken Maley

As the poets have mournfully sung,
Death takes the innocent young,
　　The rolling in money,
　　The screamingly funny,
And those who are very well hung.

W. H. AUDEN

Hearts and flowers

The valentine was a handmade pastiche of Victorian cherubs, pressed flowers and red glitter. Mary Ann Singleton took one look at it and squealed delightedly.

'Mouse! It's magnificent. Where in the world did you find those precious little . . . ?'

'Open it.' He grinned.

She turned to the inside of the magazine-size card, revealing a message in Art Nouveau script: *My Valentines Resolutions.* Underneath were ten numbered spaces.

'See,' said Michael, 'you're supposed to fill it in yourself.'

Mary Ann leaned over and pecked him on the cheek. 'I'm that screwed up, huh?'

'You bet. I don't waste time with well-adjusted people. Wanna see *my* list?'

'Aren't you mixing this up with New Year's?'

'Nah. That's nickel-dime stuff. Smoking-eating-drinking resolutions. These are the – you know – the hardcore, maybe-this-time, kiss-today-goodbye, some-enchanted-evening resolutions.'

He reached into the pocket of his Pendleton and handed her a sheet of paper:

MICHAEL TOLLIVER'S DIRTY THIRTY FOR '77

1. I will not call anyone nellie or butch, unless that is his name.
2. I will not assume that women who like me are fag hags.
3. I will stop expecting to meet Jan-Michael Vincent at the tubs.
4. I will inhale poppers only through the mouth.
5. I will not spend more than half an hour in the shower at the Y.

7

6. I will stop trying to figure out what color my handkerchief would be if I wore one.

7. I will buy a drink for a Fifties Queen sometime.

8. I will not persist in hoping that attractive men will turn out to be brainless and boring.

9. I will sign my real name at The Glory Holes.

10. I will ease back into religion by attending concerts at Grace Cathedral.

11. I will not cruise at Grace Cathedral.

12. I will not vote for *anyone* for Empress.

13. I will make friends with a straight man.

14. I will not make fun of the way he walks.

15. I will not tell him about Alexander the Great, Walt Whitman or Leonardo da Vinci.

16. I will not vote for politicians who use the term 'Gay Community.'

17. I will not cry when Mary Tyler Moore goes off the air.

18. I will not measure it, no matter who asks.

19. I will not hide the A-200.

20. I will not buy a Lacoste shirt, a Marimekko pillow, a secondhand letterman's jacket, an All-American Boy T-shirt, a razor blade necklace or a denim accessory of any kind.

21. I will learn to eat alone and like it.

22. I will not fantasize about firemen.

23. I will not tell anyone at home that I just haven't found the right girl yet.

24. I will wear a suit on Castro Street and feel comfortable about it.

25. I will not do impressions of Bette Davis, Tallulah Bankhead, Mae West or Paul Lynde.

26. I will not eat more than one It's-It in a single evening.

27. I will find myself acceptable.

28. I will meet somebody nice, away from a bar or the tubs or a roller-skating rink, and I will fall hopelessly but conventionally in love.

29. But I won't say I love you before he does.

30. The hell I won't.

Mary Ann put down the paper and looked at Michael. 'You've got thirty resolutions. How come you only gave me ten?'

He grinned. 'Things aren't so tough for you.'

'Is that right, Mr Gay Chauvinist Pig!'

She attacked the valentine with a Flair, filling in the first four blanks. 'Try *that* for starters!'

1. I will meet Mr Right this year.
2. He won't be married.
3. He won't be gay.
4. He won't be a child pornographer.

'I see,' said Michael, smiling slyly. 'Moving back to Cleveland, huh?'

Fresh start

She was *not* moving back to Cleveland. She was not running home to Mommy and Daddy. She knew that much, anyway. For all her trials, she loved it here in San Francisco, and she loved her makeshift family at Mrs Madrigal's comfy old apartment house on Barbary Lane.

So what if she was still a secretary?

So what if she had not met Mr Right . . . or even Mr Adequate?

So what if Norman Neal Williams, the one semi-romance of her first six months in the city, had turned out to be a private eye moonlighting as a child pornographer who eventually fell to his death off a seaside cliff on Christmas Eve?

And so what if she had never worked up the nerve to tell anyone but Mouse about Norman's death?

As Mouse would say: 'Almost *anything* beats the fuck out of Cleveland!'

Mouse, she realized, had become her best friend. He and his spacy-but-sweet roommate, Mona Ramsey, had been Mary Ann's mentors and sidekicks throughout

9

her sometimes glorious, sometimes harrowing initiation into the netherworld of San Francisco.

Even Brian Hawkins, an oversexed waiter whose advances had once annoyed Mary Ann, had lately begun to make clumsy yet endearing overtures of friendship.

This was *home* now – this crumbling, ivy-entwined relic called 28 Barbary Lane – and the only parental figure in Mary Ann's day-to-day existence was Anna Madrigal, a landlady whose fey charm and eccentric ways were legendary on Russian Hill.

Mrs Madrigal was the true mother of them all. She would counsel them, scold them and listen unflinchingly to their tales of amatory disaster. When all else failed (and even when it didn't), she would reward her 'children' by taping joints of home-grown grass to the doors of their apartments.

Mary Ann had learned to smoke grass like a seasoned head. Recently, in fact, she had given serious thought to the idea of smoking on her lunch hour at Halcyon Communications. Such was the agony she suffered under the new regime of Beauchamp Day, the brash young socialite who had assumed the presidency of the ad agency upon the death of his father-in-law, Edgar Halcyon.

Mary Ann had loved Mr Halcyon a great deal.

And two weeks after his untimely passing (on Christmas Eve), she learned how much he had loved *her*.

'You stay put,' she told Michael gleefully. 'I've got a valentine for *you*!'

She disappeared into the bedroom, emerging several seconds later with an envelope. Mary Ann's name was scrawled on the front in an assertive hand. The message inside was also hand written:

> *Dear Mary Ann.*
> *By now, you must need a little*

fun. The enclosed is for you
and a friend. Head for some
place sunny. And don't let
that little bastard give you any trouble.

Always
EH

'I don't get it,' said Michael. 'Who's EH? And what was in the envelope?'

Mary Ann was about to burst. 'Five thousand dollars, Mouse! From my old boss, Mr Halcyon! His lawyer gave it to me last month.'

'And this "little bastard"?'

Mary Ann smiled. 'My *new* boss, Beauchamp Day. Mouse, look: I've got two tickets for a cruise to Mexico on the *Pacific Princess*. Would you like to go with me?'

Michael stared at her, slack-mouthed. 'You're shittin' me?'

'No.' She giggled.

'Goddamn!'

'You'll go?'

'Will I *go*? When? How long?'

'In a week – for eleven days. We'd have to share a cabin, Mouse.'

Michael leaped to his feet and flung his arms around her. 'Hell, we'll seduce people in *shifts*!'

'Or find a nice bisexual.'

'Mary Ann! I'm shocked!'

'Oh, *good*!'

Michael lifted her off the floor. 'We'll get brown as a goddamn berry, and find you a lover—'

'And one for you.'

He dropped her. 'One miracle at a time, please.'

'Now, Mouse, don't be negative.'

'Just realistic.' He was still stinging from a brief affairette with Dr Jon Fielding, a handsome blond gynecologist who had eliminated Michael as lover

11

material when he discovered him participating in the jockey shorts dance contest at The Endup.

'Look,' said Mary Ann evenly, 'if *I* think you're really attractive, there must be plenty of men in *this* town who feel the same way.'

'Yeah,' said Michael ruefully. 'Size queens.'

'Oh, don't be silly!'

Sometimes Michael was sensitive about the dumbest things. He's at least five nine, thought Mary Ann. That's tall enough for anybody.

Widow's weeds

Frannie Halcyon was an absolute wreck. Eight weeks after the death of her husband, she still dragged around their cavernous old house in Hillsborough, wondering bleakly if it was finally time to apply for her real estate license.

Oh, God, how life had changed!

She was rising later now, sometimes as late as noon, in the futile hope that a shorter day might somehow seem fuller. Her languorous morning coffees on the terrace were a thing of the past, a defunct ritual that had failed her as surely and swiftly as Edgar's diseased kidneys had failed her.

Now she made do with a languorous afternoon Mai Tai.

Sometimes, of course, she drew a glimmer of comfort from the knowledge that she was soon to be a grandmother. *Twice* a grandmother, actually. Her daughter DeDe – the wife of Halcyon Communications' new president, Beauchamp Day – was about to give birth to twins.

That had been the latest report from Dr Jon Fielding, DeDe's charming young gynecologist.

DeDe, however, begrudged her mother the simple indulgence of even *discussing* her new heirs. She was downright sullen on the subject, Frannie observed. And that struck the matriarch as very strange indeed.

'And why *can't* I dote a little, DeDe?'

'Because you're *using* it, Mother.'

'Oh, piffle!'

'You're using it as an excuse to – I don't know – an excuse to keep from living your own life again.'

'I'm half a person, DeDe.'

'Daddy's *gone,* Mother. You've got to get it together.'

'Then let me start shopping for the babies. There's a *precious* place called Bebe Pierrot in Ghirardelli Square, and I'm sure I could—'

'We don't even know their sexes yet.'

'Yellow would be darling, then.'

DeDe frowned. 'I *loathe* yellow.'

'You love yellow. You've always loved yellow. DeDe, darling, what *is* the matter?'

'*Nothing.*'

'You can't lie to me, DeDe.'

'Mother, please . . . can't we just . . . ?'

'I have to feel needed, darling. Can't you see that? No one needs me anymore.' The matriarch began to sniffle.

DeDe reached out and took her hand. 'The deYoung needs you. The Legion of Honor needs you.'

Frannie smiled bitterly. 'So that's how it goes, then. When you're young, it's your family that needs you. When you're old, it's museums.'

DeDe rolled her eyes in exasperation. 'Look, if you're determined to wallow in self-pity, there's not a damn thing I can do about it. It's just such *waste,* that's all.'

Frannie's eyes were full of tears now. 'What in God's name do you expect me to do?'

'I expect you . . .' DeDe softened her tone to one of daughterly concern. 'I expect you to start being good to yourself again. Live it up a little. Join a backgammon club. Enroll in Janet Sassoon's exercise class. Get Kevin Matthews to take you to the symphony, for heaven's sake! His boyfriend is on Hydra until June.'

'I know you're right, but I—'

'Look at yourself, Mother! You've got the money . . . you ought to be taking tucks in everywhere!'

'DeDe!' Her daughter's impertinence overwhelmed her.

'Well, I mean it! Why not, for God's sake? Face, boobies, fanny – the full catastrophe! What in the world have you got to lose?'

'I simply don't think it's very dignified for a woman of my—'

'Dignified? Mother, have you seen Mabel Sussman lately? Her face is as smooth as a baby's fanny! Shugie says she found this marvelous man in Geneva who did it all with hypnosis!'

Frannie blinked in disbelief. 'There had to be *some* sort of surgery.'

'Nope. All hypnosis – or so Shugie *swears* on a stack of *Town and Country*s.' DeDe giggled wickedly. 'Wouldn't you just *die* if one of these days somebody clapped their hands or said the secret word or something and the whole damn thing fell like a soufflé!'

Frannie couldn't help but laugh.

And later that afternoon, feeling curiously clandestine, she drove into town to wander through F. A. O. Schwarz in search of a Steiff creature for the twins.

She felt better now, so she toyed with the idea that maybe DeDe was right. Maybe she *had* moped too long, longer than was healthy, longer than Edgar himself would have wanted.

As she left the store, she caught her reflection in the window of Mark Cross. She stopped in her tracks long enough to grasp the flesh under her ears and pull it tight across her cheekbones.

'All right,' she said out loud. 'All *right*!'

14

Sisters with a secret

Mona Ramsey's life was – in her own words – down to the seeds and stems.

Once a $25,000-a-year copywriter for Halcyon Communications, she had been relieved of that position following a brief, but satisfying, feminist tirade against the president of Adorable Pantyhose, the ad agency's biggest client.

Her subsequent days of leisure as Michael Tolliver's roommate had been pleasant on a superficial level, but in the long run, emotionally unfulfilling. It was *permanence* she craved. Or so she had told herself when she moved out of 28 Barbary Lane to take up residence in D'orothea Wilson's elegant Victorian house in Pacific Heights.

D'orothea was a Halcyon model, perhaps the highest-paid black model on the West Coast. She and Mona had once been lovers in New York. Their San Francisco arrangement, however, had been devoid of passion, a bloodless pact designed to alleviate the loneliness that had begun to engulf both women.

It hadn't worked out.

For one thing, Mona never quite forgave D'orothea for not being black. (Her skin color, Mona learned eventually, had been artificially induced by pigment-altering pills and ultraviolet treatments, a ruse that had rescued the model from professional obscurity.) For another, she had come to grips, however grumpily, with the fact that she missed the company of men.

'I'm a shitty heterosexual,' she had told Michael when she returned to the nest at Barbary Lane, 'but I'm a shittier dyke.'

15

Michael had understood. 'I could have told you *that*, Babycakes!'

Her last Quaalude had begun to take effect as Mona climbed the rickety wooden stairway leading up to the lane. She had spent all evening at the Cosmic Light Fellowship, but her mood was blacker than ever. She simply wasn't *centered* anymore.

What had happened to her? Why was she losing her grip? When did she first peer up from the dark, wretched pit of her life and see that the walls were unscalable?

And *why* hadn't she bought more Quaaludes?

She moved groggily through the leafy canyon of the lane, then crossed the courtyard of number 28 and entered the brown-shingled building. She rang Mrs Madrigal's buzzer, hoping that a glass of sherry and a few mellow words from the landlady might somehow banish her bummer.

Mrs Madrigal, she realized, was a special ally. And Mona was not just one of the landlady's 'children.' Mona was the only person in the apartment house whom Mrs Madrigal had actively recruited as a tenant.

And she was – she believed – the only one who knew Mrs Madrigal's secret.

That knowledge, moreover, formed a mystical bond between the two women, an unspoken sisterhood that fed Mona's soul on the bleakest of days.

But Mrs Madrigal wasn't at home, so Mona trudged upstairs to her second-floor apartment.

Michael, as she had dreaded, was also gone. Upstairs, no doubt, planning his trip with Mary Ann. He spent a lot of time with Mary Ann these days.

The phone rang just as she flipped on the light. It was her mother, calling from Minneapolis. Mona slumped into a chair and made a major effort to sound together.

'Hi, Betty,' she said evenly. She had always called

16

her mother Betty. Betty had insisted on it. Betty actually *resented* the fact that she was older than her daughter.

'Is this your . . . permanent number again?'

'Yeah.'

'I called the place in Pacific Heights. D'orothea said you'd moved back. I can't believe you'd leave that charming home in a nice neighborhood for that shabby—'

'You've never even seen it!' She's always in character, thought Mona. For Betty was a realtor, a hard-assed career woman whose husband had left her when Mona was still a baby. She didn't care much for buildings without security guards and saunas.

'Yes I have,' snapped Betty. 'You sent me a picture last summer. Does that . . . woman still run it?'

'If you mean Mrs Madrigal, yes.'

'She gives me the absolute creeps.'

'Remind me not to send you any more pictures, will you?'

'What was wrong with D'orothea's place, anyway?' Betty, of course, didn't know about the shattered relationship. She seldom thought about relationships at all.

Mona hedged. 'I couldn't handle the rent.'

'Oh, well, if *that's* the problem, I can tide you over until you're able to—'

'No. I don't want your money.'

'Just until you're able to find a job, Mona.'

'Thank you, but no.'

'She's lured you in there, Mona!'

'*Who?*'

'That woman.'

Mona blew up. 'Mrs Madrigal *offered* me an apartment after we became good friends! And that was over three years ago! Why are you suddenly so goddamned concerned about my welfare?'

Betty hesitated. 'I . . . I didn't know what she *looked* like until you sent me—'

17

'Oh, come off it!'

'She's just so . . . extreme.'

If she only knew, thought Mona. If she only knew.

Down on the roof

Brian Hawkins was thirty-three.

And *that*, he realized with a shudder as he shed his denim-and-corduroy Perry's uniform and flopped on the bed with an Oly, was as old as Jesus on Calvary.

Or the idiot in *The Sound and the Fury*.

He was treading water now. Nothing more. He was working to survive, to continue, to pay for his pork chops, and his beer and his goddamn Ivory Liquid. And no amount of laid-back, mellowed-out, half-assed California philosophizing could compensate for the emptiness he felt.

He was getting old. Alone.

Most of his mail still said 'Occupant.'

Once upon a time, of course, he had been a fiery young radical lawyer. Before that fire subsided (and relocated in his groin), he had fought the good fight for the cause of draft resisters in Toronto, blacks in Chicago, Indians in Arizona, and Mexican-Americans in Los Angeles.

Now he was waiting tables for WASPs in San Francisco.

And he loved 'chasing pussy' almost as much as he had once loved hating Nixon.

He pursued this tarnished grail through fern bars and coed bath-houses, laundromats and supermarkets and all-night junk-food restaurants, where the pickings were slim but the gratification was almost instant. There was little time to waste, he told himself. Menopause was just around the corner.

If he needed something lasting – and sometimes he felt that he did – he never stayed with anyone long enough to let that need be visible. His logic was circular but invincible: The kind of woman he wanted could not possibly be interested in the kind of man he'd become.

His libido had taken charge of everything.

It had even governed the selection of this latest apartment, this drafty, cramped little house on the roof of 28 Barbary Lane. Women, he had reasoned, would get off on its panoramic view and nursery-tale dimensions. It would work for him as an architectural aphrodisiac.

'Are you *sure* you want it?' Mrs Madrigal had asked when he requested a change of apartments. (At the time, he was living on the third floor, just across the hall from the foxy but hopelessly uptight Mary Ann Singleton.)

He had told her yes without hesitation.

The landlady's spookiness, he presumed, had to do with the apartment's former occupant, a fortyish vitamin salesman named Norman Neal Williams.

But all he knew about Williams was that he had disappeared without a trace in December.

A stiff wind shook the little house, giving Brian a morbid sense of déjà vu.

Five on the Richter, he thought.

He knew what that meant now, for he'd felt his first earthquake only the week before. A deep, demonic growling had awakened him at 2 A.M., rattling his windows and reducing him instantly to a frightened, primeval creature.

But this was only the wind, and the crunch of the Big One would be just as horrendous on the third floor as it would be on the roof. Or so he had told himself as soon as the little house became his.

His door buzzer startled him. Pulling on a sweat

shirt, he opened the door in his boxer shorts. It was Mary Ann Singleton.

'Brian, I . . . I'm really sorry to bother you this late.' The shorts had obviously flustered her.

'That's OK.'

'You're not dressed. I'll get somebody else.'

'No problem. I can throw on some pants.'

'Really, Brian, I don't need—'

'Look! I said I'd help, didn't I?'

His tone jarred her. She managed a faint smile. 'Michael and I are going to Mexico. There's a suitcase that I can't quite—'

'Hang on a second.'

He pulled on a pair of Levi's and led the way down the stairs to her apartment. He dislodged the suitcase she needed from the top shelf of her closet. 'Thanks,' she smiled. 'I can make it from here.'

His eyes locked on her. 'Can you?'

'Yes, Brian.' Her inflection was firm and faintly school teacherish. She knew what he had meant, and she was saying no. Again.

Back on the roof, he shucked the Levi's and picked up the binoculars he kept on the shelf by the bed. Facing the cottage's south window, he cursed the impenetrable Miss Singleton as he scanned the midnight cityscape.

First the green-black enigma of Lafayette Park, then the Maytag agitator of the ultramodern St Mary's Cathedral, then the Mark's obscenely oversized American flag, flailing against the inky sky like a Bircher's acid trip.

All of which was foreplay.

His real quarry was something he called the Superman Building.

Father of the year

For the first time in weeks, DeDe rose before Beauchamp.

She greeted her husband with a kiss and a croissant when he stumbled into the kitchen at seven forty-five. She was chirpy for that time of morning – excessively chirpy – so Beauchamp instinctively grew wary.

He leaned against the butcher-block countertop, rubbing his eyes. 'League meeting, or something?'

'Can't I fix breakfast for my husband?'

'You can,' he said dryly, nibbling tentatively at the croissant, 'but you don't.'

DeDe thrust two shallots into the Cuisinart. 'We're having omelets. And some of those marvelous French sausages from Marcel & Henri.' She smiled faintly. 'I . . . worry about things too much, Beauchamp, and today I . . . well, I heard those silly parrots in the eucalyptus tree outside the window, and I just thought . . . well, we're a lot luckier than most people.'

He massaged his temples, still trying to wake up. 'I *hate* those fucking parrots.'

DeDe simply stared at him.

He turned away and began to fiddle with the Mr Coffee machine. Her face was positively *suffused* with that idiotic, imploring look she used to make him feel guilty. He refused to deal with it this early in the morning.

'Beauchamp?'

He kept his back to her. 'This goddamn thing hasn't been cleaned in at least—'

'Beauchamp! Look at me!'

He turned very slowly, keeping a thin smile plastered on his face. 'Yes, my sweet?'

'Will you at least tell me . . . you're happy?'

'About what?'

She laid her hands on her swollen belly. 'About *this*, dammit!'

Silence.

She stood firm. 'Well?'

'I'm delirious.'

She moaned melodramatically and turned away from him.

'DeDe . . . there are grave responsibilities attached to parenthood.' He kept his voice calm. 'I've accepted the responsibility of raising *one* child, but with great reluctance. Forgive me, won't you, if I'm not exactly jumping for joy at the prospect of—'

'Oh, shut up!'

'There you go. Being witty again.'

'I don't need your goddamn thesis on parenthood. I need your *support*. I can't do this alone, Beauchamp. I just *can't*!'

He smirked and motioned toward her belly. 'You sure as hell didn't do *that* alone.'

'No,' she replied instantly, 'but I sure as hell didn't do it with *you*!'

They stood there over the Cuisinart, eyes locked and fangs bared. Beauchamp broke the silence with a short sardonic laugh, then slammed the counter with the flat of his hand and sank down into a Marcel Breuer chair.

'That wasn't bad, actually. For you.'

'Beauchamp . . .'

'There are *better* ways to get my attention, but all in all it wasn't half bad.'

'It's true, Beauchamp! You're *not* the father!'

Silence.

'Dammit, Beauchamp! Can't you even *add*? Look . . .' Her voice began to waver. She pulled a chair up next to him and sat down. 'I wanted to tell you a long time ago. I really did. I even considered—'

'*Who?*' he said coldly.

'I don't think we should—'

'Splinter Riley, maybe? Or how about the charming but terminally greasy Jorge Montoya-Corona?'

'You don't know him, Beauchamp.'

'How *interesting.* Do you?'

She burst into tears and ran from the kitchen. He knew she would lock herself in the bedroom and sulk until he had left the building. Then she would fill her quivering palm with dozens of multicolored tablets and down them in a single gulp.

In a time of crisis, she could never resist her M & M's.

When Beauchamp arrived at Jackson Square, Mary Ann Singleton handed him his messages.

'Also, D'orothea Wilson called about five minutes ago.'

That was all. Not Mr Day. Not even Beauchamp. He didn't have a goddamn name since this *fluffball* had become his secretary.

Beauchamp grunted. 'I don't suppose she bothered to tell you why she didn't show for that Adorable shooting at The Icehouse? She's canceled three shootings this month alone.'

'She says she doesn't . . . look right anymore.'

'What the hell does *that* mean?'

The secretary shrugged. 'Maybe she gained weight over the holidays or—'

'Or maybe she just doesn't give a good goddamn about Halcyon Communications! Maybe she wants to go to *Mexico*!' The barb stung his secretary exactly the way he hoped it would.

Her fingers began mangling a paper clip. 'Beauchamp . . . it was Mr Halcyon who wanted me to—'

'I don't need to hear this again.' He stormed into his office and slammed the door.

Then he raged in silence against the Halcyon family.

Letter from Mama

Dear Mikey,

Your Papa and I were so glad to hear about your trip to Mexico with Mary Ann. I know it will be a lot of fun for both of you. Please send us a postcard when you get a chance, and remember not to drink too much tequila. Ha ha.

Orlando has been real cold this winter, but I expect you heard all about that on Walter Cronkite. The grove down by the Bledsoes' new split-level was hurt the worst. Some of the oranges were frozen through. Papa says that's OK, though, because we can sell them for juice. I'm doing my best to help Papa, but you know how he is around harvest time. Just kidding.

Papa says for you not to worry because we're getting about $3.50 a box, and anyway overall production is up, even with the freeze and all. The only problem now is with the homosexuals.

I guess you don't know about that. It all started when the Dade County Commission passed a law in favor of homosexuals. It said you can't refuse to hire homosexuals or rent to them, and Anita Bryant spoke out against this, being a Christian mother of four and Miss America runner-up and all, and all the normal, God-fearing people in Miami backed her up 100 percent.

We didn't think too much about it, of course, because we don't have near as many homosexuals up here as they do in Miami. Papa says they like the ocean. Anyway, pretty soon this organized group of homosexuals tried to force the Citrus Commission to take Anita Bryant's commercials off TV. Can you imagine? Anita said go right ahead, if that was what she had to do to make it safe for her children to walk the streets of Miami. God bless her.

I wouldn't know so much about this, except that Etta Norris (Bubba's mother) stopped by Tuesday to watch Oral Roberts on our new color set, and she said she was signing up folks in Orlando to support Anita Bryant's group, Save Our Children, Inc. I signed right away, but Papa said he wouldn't sign because you were a grown man and no son of his needed saving from any homosexuals. I said it was the principle, and what if the homosexuals stopped drinking orange juice? He said most homosexuals didn't drink orange juice, but he signed anyway.

We had our first meeting last night in the VFW room at Fruitland Bowl-a-Rama. Etta said the important thing was to show Anita Bryant that we support her. She also said we should put in something about how we aren't prejudiced but we believe that homosexuals aren't good examples for children in school. Lolly Newton said she thought the teacher part was important too, because if the teacher is standing up there being sissy all day, the pupils are bound to turn out sissy too. Ralph Taggart seconded the motion.

Your father kept telling me to hush up and don't be a damn fool, but you know me, I had to put in my two cents worth. I stood up and said I thought we should all get down on our knees and thank the Lord that someone as famous as Anita Bryant had stepped forward to battle the forces of Sodom and Gomorrah. Etta said we should put that in the resolution, so I felt real proud.

Reverend Harker said maybe we shouldn't say anything about the rental part, because Lucy McNeil rents the room over her garage to that sissy man who sells carpets at Dixie Dell Mall. Lolly said that was OK because Lucy had done it of her own free will, and besides, it was easier when you could tell they were homosexual. That way you could warn your children.

I guess I sound like a real crusader, don't I? I hope

you don't think your old Mama's being a foolish idealist. I just believe the Lord made us all to carry out His Holy Word.

I saw Bubba at Etta's this morning. He's such a nice young man. Goodness! I can hardly believe it's been over eight years since you and him used to go camping at Cedar Creek. He asked after you. He's teaching history at the high school now and still isn't married yet, but I guess it's mighty hard to find the right girl these days.

Blackie didn't like the freeze much and just lays around the house looking tired. I'm afraid we might have to put him to sleep. He's awful old.

Take care of yourself, Mikey. We love you very much.

Mama

P.S. If you need reading for your trip, I recommend Anita Bryant's autobiography. It's called 'Mine Eyes Have Seen the Glory.'

The getaway

On the eve of their Mexican cruise, Mary Ann and Michael huddled conspiratorially over their suitcases. 'Maybe,' grinned Michael, 'if we rolled it up in some Kleenex and stuffed it in your bra . . .'

'That's not funny, Mouse.'

'Well, look: we don't have to take it off the ship. It's not like we'll be smoking it on the street in Acapulco. Hell, we won't even see a customs agent until we get back to LA.'

Mary Ann sighed and sat down on the edge of the bed. 'I used to be a Future Homemaker of America, Mouse.'

'So?'

'So now I'm smuggling dope into Mexico.'

'And traveling with' – he lowered his voice to a sinister basso – 'a known homosexual.'

She smiled faintly. 'That too.'

He stared at her for a moment to determine exactly how seriously she had taken him. There were times, even now, when his irony came perilously close to describing the way she felt about things. She winked at him, however, so he continued packing.

'I love that expression,' he said, without looking up.

'What?'

'"Known homosexual." I mean, you *never* hear about known Southern Baptists, do you? Or known insurance salesmen. And when you're not a known homosexual, you're an *admitted* one. "Mr Farquar, an admitted stockbroker, was found stabbed to death in Golden Gate Park early this—"'

'Mouse, you're giving me the creeps!'

'Sorry.'

She reached over and squeezed his hand. 'I didn't mean to bark at you. It's just . . . well, I'm still a little jumpy about dead people, that's all.'

He started to say, 'I can dig it,' but thought better of it. Instead, he held on to her hand and reassured her for the third or fourth time that week. 'It'll get better, Babycakes. It's only been two months.'

Her eyes became moist. 'You don't think we're . . . escaping or anything?'

'From what?'

She brushed a tear from her eye, shrugged and suggested feebly: 'The law?'

'You haven't *broken* any law, Mary Ann.'

'I didn't report his death.'

He fought to be patient with her. They had hashed this out so many times before that the conversation had become ritual. 'That guy', said Michael softly, 'was a certified prick. He was a child pornographer, for

27.

Christ's sake. You didn't *push* him off that cliff, Mary Ann. His death was an accident. Besides, if you had reported his death, you would have been obligated to tell the police that he was investigating Mrs Madrigal. And we *both* love Mrs Madrigal too much for that, no matter *what* was in that file.'

The very mention of the file made Mary Ann shudder. 'I never should have burned it, Mouse.'

So Michael ran through *that* again. Burning the file, he told her, had been Mary Ann's most intelligent move. By destroying the private eye's dossier on Mrs Madrigal, Mary Ann had scored a twofold triumph: She had kept herself from being privy to information she might have been obligated to pass along to the police. And she kept the file out of the hands of the police.

The police had turned up at 28 Barbary Lane as soon as Mrs Madrigal reported her tenant missing. Their investigation appeared to have been routine and short-lived. Norman Neal Williams had been a transient, they learned, an itinerant vitamin salesman with no known relatives. His involvement in the child-porn racket surfaced immediately, though Mary Ann feigned ignorance of it.

She had 'gone out with him' several times, she told police. She hadn't known him well. He had seemed 'a little weird' to her at times. And yes, it seemed possible he had moved to another town.

When the police had gone, Mary Ann had summoned Michael to her apartment, where they pondered the real mysteries of this terrible chapter in her life.

Did the police know that Norman Neal Williams had been a private eye?

Did Mrs Madrigal know that she had been the subject of Williams' investigation?

Would Williams' body turn up in the bay?

And why would anyone want to investigate a

28

woman as warm and compassionate and . . . harmless as Anna Madrigal?

Mexico, of course, *was* an escape, but not the sort that Mary Ann had meant. Depression and morbidity had settled into her bones like mildew. She would *bake* it out, she decided, reverting to her adolescent solution for everything.

She tucked a bottle of Coppertone into a side pocket of her American Tourister. 'You know what?' she said, her voice ringing with pep-rally optimism.

'What?'

'This trip is gonna work for me. I'm gonna meet somebody, Mouse. I know it.'

'A man, you mean?'

'Not that you aren't the best company in the world, Mouse, but I really—'

'Look, you don't have to explain *that* one. I've got this dynamite plan, anyway. I spot a guy, right? Lounging out by the ship's pool, maybe, or . . . whatever, and I saunter up kind of casual like, with you on my arm all tanned and gorgeous, so that he's *bound* to be eating his heart out, and then I say in my very *butchest* Lee Majors voice, "Hi, guy, I'm Michael Tolliver and this is Mary Ann Singleton. Which one of us would you like?"'

Mary Ann giggled. 'What if he doesn't want either one of us?'

'Then,' said Michael matter-of-factly, 'you push him off the first available cliff in Acapulco.'

Mona flees

After Mona had driven Mary Ann and Michael to the airport, she returned to Barbary Lane and fell into a cosmic funk.

She felt grossly disoriented, partially because of her mother's weird phone call, and partially because two of her friends had managed to break the bonds of this incestuous backwater Babylon called San Francisco.

That was what she needed, really. Fresh territory. Blue skies. Communion with the Eternal. A chance to restructure her life into something that would bring her the inner tranquillity she so desperately wanted.

She mapped out a plan of action in less than ten minutes, leaving a terse note on Mrs Madrigal's door:

> Mrs M,
> I'll be gone for a while.
> Please don't worry. I
> need to breathe.
> Love,
> Mona

She made *her* escape by cable car, irked by the bitter irony of it all. Wouldn't Tony Bennett be tickled to know that Mona Ramsey, aging freak and transcendental cynic, had been forced to flee Everybody's Favorite City on one of these cloyingly cute tourist trolleys?

At Powell and Market she disembarked, separating herself from the double-knit masses as soon as possible. She strode up Market to Seventh, and stopped with a sigh in front of the Greyhound bus station.

After three minutes' consideration, she bought a ticket to Reno, deciding on the spot that sun and sky and desert might somehow offer new horizons. The bus, they told her, would leave shortly after midnight.

For the rest of the afternoon she sat in Union Square, where the drunks and derelicts and burned-out hippies could only reinforce her decision to leave. Then, as soon as night fell, she smoked a potent mixture of grass and angel dust and drifted back to the bus station.

She was eating a cheese sandwich, when a garishly painted crone – eighty if a day – tried to make conversation with her in the snack bar.

'Where ya headin', dolly?'

'Reno,' she said quietly.

'One stop after me. You takin' the midnight bus?'

Mona nodded, wondering if the angel dust had made this woman more grotesque than she really was.

'How 'bout sitting with me, then? I get real nervous on the bus, what with the perverts and all?'

'Well, I'm not sure I'd be much—'

'I won't bother you none. I won't say nothin' unless you want me to.'

Something about that touched Mona. 'Sure,' she said finally. 'It's a deal.'

The old woman grinned. 'What's your name, dolly?'

'Mo . . . Judy.'

'Mine's Mother Mucca.'

'Mother . . . ?'

'Mucca. It's a kind of a nickname. I'm from Winne-mucca, see?' She cackled gleefully. 'It's a long story, and I don't see no point in . . . Say, dolly, are you OK?'

'Yes.'

'You look kinda fucked up.'

'What?' A terrible sea roar was resounding in her head, as if someone had lashed a giant conch shell to her ear.

'I said you looked fucked up. Your eyes are all . . . You ain't been smokin' no reefers have you, dolly?'

Mona nodded. 'Sort of.'

'Meanin'?'

'I don't think you'd—'

'Somethin' in it?'

'Ever heard of angel dust?'

Mother Mucca's hand came down on the counter so hard that several sleepy diners looked up from their coffee. 'Holy shit! That stuff is for puttin' elephants to sleep, girl! If you don't know any better than to fuck yourself up with an animal tranquilizer, you ain't got no business ridin'—'

Mona lurched to her feet. 'I don't have to sit here and listen—'

A bangled talon of a hand clamped onto her wrist and pulled her back down.

'The fuck you don't!' shrieked Mother Mucca.

Animal magnetism

'Some people drink to forget,' said Mrs Madrigal, basking in the sun of her courtyard. 'Personally, I smoke to remember.' She took a toke of her new Colombian and handed the joint to Brian.

'Like what?' he asked.

'Oh . . . old lovers, train rides, the taste of fountain Cokes when I was a kid. Grass is a lovely, sentimental . . . *Reader's Digest* kind of a thing. I can't understand why the bourgeoisie doesn't approve of it.'

Brian smiled, stretching his legs out on the beach towel. 'You've been smoking long?'

'Not by my standards. Oh, I think . . . since you were a teenager, probably.'

'That's not long.'

She smiled. 'I thought you might say that.'

'Do you remember the first time?'

'No. I remember the third time, though.'

'The first time didn't work?'

'No. It worked.' She chuckled. 'Don't you hate people who say that?' She mimicked the voice of a middle-aged matron. 'The children *insisted* I smoke pot, so I tried it, Madge, and it didn't do a *thing* for me, not one thing.'

Brian laughed. 'Sometimes it's true, though. My first time didn't work.'

'So?' The landlady shrugged. 'Your first time at sex doesn't *work*. It's still the first time, though. Isn't that enough?'

'I guess so.'

'There's nothing that beats the high of a first time. *Nothing*.'

'Something tells me you've had a lot of first times.'

'I try to. And you're changing the subject.'

'Sorry. I'm ripped.'

'I was going to tell you about my third time.'

'Oh, right.'

'The third time', said Mrs Madrigal, adjusting the sleeves of her kimono, 'happened at the San Francisco Zoo just after Bobby Kennedy was killed.'

'Bummer, huh?'

'No . . . I mean, I didn't get stoned because of that. He had just been killed, that's all. Anyway, I knew this lovely little man at the zoo who was in charge of the monkeys. Actually, that's the wrong term. He was more like *one of* the monkeys. He had rather long arms and he was quite hairy and the monkeys simply *adored* him. I adored him too. He was a marvelous backgammon player.

'Well, on this particular day, we had a nice long chat in this funny causeway thing that led from the gorilla quarters to the cage where the gorillas go to diddle with themselves in public—'

Brian chuckled.

Mrs Madrigal raised an eyebrow. 'Well, isn't that what zoos are for? Why else do people watch gorillas?'

'I see what you mean.'

'So there we were, standing in this causev `y, chatting pleasantly, when this rather formidable-looking lady gorilla strolled up and joined our little group. She stood next to my zookeeper friend and flung an arm across his shoulder, like an old school chum or something. Then my friend said, "Oh, I almost forgot," and pulled a joint out of his shirt pocket. He lit the joint, took a toke off it and handed it to the gorilla—'

'C'mon!'

'So help me god! And *then*, if you please, the

gorilla took a long hit and handed the joint to me!'

'Jesus. What did you do?'

'I am not *rude*, dear boy. I accepted it graciously, without Bogarting, and passed it back to my friend. The gorilla stayed for two more hits, then promenaded down the causeway to greet her public. She was a very mellow lady by then.'

'She did this all the time?'

'Every day. It helped her cope, I suppose.'

'Is she still there?'

Mrs Madrigal tapped a forefinger against pursed lips. 'You know, I'm not really sure. I often wonder if she's still alive. Gorillas can live to be quite old, I understand. I'd rather like to see her again.'

'Why?'

'Oh . . . I guess, because we have a lot in common. She was a tough old cookie, and she had fun the best way she knew how. And . . . because she learned a lot late in life.'

'So what have you learned?'

She smiled at him reprovingly. 'I've learned how snoopy you get when you're loaded.'

'I wasn't asking for your life story.'

'What a pity. You should sometime. But not when *I'm* loaded.'

'Why?'

'Because, dear . . . I *might* tell you the truth.'

The kindest cut

Emma was getting old, Frannie noted wistfully, as the rail-thin black maid tottered into the master bedroom with a breakfast tray in her hands.

'Open the drapes, Miss Frances?'

Miss Frances! That was what made Emma an

34

absolute gem, the last of her species. As long as she had worked at Halcyon Hill, it had been Miss Frances, Miss DeDe, Mr Edgar . . .

'No, thank you, Emma. Just leave the tray on the table, please.'

'Yes'm.'

'Emma?'

'Ma'am?'

'Do you think I'm . . . Sit down, will you, please, Emma?'

Emma complied, perching delicately on the edge of a button-tufted lady chair near the bed. 'You aren't . . . sick, Miss Frances?'

'No . . .'

'Mr Edgar's gone, Miss Frances. You gotta live with that now. He's passed on to the bosom of Jesus, and there's not a livin' thing in this whole blessed world that can bring him back until the final judgment of the Lord delivers His people from—'

Frannie cut her off with a jingle of the bedside bell. 'Emma, dear . . . you're giving me a headache.'

'Yes'm.'

'Now, what I'd like to know is . . . Emma, I trust your opinion a great deal. I think you know that, and . . . Do you think I need a face-lift, Emma?'

Silence.

'You *do* know what a face-lift is, Emma?'

The maid nodded sullenly. 'Cuttin'.'

'No . . . well, yes, that's part of it, but it's a complete cosmetic process that's really quite common these days. I mean, *lots* of ladies—'

'White ladies.'

'Don't be impertinent, Emma.'

A quarter century of faithful employment at Halcyon Hill entitled Emma to the scowl with which she now confronted her mistress.

'Miss Frances, the Lord gave you a perfectly fine face, and if the Lord had intended for—'

'Oh, poo, Emma! The Lord doesn't have to go to Opera Guild meetings!'

'Ma'am?'

'I'm so *old*, Emma. And everybody I know looks like ... Nancy Kissinger! I'm nothing but an old turkey gobbler!' She pinched the flesh along her cheekbone. 'Look at that, Emma!'

Emma's expression was dour. 'Mr Edgar wouldn't like that kind of talk.'

Frannie rolled over in bed and pushed out her lower lip. 'Mr Edgar is dead,' she said dully.

When Emma was doing the laundry, Frannie locked the bedroom door and phoned Vita Keating. The furtiveness of this act made her realize that, even at fifty-nine, she was not an adult. She had always been answerable to *someone*.

Edgar, however, was gone now; Emma was all she had left.

Vita, thought Frannie, had never known that kind of emotional servitude. Vita was a trailblazer, a vigorous independent whose nineteen-fifty-something Miss Oklahoma title had spurred her on to runner-up stardom in Atlantic City and a Republican husband in San Francisco.

A hostess of impeccable credentials, Vita sometimes shocked her stuffier peers by shattering long-established social traditions in the city: she was, after all, the *first* socially registered localite to pair denim place mats with Waterford crystal. And she did the cutest things with bandannas.

Who else but Vita had the panache to show up at the Cerebral Palsy Ball wearing a gingham granny dress and twirling a lasso? She was *such* fun.

Naturally, she laughed heartily when Frannie blurted out her request.

'My face man? God, honey, for all I know, he's bottling sheep semen in Switzerland. His last patient was a *total* washout – some poor woman in Santa Barbara who ended up looking like the Phantom of the Opera.'

Frannie couldn't hide her disappointment. 'I see,' she said glumly.

'Have you thought about the shots,' chirped Vita.

'The shots?'

'The sheep semen, honey.'

'Vita!'

'Well, *I* couldn't agree with you more, but Kitty Cipriani says it's made her a new woman. Personally, I think someone's pulling the wool over her eyes!' Vita roared with laughter, and Frannie, despite her ever-blackening mood, joined in with her.

Finally, Vita said abruptly, 'How old are you, Frannie?'

The question stung more than it might normally have. Vita was Frannie's junior by at least fifteen years. 'I'm asking for a reason,' Vita added apologetically.

'Fifty-four,' said Frannie.

'Oh. Too bad.'

'Don't rub it in, Vita.'

'No, honey. I mean, it would help if you were sixty.'

'Why on God's green earth would that help?'

Vita chuckled throatily. 'I won't tell you unless you tell me your real age.'

Frannie hesitated for a moment and then told her.

'Ooh, boy,' said Vita. 'Ooooh, *boy*!'

'Vita, what in the world are . . . ?'

'Just you wait, Frannie Halcyon! Just you wait!'

The cruise begins

The agonies of last-minute packing, a lingering cold and a nerve-jangling PSA flight to Los Angeles all but disappeared when Mary caught her first glimpse of the *Pacific Princess*.

'Oh, Mouse! It's so *white*!'

Michael poked the flesh of his forearm. 'We'll blend right in, won't we?'

Mary Ann didn't answer, lost in the majesty of the huge, moonlit ship. There was something scary yet exhilarating about this moment. She felt like a sky-diver, hurtling recklessly through space, knowing that *this* time would matter, this time was real, this time her chute had to open.

The cabdriver looked over his shoulder at the couple in the back seat. 'You folks married?'

'Shacked up,' said Michael, provoking the expected glare from Mary Ann.

'Well.' The driver chuckled. 'I guess you seen *The Love Boat*?'

Michael nodded. 'Movie for TV, right?'

'Yeah. Bert Convy. Lyle Waggoner. Celeste Holm . . .'

'All the biggies.'

The driver nodded. 'Filmed it right there. On the *Pacific Princess*. Pretty sexy stuff.'

'Mmm. I remember,' said Michael, smirking privately at Mary Ann. 'Celeste Holm was a plump but lovable matron who thought she was washed up with men, until she met Craig Stevens on the cruise. Craig had been her boyfriend years before, and Celeste . . . well, the poor thing was *petrified* that Craig would find out what a chubbette she'd become.'

'Did he?' asked Mary Ann.

'Nope. Happy ending. Craig turned out to be blind.'

'You made that up, Mouse.'

'Scout's honor! And they were *married* at the end. Isn't that right driver?'

'Yep.'

'Apparently', shrugged Michael, 'ol' Craig couldn't *feel*, either.'

*   *   *

The ship's photographer surprised them on the gangplank, shouting out a jovial, 'Smile, young lovers!'

Michael obliged and clamped his hand over Mary Ann's right breast.

'Christ!' he said, as they boarded the ship. 'Is this a cruise or a senior prom?'

'Mouse, would you try to be just a *little* respectable?'

'For eleven whole days?'

'It's a *British* ship, Mouse.'

'Ah, yes! But with *Italian* stewards.' He held his forefingers erect, several feet apart.

Mary Ann flushed, then giggled. '*Straight* Italian stewards,' she corrected him.

'You *wish*,' said Michael.

Their stateroom was on the Promenade Deck, deluxe accommodation with twin beds, wood-grain cabinetry, comfortable chairs, and a tub in the bathroom. A bottle of chilled champagne awaited them.

Mary Ann proposed the first toast. 'To Mr Halcyon. God bless Mr Halcyon.'

'Right on. God bless Mr Halcyon.'

'And' – she filled their glasses again – 'to . . . to adventure on the high seas!'

'And romance.'

'And romance!'

'To Mrs Madrigal . . . and marijuana . . . and the munchies . . . and to every goddamn person in Florida except Anita Bryant!'

'Yeah!'

'But most of all', said Michael, turning mock-grave suddenly, 'to that well-bred, debonaire, but incredibly hunky number who gave the eye to *one* of us when we came on board tonight.'

'Where? Who?'

'How do I know who? I just got here, woman. You *saw* him, didn't you?'

'I don't think so.'

Michael rolled his eyes in exasperation. 'He never stopped staring at us!'

'A passenger?'

'Yep.'

'Looking at *us*?'

'You got it, girl.'

Mary Ann bit the tip of her forefinger. 'Do you think he was blind?'

Michael whooped and raised his glass. 'OK, then . . . to blindness!'

'To blindness,' echoed Mary Ann.

Mother Mucca's proposition

Mona woke from an uneasy sleep when the Greyhound pulled into Truckee, California, just before dawn. She was sure her tongue had turned into a dead gopher. The bizarre old woman next to her patted her hand.

'This ain't it, dolly. Go back to sleep.'

It? What was It? Where was It?

'It's OK, dolly. Mother Mucca's here. I'm lookin' out for ya.'

'Look, lady. I—'

'Mother Mucca.'

'OK. I appreciate your help, but—'

'That angel dust'll fuck you up every time. You shoulda heard yourself talkin' in your sleep, dolly!'

'I don't . . . what did I say?'

'I don't know. Crazy stuff. Somethin' about mice.'

'Mice?'

'Somethin' like that. Somethin' like: "Where did the mouse go? I can't find the mouse." Then you started hollerin' for your daddy. It was goddamn spooky, dolly.'

Mona rubbed her eyes and watched the zombie-faced passengers shuffle out for coffee in the Truckee station. They looked like haggard infantrymen bracing for a predawn assault.

What in the name of Buddha was she doing here?

When Mother Mucca insisted on buying breakfast, Mona was too weak to refuse. Besides, the old biddy seemed kind of together, even if she *did* look like a refugee from a Fellini movie.

'I had a girl named Judy once.'

'What?'

'You said your name was Judy, didn't you?'

Mona nodded, opting to remain as anonymous as possible. She'd had all she could take of Mona Ramsey.

'Judy was a peach,' continued Mother Mucca. 'I guess she stayed with me longer'n any of 'em.' She shook her head, smiling, lost in rosy recollection. 'Yessir, she was a peach!'

Mona found herself warming to her. 'You had lots of children?'

'Children?' She spat out the word.

'You said . . .'

Mother Mucca began to cackle again. 'You're a lot dumber'n you look, dolly. I'm talkin' about the best damn whorehouse in Winnemucca!'

Mona was jarred, but instantly fascinated. Of course! A genuine Nevada madam! A rawboned relic of the West's first group encounter enterprise!

'You . . . ? How long have you . . . ?'

'Oh, Lord, dolly! Too fuckin' long!'

They both laughed exuberantly, sharing the same emotion for the first time since they'd met. Mona found herself riveted by the sheer, unembarrassed ballsiness of this extraordinarily ugly old woman.

'What brought you to San Francisco?' she asked.

'Hookers union meeting. Coyote.'

Mona nodded knowledgeably. One of the cardinal

41

earmarks of North Beach Chic was an unflinching familiarity with Margo St James and her prostitutes' union.

'You know Margo?' asked Mother Mucca.

'Oh, yes,' lied Mona. She had, however, *seen* the woman several times, breakfasting on coffee and croissants at Malvina's.

Mother Mucca arched a painted eyebrow. 'She's a lot classier'n me, huh, dolly?'

'I think you're very classy.'

Mother Mucca ducked her head and blew into her coffee.

'I do,' Mona persisted. 'Really. You're a very ... together person.'

'You're a damn liar, too.' She reached over suddenly and squeezed Mona's arm above the elbow. For a moment, it seemed that her crusty veneer might crack, but then she cleared her throat abruptly and continued in a tone that was tougher than ever.

'Well, dolly! You ain't told me why you're headin' to Reno with a head full o' angel dust!'

'There's nothing special about Reno.'

The old woman snorted. 'You're right about *that*!'

Mona laughed. 'I just wanted – I don't know – to get away for a while. I've never seen the desert.'

'We got plenty o' that in Winnemucca.'

Mona looked down at her hash browns, avoiding what seemed to be an invitation of sorts.

'It's a big place, dolly. I need some help with the phones. It's real clean and pretty too. I think you'd be kinda surprised.'

'I'm sure it's a nice—'

'Hell, dolly! I'm not white-slavin' ya or anything! You'll keep me company, that's all. You can leave whenever you want to.'

'I just don't think I'm—'

'What do you do, anyway?'

'What?'

'For a livin'.'

42

'I'm . . . I used to be an advertising copywriter.'

Mother Mucca roared. 'Well, don't be so fuckin' uppity, then!'

Mona grinned and dropped her napkin on her plate. 'The bus is leaving, Mother Mucca.'

'You won't do it, then?'

'Nope,' said Mona, chewing on the knuckle of her forefinger. 'Not unless I can have my own waterbed.'

Life among the A-Gays

For the Hampton-Giddes, the mechanics of party-giving were as intricate as the workings of Arch Gidde's new Silver Shadow Rolls.

After careful scrutiny, prospective guests were divided into four lists:

The A List.

The B List.

The A-Gay List.

The B-Gay List.

The Hampton-Giddes knew no C people, gay or otherwise.

As a rule, the A List was comprised of the Beautiful and the Entrenched, the kind of people who might be asked about their favorite junk-food or slumming spot in Merla Zellerbach's column in the *Chronicle*.

There was, of course, a sprinkling of A-Gays on the A List, but they were expected to behave themselves. An A-Gay who turned campy during after-dinner A List charades would find himself banished, posthaste, to the purgatory of the B-Gays.

The B-Gays, poor wretches, didn't even get to *play* charades.

The range and intensity of cocktail chatter at the

Hampton-Giddes' depended largely on the list being utilized.

A List people could talk about the arts, politics and the suede walls in the master bedroom.

B Listers could talk about the arts, politics, the suede walls in the master bedroom, and the people on the A List.

The A-Gays could talk about whoever was tooting coke in the bathroom.

The B-Gays, being largely decorative, were not expected to talk.

'Binky *swears* it's the truth,' said William Deveraux Hill III, on a night when the Hampton-Giddes' Seacliff mansion was virtually swarming with A-Gays.

'*Chinese?*' hissed Charles Hillary Lord.

'Twins!'

'A *litter*!' exclaimed Archibald Anson Gidde, butting in.

'I can't *stand* it!'

'*You* can't? Honey, Miss Gidde over there practically *ruined* her nails on the Princess phone this morning, just spreading the news.'

'I did *not*.' The host was indignant.

'You told *me*.'

'Well, that was all.'

'Stoker says you told him too.'

'She lies!'

Charles Hillary Lord needed more dish. 'Christ, Billy, an *Ornamental*? DeDe's been doing it with an *Ornamental*?'

'They have *teeny* pee-pees.' This from Archibald Anson Gidde.

'I think you're *all* disgustingly prejudiced,' said Anthony Latimer Hughes, joining the group.

'Oh, Mary! You're *not* having another *Chinoiserie* period, are you, darling?' Gidde again.

'There are two things one should know about San

Francisco,' interjected Charles Hillary Lord. 'Never meet *anyone* at the Top of the Mark. And never walk through Chinatown in the rain.'

'Why?' chorused everyone.

'Because they're so *short*. Their umbrellas will blind a white man!'

Across the room huddling under the Claes Oldenburg, Edward Paxton Stoker, Jr, swapped pleasantries with his host, Richard Evan Hampton.

'I wish', said the guest, 'that Jon Fielding were here.'

'Oh, pullease!' Rick Hampton had never fully recovered from the fall soiree at which Jon Fielding had suddenly exploded, exiting in a terrible huff. 'You won't find that bitch on any guest list of *mine*, Edward.'

'But he *is* DeDe's gynecologist, and I'm sure he—'

'*And* an Occasional Piece for Beauchamp.'

'Not any more he isn't.'

'*Really?*'

'The doctor, as we *all* know he is wont to do, got *very* sanctimonious all of a sudden and gave our Beauchamp the old heave-ho. Beauchamp was *livid*.'

'I'd love to hear Fielding's version of it!'

'You'll have to wait a while, I'm afraid. He's on the way to Acapulco.'

'What on earth for?'

'What else? A gynecologists' convention.'

The richer – and older – half of the Hampton-Giddes rolled his eyes laboriously. 'Acapulco has gotten *so* tacky these days.'

Fantasy on the fantail

Somewhere off the coast of Mexico, a dazzling midday sun found dozens of willing worshipers on the fantail

of the *Pacific Princess.* Mary Ann was on her stomach
– her bikini top untied – when an unannounced hand
glopped something gooey on her back.

'Mouse?'

Silence.

'Mouse!'

'I do not know thees Mouse, signorina. I am but
a seemple Italian dining room steward who wants
to make ze whoopee weez zee beyootiful, horny
American girls!'

'You smoked that joint, didn't you?'

Michael sat down next to her and sighed dramatically. 'I *wish* you'd learn to fantasize.'

'What is that stuff, anyway?'

'What stuff? Oh . . . tortuga cream. The room steward gave it to me. He says they make it in Mazatlán.'

'It smells yummy.'

'Uh huh. Ground-up turtles.'

'Mouse!'

'Well, that's what he *said.*'

'Ick!'

'What the hell do you think Polly Bergan uses? Rose
petals?'

Mary Ann sat up, blinking into the sun, holding her
bikini top in place with her right arm.

'Tie me up, will you?'

'Bondage *already*? You haven't tried bingo yet. And
there's a swell seniors mambo class this afternoon in
the Carrousel Lounge, if you'd care to—'

'Mouse . . . don't look now, but he just dove into the
pool.'

'Who?'

'Our Mystery Man. The guy you saw when we were
boarding.'

'The one who was cruising us?'

Mary Ann corrected him. 'One of us.'

'Maybe he's into three-ways.'

'Mouse, do you think he's gay?'

'Well . . . his backstroke *is* a little nellie.'

'Mouse, I'm serious.'

'Then *ask* him, dummy! Invite him over for a Pina Colada!'

Mary Ann turned and studied the strong white body thrashing through the green water of the pool. He was a strawberry blond, she noticed, and he shook his head like a wet collie when he surfaced at the ladder.

She looked back at Michael. 'You don't think I'll do it, do you?'

Michael just grinned at her, maddeningly.

'OK. Just watch me!'

The wet collie was stretched out on a towel at the pool's edge. Mary Ann approached as casually as possible, her eyes fixed on the surface of the water. Her intent was to look vigorous and liberated, like Candice Bergen out for a swim after a rough day of photographing the African wilds.

The collie looked up and smiled. 'The only way to do it is to close your eyes and jump.'

'Is it cold?' Mary Ann asked.

Not too swift. Very un-Candy Bergen.

'Go ahead,' he urged. 'You can take it.'

She shrugged her shoulders and mugged, hoping it wasn't too late to try for a Marlo Thomas effect. A tolerant smile spread over the collie's face when she held her breath and jumped.

It was a funny little hatbox of a pool, not really wide enough for swimming laps. The cold ocean water was invigorating, but impossible to take for long. Shivering, she reached for the ladder.

The collie extended his hand. 'The goose bumps are very becoming.'

'Thanks,' she said, smiling.

'Will you join me for a drink? You and your husband, that is.'

'My . . . ? Oh, that's not my . . .' She turned and

looked at Michael, who was smirking at her. He gave his imitation of Queen Elizabeth's royal wave. 'Michael's just a friend.'

'That's nice,' said the collie.

For whom? thought Mary Ann. Me or Michael?

The collie introduced himself to both of them. His name was Burke Andrew. He was traveling alone on the cruise. He shook Michael's hand firmly and excused himself to get the drinks.

'Well,' said Mary Ann. 'Is he?'

'How the hell should I know? There hasn't been a secret queer handshake since 1956.'

'He's gorgeous, isn't he?'

Michael shrugged. 'If you like big thighs.'

Staring out to sea, Mary Ann sighed. 'I think he likes me, Mouse. Help me figure out what's wrong with him.'

The Superman Building

The irony, thought Brian, as he dragged back to Barbary Lane at midnight, was that he could have gone home with her.

Easily.

She had practically *drooled* on him, for Christ's sake, jammed up against him there in the brutal, nuclear glare of Henry Africa's Tiffany lamps. He could've bagged her without batting an eye.

So why *hadn't* he? What perverse new quirk of his personality had prompted him to sabotage a sure thing and scuttle his butt back to his little house on the roof?

The scene in the bar had gone like this:

'I still can't get over Freddie Prinze.'

It figures, he thought. A Farrah Fawcett-Majors

fright wig. A Bernadette Peters pout. She gets her material from the tube. In a minute, she'll be talking about *Roots*.

'I mean, he was so *young*, and . . . well, even if he *was* taking drugs and all, I don't see why that would depress him enough to . . . God, it's just such a *bummer* . . . and he was doing so much for the Chicano people.'

Brian didn't look up from his beer. 'He was Puerto Rican,' he pointed out.

'Besides, cocaine isn't supposed to . . . He was?'

'Yep.'

'I had a Puerto Rican roommate once. I got her through the Ethnic Studies Program at college.'

He sipped his Oly, poker-faced. 'She work out?'

'It was really educational.'

'Good.'

'Her name was Cecilia.'

'Nice name.'

'Cecilia Lopez.'

'Mmm. I sent off for a spider monkey once when I was eleven or twelve.'

'I'm sorry. I don't . . .'

'Those things in the back of comic books. Darling Pet Monkey. Fits in a Teacup . . .'

'But what does that . . . ?'

'Her name was Cecilia too.'

'Oh.'

'She was dead when I got her. All packed up in her little crate. It nearly killed me.'

'How awful! Was . . . whose fault was it?'

'Nobody's really.'

She nodded solemnly.

'It was . . . suicide!'

She looked at him morosely.

'Drugs,' he explained. 'And she was so *young*.'

She reached out to lay her hand on his, but he rose abruptly and slapped some money on the bar.

'I'm sorry,' he said. 'I'm too depressed to fuck tonight.'

The Superman Building was a towering Deco apartment house at the corner of Green and Leavenworth. Brian loved it because it reminded him of the Daily Planet building in the old television series.

Able to leap tall buildings in a single bound . . .

He also loved it because it afforded him a kind of power that sometimes bordered on the erotic.

Tonight, as he shucked his Levi's and rugby shirt, he noted that there were still six or eight lights burning in the Superman Building.

He lifted his binoculars and studied the sixth floor for several minutes, concentrating on a large corner apartment. A dumpy-looking woman with short hair and a red sweater moved sluggishly from room to room, plumping pillows.

At midnight?

A lover arriving? Not likely. An early departure in the morning? Maybe, but what guest could be *that* important? It was probably a simple case of boredom. Boredom or nervousness . . . or insanity.

Bored himself, he shifted his gaze to the – what – eighth floor? There, against a well-lighted window, a thin, balding man was lifting his foot slowly to meet his outstretched arm.

The movement seemed too expressive for exercise, too erratic for dance. Some sort of martial art, maybe . . . or maybe the whole goddamn building was full of loonies.

If he wasn't careful, he'd start making up names for these people. Like Jimmy Stewart did in *Rear Window*.

A light came on.

He raised the binoculars again and zeroed in on an eleventh-floor room that was suffused with a dim, rosy light. Seconds later, a woman appeared.

She stood near the window in a long gown of some sort, a dark form against the fleshy warmth of her room. She was motionless for a moment, then her hands went down to her waist and up again suddenly to her face.

She was wearing binoculars.

And she was looking at Brian.

The house

At dawn the desert around Winnemucca was gray and jagged-looking, as if built from shattered concrete, fragments perhaps of a pre-Columbian freeway.

Or so it seemed to Mona from the window of the battered Ford Ranchero that bore her swiftly and unceremoniously from the bus station to a place called the Blue Moon Lodge.

'Well, that's her,' bellowed Mother Mucca, nodding through the windshield to the one-story stucco building squatting in the distance.

'Nice,' said Mona.

'Yep,' said Mother Mucca.

'You had it long?'

'Sixty years long enough for ya?'

Mona whistled.

The octogenarian emitted a gravelly chuckle. 'Mother Mucca is an *old* motherfucker!'

Before Mona could muster a comment about the Young at Heart, the Ranchero swung abruptly into a dusty parking lot adjacent to the brothel. Mother Mucca leaned on the horn.

'Now where the hell is Bobbi?'

An aluminium door banged open, revealing a nervous-looking blond woman in her mid-twenties. She was wearing cut-off Levi's and a pink Qiana blouse knotted at the waist. Hobbling slightly, she ran out to meet the car.

'Welcome back,' she beamed.

'What the hell happened to your feet?'

'Nothin'.'

Mother Mucca climbed out of the Ranchero, scowling like a cigar store Indian. 'Nothin', huh?'

'Mother Mucca, I didn't let him—'

'Now you listen to me, dolly! If you turn one more trick with the crazy-ass Elko shitkicker, I'll boot your ass outa here so fast you'll wish you never . . . You ain't broke nothin', have ya?'

Bobbi shook her head.

'Fetch the bags, then. This here's Judy.' She jerked her head toward Mona. 'Judy's gonna stay and work the phones for a few days.'

The two young women nodded to each other.

'Give her Tanya's room,' said Mother Mucca, mellowing a little now. 'But take out the swing first.'

Their first stop was the kitchen, where Mother Mucca swilled half a quart of milk and toasted Pop-Tarts for the two of them.

'She's a sweet little thing, ain't she?'

'Who?'

'Bobbi.'

'Oh . . . yes. She seems very nice.'

'Fucked up, though. Loco as they come. You gotta watch her like a mother hen. Hell, when I found that dolly she'd sunk plumb to the bottom. She couldn't go no lower.'

Mona shook her head sympathetically. 'Heavy drugs?'

'Nope. Worse. Key punch operator.'

Mona's room looked out on the desert, the last of a series of rooms opening, motel-style, on a common sidewalk.

Her furnishings consisted of a bed (neither water nor brass), a green vinyl butterfly chair, a Formica-topped night stand, and an Eisenhower-era vanity displaying, among other things, an Autograph Hound (Tanya's?), a plastic fern and an Avon cologne bottle shaped like a stage-coach.

Mona was face down on the bed – wondering whether a week in a whorehouse would seriously screw up your karma – when Bobbi entered the room.

'Knock, knock,' she said sweetly.

Mona rolled over, rubbing her eyes. 'Oh . . . hi.'

'I brought you some towels.'

'Thanks.'

'You settled in now?'

'Yeah. Thanks, Bobbi.'

She smiled. 'Sure, Judy.'

Mona returned the smile, feeling an odd sense of communion with this simple creature.

'You'll like Mother Mucca,' said Bobbi softly. 'She talks real mean, but she's not that way at all. She loves us all like daughters.'

'I guess she never had any of her own, huh?'

'No. No daughters. She had a son once.'

'What happened to him?'

'He ran away, they say. When he was a teen-ager. A long time ago.'

Land ho!

Breakfast on the *Pacific Princess*. The Aloha Deck dining room was humming with sun-flushed passengers, eager for their first glimpse of Puerto Vallarta. Mary Ann made her entrance without Michael, who was still showering.

'Well,' boomed Arnold Littlefield, dousing his

scrambled eggs with ketchup, 'the hubby stood you up, huh?'

Arnold and his wife, Melba, shared a table with Mary Ann and Michael. The Littlefields were fortyish and always wore matching clothes. Today, in deference to their destination, they were sporting identical Mexican flour sacks outfits. They were from Dublin. Dublin, California.

'He always takes longer than I do,' said Mary Ann breezily, as she sat down. It was easier, by far, to pass off Michael as her husband than to explain what Michael called 'our bizarre but weird relationship.'

'Right on,' said Melba, with a mouthful of bacon. 'Men are much fussier than girls.'

Mary Ann nodded, grateful that Michael wasn't around to comment on *that* one.

She ordered a huge breakfast, then remembered Burke Andrew and canceled the waffles. She was downing her orange juice when Michael appeared, looking spirited and squeaky clean.

He was wearing Adidas, Levi's and a white T-shirt emblazoned with a can of Crisco.

'Apologies, apologies.' He grinned, nodding toward the Littlefields as he sat down.

'No sweat,' said Arnold. 'You better keep an eye on the little lady, though.' He winked at Mary Ann. 'She's too pretty to be let out without a leash.'

'Arnold!' That was Melba.

'Well, Mike knows that. Don't you, Mike?'

'Can't let her out of my sight for a minute.'

Melba elbowed her husband. 'You don't ever say that about *me*, Arnold!'

'Well, these kids are younger than us and you remember how it was when . . . Say, Mike, how long you been with Crisco?'

'What?' Michael had been cruising a waiter at the next table.

'Your shirt. You affiliated with Crisco?'

Mary Ann thought of crawling into her oatmeal.

'Yeah,' Michael answered soberly. 'I've been ... in Crisco – oh, I don't know – four, five years.'

'Sales?'

'No. Public relations.'

'Mouse . . .'

Michael winked at Arnold. 'The little woman doesn't like me to talk business at the table.'

'Right on,' said Melba, siding with Mary Ann. 'Arnold talks about aluminium honeycomb until he's blue in the face. And it's *so* boring!'

'It may be boring to you, Melba, but it's not boring to *some* people, not if that's the way they choose to make their living! You don't think Crisco is boring, do you, Mike?'

'Hell, no,' said Michael assertively.

From the Promenade Deck, the white sands and palm trees of Puerto Vallarta seemed almost within reach. Mary Ann leaned against the rail and watched the taxi drivers and serape salesmen who had already begun to swarm across the landing.

'Where shall we go, Mouse?'

'I don't know. Down the beach, I guess.'

'We don't have any Mexican money.'

'The purser said they'll take ... Hang on. Here he comes!'

'Who?'

'The mysterious but hunky Mr Andrews.'

Mary Ann wheeled around to see the strawberry blond striding down the deck toward her. 'It's *Andrew*,' she corrected Michael quickly. 'No *s*.'

Michael shrugged. 'His *s* looks fine to me.'

Mary Ann missed the joke; Burke Andrew was beaming at her. 'I've been looking for you two,' he said.

Both of us? thought Mary Ann.

Baby talk

Even three Scotches at the University Club couldn't take Beauchamp's mind off the letter he carried in the breast pocket of his Brioni.

'Well,' said Peter Cipriani, joining the young executive on the terrace, 'so life *isn't* a cabaret, old chum?'

Beauchamp scowled. 'Not even *half* the time.'

'It could be worse.'

'How?'

'You could be *me, mon petit.* You could be doomed to dinner tonight at Langston's house.'

Beauchamp glanced at him ruefully over the rim of his glass. 'What's on the menu tonight? Antique pheasant?'

'Worse – oh, worse!'

'Victorian venison?'

Peter shook his head soberly. 'The rumor – God help us – is Edwardian elk! Heaven *knows* how long that creature's been in his freezer. Miss Langston hasn't felled an elk since the late sixties!'

What a pisser, thought Beauchamp bitterly as he rode the elevator to his Telegraph Hill penthouse. Other people's problems were laughable next to his.

DeDe was in the library, curled up on the camelback sofa with a copy of Rosemary Rogers' *Sweet Savage Love.* Her free hand was partially submerged in a cloisonné bowl full of M & M's. Beauchamp glared at her from the doorway.

'Behold! The Total Woman!'

'I've had a long day, Beauchamp.'

He dropped his attaché case and headed for the bar. 'I'll bet you have.'

'What the hell's that supposed to mean?'

He kept his back to her as he filled a shot glass with J & B. 'It must be *murder* finding a super jumbo bag of M & M's. You drive all the way to Woolworth's?'

'Very funny.'

'If *fat* amuses you, go right ahead and yuck.'

'May I remind you I'm carrying *two* babies!'

'I know,' he said, downing his Scotch. 'Plain and Peanut.'

Dinner that evening was cold quiche and salad. They ate in glacial silence, avoiding each other's eyes, waiting petulantly for the moment they both knew would come.

'We have to talk,' Beauchamp said finally.

'About what?'

'You know goddamn well about what!'

'Beauchamp . . . I'm tired of talking about it. I don't blame you for being upset. I really don't. But I'm having these babies and I can't take this . . . harassment anymore.' She looked him squarely in the eyes. 'I've thought about this a long time. I've decided to move to Mother's.'

'Brilliant. Just brilliant.'

'I don't know whether it's brilliant or not, but at least I'll be—'

'Look, goddammit! You've got some explaining to do. You're not running home to Mommy until I get a few answers.' He fumbled in his pocket for the letter, thrusting it into her hands. 'This charming anonymous missive came to me at the office today!'

DeDe's hands shook as she removed a sheet of notebook paper from the envelope. The message, printed in yellow with a felt-tip pen, consisted of eight words:

WHY DON'T YOU NAME THEM YIN AND YANG?

'Now,' said Beauchamp ominously, 'will you please tell me what the hell that means?'

DeDe stared at the horrible note for several seconds, stalling for time, commanding herself to stay calm. The cycle, she realized, was complete. From her best friend Binky, to Carson Callas the gossip columnist, to the city at large, the ignominious truth had spread. She was bearing the children of a Telegraph Hill grocery boy!

She laid the letter on the table, face down. 'That's disgusting,' she said quietly.

'Answer the question, DeDe.'

'Beauchamp, please . . .'

He was poised like a cobra.

'Oh, fuck it, Beauchamp! The babies' father is Chinese!'

The landlady's lesson

When he had finished his shift at Perry's, Brian went straight home to Barbary Lane. Mrs Madrigal was perched on a stepladder in the hallway, replacing a light bulb. Up there, in her sixty-watt aura, she shone like a B-movie madonna about to descend on an unsuspecting French village.

'Welcome to Manderley,' she mugged. 'I'm Mrs Danvers. I'm sure you'll be very happy here.'

Brian laughed. 'Feeling gothic tonight?'

'My dear! Aren't you? This place is a veritable *tomb*, what with Mary Ann and Michael in Mexico and Mona God knows *where* – and you out there terrorizing half the female population.'

'I was working.'

'Mmm. It *is* work, isn't it?'

He bridled at her teasing, but let it go. She had cast

him as the aging Don Juan of her Barbary Lane family, and the label seemed as apt as any at this point. 'Well,' he sighed, 'I guess I'd better go confront my kitchen sink. It's beginning to grow penicillin, I think.'

'Brian?'

'Yeah?'

'Would you care to smoke a quick joint with an old lady?' Her huge blue eyes blinked at him unembarrassedly.

'Sure,' he smiled. 'I'll bring the joint, if you bring the old lady.'

Her apartment seemed fussier than ever, as if the doilies and tassels had taken to breeding in their unguarded moments. Still flanking the archway to the dining room were the two marble statues that had fascinated Brian on his very first visit to the landlady's home: a boy with a thorn in his foot and a woman with a water jug.

Mrs Madrigal sat on the ancient velvet sofa, curling her feet up under her kimono in a movement that seemed surprisingly girlish. She took a short toke off the joint and handed it to her tenant. 'So who is she, dear?'

'Who?'

'The creature who's driving my carefree boy to utter distraction.'

Brian held the smoke in his lungs for as long as possible. 'I think you've got the wrong carefree boy.'

'Have I?'

Her eyes were on him again, offering refuge.

'Mrs Madrigal, it's late and I don't feel like playing games.' His abruptness embarrassed him, so he laughed and added: 'Of course, if you *know* any . . . creatures, I could use another notch or two in my gun!'

'Brian, Brian . . . that isn't *you*, dear.'

He snapped at her. 'Would you just lay off with the—'

59

'I *worry* about you, dear. Hell, I know I'm a nosy old biddy, but look, I've got nothing better to do. I mean, if you ever want somebody just to *talk* to . . .' She leaned forward slightly and smiled like a stoned Mona Lisa. 'May I give you some unsolicited advice?'

He nodded, feeling more uncomfortable by the second.

'The next time you meet a girl – someone that you really like – pretend that you're a war hero and that all your basic plumbing got shot off in the war.'

Brian grinned incredulously. 'What?'

'I'm perfectly serious, dear. Don't tell a soul – especially *her*, for heaven's sake – but pretend to yourself that this dreadful thing has happened and the *only* way you can communicate your feelings is through your eyes, your heart.'

'And what if she wants to go home with me?'

'You *can't*, dear. You've lost your wee-wee, remember? All you can do is smile bravely and invite her to dinner the next night – or maybe a nice walk in the park. She'll accept, too. I promise she will.'

Brian took a long drag on the joint. 'So how long . . . ?' He exhaled in midsentence, making sure he maintained an expression of amused tolerance. 'How long am I supposed to keep pretending?'

'As long as possible. Until she asks you.'

'Asks me what?'

'If you were wounded in the war, of course.'

'And what do I tell her?'

'The truth, dear. That everything's intact. It'll be a *lovely* surprise for her.'

He folded his arms across his chest and smiled at her.

'And', she said, raising her forefinger, '*you'll* have a nice surprise too.'

'What?'

'You'll *know* the poor dear, Brian. And you might even *like* her by then.'

Minutes later, as he stood in the window of his little house on the roof, he marveled at how well Mrs Madrigal could read him, how swiftly she had detected 'the creature who's driving my carefree boy to utter distraction.'

Did it show on his face now? Did the pupils dilate from the sheer, loin-twitching force of the fantasy? What set of the jaw or tic of the eye betrayed the passion that had begun to consume him?

At two minutes before midnight he lifted his binoculars to his face and focused on the eleventh floor of the Superman Building.

She appeared, as he prayed she would, on the hour.

And he heard himself whimper when their binoculars locked in mid-air.

Bobbi

Exhausted by the drugs and the long bus ride, Mona crashed after breakfast at the Blue Moon Lodge. The broiling midday sun had already forced her to kick off the covers when Bobbi knocked on the door of her cinder-block cubicle.

'Knock, knock,' she said.

Mona groaned silently. How long would she be able to endure the puppy love of this sugar-coated tart?

'Hi Judy. Mother Mucca asked me to show you how the phones work.'

Arrggh. The phones. This was a job, wasn't it? She was paying her way on this acidless trip. Dragging herself into a semi-upright position, she leaned against the headboard and rubbed her eyes. 'Three minutes, OK?'

She staggered into the tiny bathroom and splashed

water on her face. It would only be for a week, she reassured herself, and prostitution was legal in Nevada. Besides, if she ever decided to take up copywriting again, *this* gig would look stunning on a résumé.

Two large metal hooks in the ceiling caught her eye as she left the bathroom.

'What's that for?' she asked Bobbi.

'What?'

'Those hooks.'

'Oh. This used to be Tanya's room.'

Gotcha. Thanks a helluva lot. 'Tanya did something with hooks?'

Bobbi giggled, as if Mona were a new kid on the block who didn't know the first thing about hopscotch. 'That's where she hung the swing.'

Should I ask about that? thought Mona. Yes. I'm a receptionist in a whorehouse. I should know about swings. 'The swing was part of . . . her routine?'

Bobbi nodded. 'Water sports. She was real famous for it.'

'You mean . . . ? I don't get it.'

'Oh, silly,' chirped Bobbi. 'She *tinkled* on them from up there. While she was swinging, see?'

'I think I saw her on *The Gong Show* once.'

'Huh?'

'Nothing. What happened to her, anyway?'

'Tanya? She switched to a house in Elko.'

'Was that good?'

Bobbi shrugged. 'For her, I guess. Mother Mucca was plenty pissed. But Tanya'll be back, probably. There aren't that many good houses in these parts. Elko, Winnemucca, Wells . . . that's about it.'

Mona suppressed a smirk. This dippy child who said tinkled when she meant pissed and pissed when she meant angry could still distinguish between a respectable and an unrespectable whorehouse. 'Where are the crummy ones?' Mona asked.

Bobbi pursed her lips thoughtfully, obviously delighted with her role as the Duncan Hines of whorehouses. 'Oh . . . Mina, I guess, and Eureka and Battle Mountain. Battle Mountain is definitely the pits. When a girl hits that circuit . . . well, she might as well hang it up.'

Bobbi's income, Mona learned, was about three hundred dollars a week. That was *after* Mother Mucca had taken her cut and Bobbi had paid her room and board.

All of the girls at the Blue Moon Lodge were required to work three weeks straight before taking a week off. The state saw to it that they were issued a work permit, fingerprinted, photographed and examined by a doctor prior to setting up shop – or swings.

The most profitable season, according to Bobbi, was summer, when transcontinental traffic on Interstate 80 was heavier, and a period between mid-September and mid-October, when deer hunters invaded the area.

In accordance with the Municipal Code of Winnemucca, the girls of the Blue Moon Lodge took turns in exercising their privilege to go into town for shopping, movies and medical attention.

There was also a law that forbade a woman from working in a Winnemucca brothel if a member of her family resided in the county.

'C'mon,' bubbled Bobbi, as soon as Mona pulled herself together. 'I wanna show you something neat.'

Mona braced herself for the abomination. A rubber room, perhaps? A mirrored ceiling? A sex-crazed donkey? A crotchless Naugahyde wet suit by Frederick's of Hollywood?

Bobbi led the way out of the cubicle into the sunshine. The warm desert air made Mona acutely aware of the original purpose of her escape from San Francisco. Communion with Nature. Harmony with the Elements.

But no . . . oh, no. That was not Buddha's Design.

Buddha, for some goddamn reason, wanted her to have a room with hooks in the ceiling.

Their destination was Bobbi's cubicle, a space identical to Mona's, three doors closer to the main building. Bobbi swung open the door with a flourish.

'Over there,' she exclaimed, 'on the shelf above the bed.'

Mona's jaw went slack.

'Dolls of All Nations,' said Bobbi. 'I've been collecting since I was twelve.'

'They're . . . very nice,' said Mona.

The child-whore beamed proudly. 'Their faces are really all the same, but . . . well, I guess you can't have everything.'

'No.'

'You can touch 'em if you want.'

Mona went to the shelf and pretended to examine one of the dolls. 'Very pretty,' she said quietly.

'You picked my favorite. Norway.'

'Yeah?'

'Do you think girls in Norway really have dresses like . . . ? Is something the matter, Judy?'

'No, I . . . I was just distracted for a minute.'

Moments later, Mona excused herself and returned to her own cubicle, where she locked herself in the bathroom and cried for a while.

Angel dust did that to her sometimes.

Day of the iguana

Underneath a thatched umbrella at the Posada Vallarta, the unlikely threesome sipped Coco Locos and gazed out at the bluest of oceans.

'This is nice,' said Burke, stretching his arms above

his head. 'I'm glad you two let me join you. I don't exactly . . . relate to most of the people on the ship.'

Michael grinned over the top of his coconut. 'You don't get off on blue rinse?'

'Blue what?'

'Old ladies,' translated Mary Ann.

'Oh.' He laughed warmly, looking first at Mary Ann, then at Michael. 'I guess I'm a little out of it, huh?'

Mary Ann shook her head. 'Mouse talks in code, Burke. Half the time, I don't have the slightest idea what he's talking about.'

'How long have you two . . . known each other?'

Michael glanced at Mary Ann. 'How long ago was the Safeway? Nine months? A year?'

'Yeah. I guess.'

'We met in a grocery store,' explained Michael. 'Mary Ann was trying to pick up my boyfriend.'

Burke blinked. 'You . . .'

'Gay as a goose,' said Michael. He stood up, smiling, adjusting his blue satin Rocky shorts. 'I'm gonna take a hike. I'll give you two exactly an hour to get it on.'

Mary Ann turned and watched Michael sprint recklessly to the surf. Her smile to Burke was amused and apologetic. 'I can't do anything with him,' she said.

'Apparently,' laughed Burke.

She laughed with him. 'I didn't mean it like *that*.'

'He seems very nice, actually.'

'He is. I love him a lot.'

'But he's not your . . .'

She shook her head, then giggled. 'He says he thinks of himself as my pimp service.' Her smile faded when she saw Burke's expression. 'Did that sound gross?'

'Not at all. I just . . . well, I've never met anybody like you two.'

Mary Ann pored over his face for a moment, assessing the firm jaw and the full mouth and the baffling naïveté of those wide-spaced gray eyes. Was anybody *that* innocent anymore?

65

'Where are you from, Burke?'

He looked back at her for a moment, then traced the rim of his coconut with his forefinger. 'All over, really.'

'Oh. Well, then, most recently.'

'Uh . . . San Francisco.'

'Great! So am I! Where do you live?'

'Actually, I'm from Nantucket. I mean, my parents live there now, and I'm staying with them. I used to live in San Francisco for a while, but I don't anymore.'

'Where did you stay when you were—'

He pushed his chair back abruptly. 'Would you like a swim or something? I feel like we should use that hour.'

She smiled at him. 'You're right. Let's go.'

They strolled up the beach in the direction of town, stopping occasionally to romp in the surf or gasp at the billowing parasails soaring through a cloudless sky. Burke took it all in with unembarrassed wonder, as gleefully open as a child catching his first glimpse of the sea.

He was gentle, Mary Ann observed, gentle in a primitive, manly sort of way. And manly without being macho. It was impossible to imagine him hustling Kelly Girls at Thomas Lord's. When a peddler appeared, draped in a hideous necklace of stuffed iguanas, Burke reached immediately for his wallet.

'Which one do you want?'

'Ick! You're not serious?'

'One of those shirts, then? With the embroidery?'

'Burke . . . you don't have to buy me anything.'

He wrinkled his brow solemnly. 'How will you remember me if you don't have an iguana?'

Smiling, she laid her hand on his back at the spot where a patch of golden hair peeped over the top of his swim trunks.

'I'll remember,' she said. 'Don't you worry about that.'

Desperate straights

When DeDe Halcyon Day was ten years old, her parents sent her to camp at Huntington Lake. For six excruciating weeks, she hurt as only a fat child can hurt when forced to paddle canoes, stitch wallets and sing songs to the tune of 'O Tannenbaum.'

The end came as a merciful release, an escape from the tyranny of children into the comfortable, protective sanctuary of Halcyon Hill.

She felt something of that now, something of that ancient longing for home, as she packed her Gucci luggage and prepared herself mentally for Hillsborough.

She wanted Beauchamp behind her.

She wanted him to be like poison-oak and short-sheeted beds and pretty preteens who made jokes about Kotex.

She wanted him gone.

But Beauchamp persisted:

'This isn't doing a goddamn bit of good, you know!'

She ignored him, continuing to pack.

'OK. So you run home to Mommy. Then what? What the hell do you think people are gonna say when those babies are born?'

'I don't care what they say.'

'How very *au courant* of you!'

DeDe's voice remained calm. 'I want them, Beauchamp.'

'Do you think their father wants them? What the fuck's he gonna do, anyway? Strap 'em on the back of his delivery bike?'

'Leave him out of this.'

'Oh, heavens, yes! For Christ's sake don't offend his delicate Asian sensibilities. All *he* ever did was take an innocent ethnic poke at my—'

'Shut up, Beauchamp!'

He was snarling now. 'Why don't you just drop the Pearl Buck routine, Miss Tightass! You couldn't give a flying fuck about those babies and you know it!'

'That's not true.'

'Half your friends have had abortions, DeDe.'

'Not in the sixth month.'

'It's a simple salt injection. It's no more complicated than—'

'I don't want to talk about this anymore.'

He mimicked her tone. '"I don't want to talk about this anymore." Shit! Do you even give a rat's ass about all the humiliation you're going to put me through? Do you give a good goddamn about Halcyon Communications – your *own father's* business?' His voice lowered dramatically, becoming almost plaintive. 'Jesus, DeDe, we're up for the PU club this year.'

'You, Beauchamp. Not me.'

'It's the same goddamn thing.'

Looking up from her suitcase, she mustered a faint smile. 'Not anymore it isn't,' she said.

He glared at her murderously for several seconds, then slammed the bedroom door and stormed out of the house.

Hunched over his desk at Halcyon Communications, Beauchamp spent the rest of that Saturday afternoon immersed in the new campaign for Tidy-Teen Tampettes. The work allowed his thoughts to solidify, so that by six o'clock he had settled on another approach to his problem.

He phoned a number in West Portal.

'Yeah?' growled a voice at the other end. Its fuzziness, Beauchamp knew from experience, was not caused by postnasal drip.

'Bruno?'

'Yeah, yeah.'

'It's Beauchamp Day.'

'Oh. Yeah. More snow already?'

'No. Well, maybe that too. I've got kind of a special request this time.'

'I got some Purple Haze now. And some dynamite Black Beauties.'

'No. This is different. Remember that friend of yours who . . . settles differences?'

Silence.

'It's not what you think. Nothing heavy. I just need . . . well, it's kind of special . . . I mean, a special situation.'

'It'll cost ya.'

'I know. When can we talk?'

'Tonight? Eight o'clock?'

'Where?'

'Uh . . . the Doggie Diner. On Van Ness.'

'Right. The Doggie Diner on Van Ness at eight o'clock.'

'No snow, huh?'

'No, Bruno. Not tonight.'

Lady Eleven

Against his better instincts, Brian Hawkins made up a name for the woman in the Superman Building.

Lady Eleven.

This wasn't some sort of sicko fantasy trip, he told himself. She was *there*, like Everest, a nightly reality as fixed and inevitable as the clang of the cable cars or the toot of the foghorns on the bay. It seemed only natural to give her a name.

She would appear, invariably, on the stroke (could a

digital clock strike?) of midnight, assuming her stance against the dim pinkish glow of her bedroom. After that she would scarcely move, except to raise and lower her binoculars and to make an unceremonious exit less than twenty minutes later.

She would never acknowledge Brian's presence, nor would she shift her gaze from the window of his little rooftop house. Viewed with the naked eye, she was nothing more than a dark blemish against the distant rectangle of light. With the field glasses, however, it was possible to discern her features.

A long, full-lipped face framed by hair that was . . . dark brown? The color was impossible to determine, but Brian settled on auburn.

Her hair fell lower than her shoulders and appeared to be tied in the back. Her robe was light-colored and undramatic, terry cloth maybe, and it revealed little about the rest of her body.

There was something about Lady Eleven's look that suggested she had just stepped from a shower.

Brian always wondered if her hair was wet and smelled of Herbal Essence.

This was the sixth night.

When Brian returned from Perry's, he couldn't help but remind himself again how radically his behavior patterns had changed. It was eleven o'clock, for Christ's sake, and he was home!

Furthermore, he found that he was showering after work now. Tonight he spent even longer than usual in the bathroom, primping like a college freshman about to immerse himself in a sorority mixer.

After brushing his teeth and shaving (shaving?), he slipped into his terry cloth bathrobe and sat in an easy chair by the south window with a dogeared copy of *Oui*.

Only seven minutes to go.

*　　*　　*

The sky around the rooftop house was alive with Wagnerian tumult. Hoky white clouds, phony as angel's hair props, drifted past the ghostly monolith of the Superman Building. At 11.56 a light appeared on the eleventh floor.

The light.

Brian dropped the magazine and moved to the window. He picked up the binoculars and focused on the lair of Lady Eleven. She wasn't in sight yet; there was no movement in her bedroom.

Nor was she in sight at midnight.

She had stood him up.

Brian remained at the window, numbed by disappointment and betrayal, like a child who had been awakened suddenly from a summer dream about Christmas morning. Then, gradually, his face began to burn with rage as he leaned there immobile against the cold windowpane (a window he had Windexed just that morning) and cursed the secret siren who had made him shave at midnight.

It would always be like this, wouldn't it? The ones you wanted could sense it with cunning, primeval precision. Your lust, not its fulfillment, was all these women required. And as soon as they felt it, as soon as they experienced the first acrid waft of your musk in their nostrils, they were gone from your life forever.

But then – sweet Jesus! – she appeared.

Poised and majestic as a figurehead on the great white clipper ship of the Superman Building, Lady Eleven materialized in her window and lifted her binoculars to her face. Brian matched her pose.

And then he caught his breath.

For now she was holding the binoculars with her right hand . . . and using her left hand to unknot the cord of her bathrobe.

As the robe slipped to the floor, so did Brian's.

On that sixth enchanted evening, across a crowded city.

On-the-job training

Mona's first afternoon at the Blue Moon Lodge was disappointingly uneventful. The phone rang only twice. The first call was from a man who wanted to know if Monique still worked there. A quick aside with Mother Mucca revealed that she did not.

'She left last month,' the madam explained. 'She's a directory assistance operator in Reno.'

'What do I tell this guy, then?'

'Tell him Doreen knows that bit too.'

'What bit?'

'Don't be so goddamn nosy!'

Mona frowned and picked up the receiver again. 'Uh . . . Monique isn't here anymore, but Doreen . . . knows how to do that too.'

The customer hesitated. 'The whole thing?'

'Uh huh.'

'With the rabbit's foot and all?'

'Uh . . . one moment, please.'

Mother Mucca was looking irritated. 'Don't you know the first damn thing about—'

'He's asking about a goddamn rabbit's foot!'

The old woman's mouth puckered into a pout. 'Don't you talk nasty to your elders, dolly! I'll wash your fuckin' mouth out with soap!'

Mona softened her tone. 'What about the rabbit's foot?'

Mother Mucca shrugged. 'Doreen can do it.'

Mona returned to the customer. 'Yes, she can do the . . . rabbit's foot thing.'

'All the way?'

'Yes. Satisfaction guaranteed.'

'The girls in Battle Mountain fake it, ya know?'

'Maybe so,' snapped Mona, 'but this isn't Battle Mountain. This is the Blue Moon Lodge!'

Mother Mucca beamed, squeezing Mona's arm. 'Atta girl, Judy! Atta girl!'

And the glow Mona felt came from pure, unadulterated pride.

One by one, the girls of the Blue Moon Lodge began to straggle into the parlor. There were seven in all, including Bobbi. The oldest seemed to be in her mid-thirties. She had ratted hair and thin lips and looked like a gospel singer from the Billy Graham Crusade.

'You're Judy, ain't ya? I'm Charlene.'

Charlene, Bobbi, Doreen, Bonnie, Debby, Marnie and Sherry. Jesus, thought Mona. What the hell are they. Hookers or Mouseketeers?

Charlene was checking her out. 'Mother Mucca says you're workin' the phones this week.'

'Yeah, just – you know – for the experience.'

That was wrong, all wrong. Patronizing as hell. Charlene knew it, too. 'You ain't writin' one o' them – whatchacallit – college papers?'

'No.'

'Good.' She knelt, stretching her lime-sherbet Capri pants to the limit, and turned on a mammoth color television set. Mona noticed for the first time that the top of the set was adorned with a Plasticine bust of JFK.

Most of the girls were watching Merv Griffin when the second customer call came in.

'Who's this?' asked a well-modulated voice.

'I'm Mo . . . I'm working here this week.'

'Oh.'

'Mother Mucca has authorized me to—'

'I think I'd better talk to her, please.'

Mona was piqued. 'Sir, if you would like to make an appointment, I'll be glad—'

Sensing a problem, Mother Mucca moved to Mona's side. 'He givin' you trouble, Judy?'

'He insists on talking to you.'

The madam took the phone. 'Yeah, this is . . . Oh, yes, sir . . . No, she's a new girl. I've . . . Yes, sir, she can be trusted completely . . . Yes, sir . . . Of course, sir . . . No, that's not short notice at all . . . I'll take the usual precautions . . . Fine, sir . . . Goodbye and thank you very much.'

The old woman hung up the phone, curiously subdued. The gentility she had mustered for the conversation left Mona somewhat stunned.

'Charlene,' said Mother Mucca.

'Yeah?'

'Get rid o' the other johns tonight.'

'Huh?'

'You heard me. Get rid of 'em. Call 'em up or reschedule 'em or somethin', but get rid of 'em.'

'Was that . . . ?'

Mother Mucca nodded. 'He's flyin' in from Sacramento.'

Charlene whistled softly. 'Which girl did he ask for?'

'He didn't.'

'Huh?'

'He wants a new one.'

Cravings

Under way again, the *Pacific Princess* steamed south toward Manzanillo, washed in the light of a full moon. Shortly after eight o'clock Mary Ann emerged from her bath and anointed her body with turtle lotion.

In less than an hour she would be having her first real date with Burke.

'Am I getting brown yet, Mouse?'

'What? Oh, yeah . . . fine.'

'Watcha reading?'

'Holy shit!'

'It must be good.'

He whistled in disbelief, still hunched over his book. Mary Ann grew impatient. 'Mouse . . . show me!'

Michael held up the paperback. It was entitled *Cruise Ships – The Inside Story*. 'I bought this damn thing down in the gift shop. I mean, they were actually pushing it!'

He read to her: ' "There are two categories of aggressive women among cruise passengers. There are those who are after the medals and those who just like tramping around." '

'That's the most sexist thing I've ever—'

' "The former like to aim at officers. The latter like nothing better than to disappear into crew quarters and spend the rest of the voyage in a variety of arms." '

'Well, variety is the—'

'Wait. Here comes the good part: "Occasionally, wealthy and lonely male homosexuals—" '

'You're making that up!'

'Listen, will you? "Occasionally, wealthy and lonely male homosexuals will appear on a cruise, attempting to buy the favour of crew members. It is an easy task." '

'Let me see that!'

He held the book so she could see it and continued to read. ' "A generous tip will carry the request to a willing crew member. Sometime later, the cabin phone will ring and a deal will be struck." '

'Leave it to you to find that.'

'Well, don't get snotty, just because *you've* found Mr Right already.'

Like a long-married couple, they sensed a pun together and spoke it in unison. 'All right, already!'

She tried on three blouses, unable to settle on the best complement for her beige slacks.

'Stick with the blue,' said Michael. 'That orange thing makes you look like Ann-Margret.'

'Maybe I *want* to look like Ann-Margret.'

Michael sighed laboriously. 'All right. If you *seriously* think that nice Nantucket boy is hot for the kitten-with-a-whip type, go right ahead and—'

Mary Ann threw off the blouse and scowled at him. 'You're worse than Debbie Nelson!'

'Thank you. Who's Debbie Nelson?'

'My freshman roommate.'

'The blue is very wholesome.'

'Screw wholesome.'

Michael pretended to be aghast. 'Wash your mouth out, young lady!' He buttoned up the blue blouse. 'There. Look at yourself. Isn't that better?'

'My mother hired you, didn't she? You're a plant.'

'A pansy, to be specific.'

'Look, don't you think that cream blouse might—'

Michael ignored her. 'Blow,' he ordered.

'What?'

'Blow in my face. You had two slices of garlic bread tonight.'

'Mouse! I am perfectly capable—'

'Strong men have turned queer over two slices of garlic bread!'

She blew.

Leaving the stateroom, she turned and winked at him. 'Don't wait up for me Babycakes!'

He stuck his tongue out at her.

'Thank you, Mouse. I love you.'

'Save the schmaltz for Thunder Thighs.'

'What are you gonna do?'

'Right now it's a tossup between shuffleboard and self-abuse.'

She laughed. 'There's a Cole Porter revue in the Carrousel—'

'Will you get outa here!'

*　　*　　*

He read for an hour, then wandered out onto the Promenade Deck, where he leaned on the rail, watching the ocean. Up here, away from the white vinyl shoes and harlequin glasses, it was easier to visualize the kind of sea cruise that inhabited his dreams: Noel Coward and Gertie Lawrence. Eccentric dowagers and rakish gigolos and steamer trunks stuffed with stowaways . . .

Romantic self-delusion, all of it. Like his hope for a lover, really. A futile, if harmless, fantasy that did little more than distract him from the imperturbable, central fact of his life: He was alone in this world. And he would always be alone.

Some people – the happy ones, probably – could deal with that knowledge the way they dealt with the weather. They skimmed along the surface of life exulting in their self-sufficiency, and because of it, they were *never* alone. Michael knew about those people, for he had tried to mimic them.

The ruse, however, rarely worked. The hunger always showed in his eyes.

Back in the stateroom, he smoked a joint and worked up the nerve to push the steward's button on the telephone. The steward appeared five minutes later.

'Yes, sir?'

'Hi, George.'

'Good evening, Mr Tolliver. What can I do for you?'

'Yes. Well, I'd like . . . I mean, if you don't mind . . .' He reached for his wallet. 'George, I'd like you to have this.' He handed the steward a ten-dollar bill.

'Very kind, sir.'

'George, would you . . . ? I understand it's possible for you to make arrangements . . . Do you think you could bring me some ice cream?'

'Certainly, sir. What flavor?'

77

'I don't . . . Chocolate, I guess.'

The steward smiled, pocketing the bill. 'One of those late-night cravings, eh?'

'Yeah,' said Michael. 'The worst.'

Vita saves the day

The artifacts of DeDe's maidenhood still haunted her old bedroom at Halcyon Hill. A tattered Beatles poster. A Steiff giraffe from F. A. O. Schwarz. A swizzle stick from the Tonga Room. A jar of dried rose petals from Cotillion days.

Nothing had been altered, nothing touched, as if the occupant of this artless little pink-and-green room had perished in a plane crash, and a grieving, obsessive survivor had preserved it as a shrine for posterity.

In a way, of course, she had died.

In Mother's eyes, at least.

'Darling, I'm sorry. None of it makes any sense to me.'

'It's between me and Beauchamp, Mother.'

'I could help, if you'd just let me.'

'No, you can't. Nobody can.'

'I'm your *mother*, darling. Surely there's—'

'Just drop it.'

'Have you told Binky?'

DeDe's anger rose. 'What the hell's that got to do with it?'

'I just wondered.'

'You just wondered if any of those leathery old bitches at the Francesca Club are gonna be gossiping about your precious, darling daughter!'

'DeDe!'

'You think the separation's gonna hit Carson Callas's

78

column tomorrow, and you won't be able to hold your head up at the Cow Hollow Inn. Well, too bad, Mother! Too goddamn bad!'

Frannie Halcyon sat on the edge of her daughter's bed and stared numbly at the wall. 'I've never heard you talk this way, DeDe.'

'No. I guess not.'

'Is it the pregnancy? Sometimes that can—'

'No.'

'You ought to be radiant, darling. When I was expecting you, I felt so—'

'Mother, please don't start on this again.'

'But why *now*, darling? Why would you leave Beauchamp only *weeks* before—'

'Look, I can't help it. I can't help it if I don't feel radiant. I can't help a goddamn thing about Beauchamp. I'm having the babies. I want them. Isn't that enough, Mother?'

Frannie's brow wrinkled. 'Why on earth shouldn't you want them?'

Silence.

'DeDe?'

'I've got a headache, Mother.'

Frannie sighed, kissed her on the cheek and stood up. 'I love you, but you don't seem like my child anymore. I think I know . . . how Catherine Hearst must feel.'

The matriarch of Halcyon Hill was mixing a Mai Tai when the phone rang.

'Mrs Halcyon?'

'Yes.'

'My name is Helena Parrish. I was referred to you by Vita Keating.'

Frannie braced herself for another well-bred pitch to join the board of another museum. 'Oh . . . yes,' she said cautiously.

'I'll get straight to the point, Mrs Halcyon. I have

79

been asked to approach you concerning your interest in affiliating with Pinus.'

Frannie wasn't sure she had heard right.

'You're not familiar with us, perhaps?'

'No, I . . . Well, of course, I've *heard* of . . . Excuse me, if this is one of Vita's jokes, I don't think it's . . .'

The caller chuckled throatily. 'It's no joke, Mrs Halcyon.'

'I . . . I see.'

'Do you suppose we could get together for a little chat sometime soon?'

'Yes. Well, of course.'

'How's tomorrow?'

'Fine. Uh . . . shall we meet somewhere for lunch?'

'Actually, we prefer to keep a lower profile. May I call on you at Halcyon Hill?'

'Certainly. When?'

'Oh . . . twoish?'

'Lovely.'

'Good. Ta-ta, then.'

'Ta-ta,' said Frannie, feeling her heart rise to her throat.

Looking for a lady

Brian spent the morning in Washington Square, sunning his body for a person who would probably never know the difference. As he trudged back up Union Street to Barbary Lane, he suddenly decided that it was time to confront his fantasy face to face.

He turned off Union at Leavenworth and walked a block up the hill to Green Street, where the Superman Building shimmered magically in the sunshine.

Up close, its modern hieroglyphics seemed to take a kind of mystical significance, as if they themselves concealed the secret identity of Lady Eleven.

As Brian approached, a Luxor cab deposited a passenger on the sidewalk. An LOL. And she was headed for the door of the Superman Building.

'Excuse me, ma'am?'

'Yes?'

'I'm looking for a friend of mine who lives here. It's kind of embarrassing, actually. I've forgotten her name. She lives on the eleventh floor. She's about my age, with longish hair and—'

The old woman's face slammed shut on him. Brian was certain she carried Mace in her purse. 'The names are by the buzzers,' she snarled.

'Oh. Yes, I see.'

He walked to the buzzers, feeling the woman's eyes on him all the time. He stood there for a moment, pretending to survey the names. Then he turned around and faced his white-gloved accuser.

'I'm not a rapist, lady.'

The old woman glared at him, drew herself up and stormed into the building. She spoke several words to the security guard, who turned and studied Brian, then said something to the LOL.

Brian continued to scan the names, hoping his nonchalance didn't appear too hoky. He was burning with guilt and hated himself for it.

There were six names listed on the eleventh floor: Jenkins, Lee, Mosely, Patterson, Fuentes and Matsumoto. A big goddamn help.

Maybe if he left a note with the guard . . . No, the asshole was already giving him the evil eye. And there was no *way* he could lurk around the lobby until Lady Eleven showed up. On the other hand, if he . . .

'Can I help you?' The guard had moved in. Trying his damnedest to look like Karl Malden.

'Well, I'm looking for a young woman.'

The guard's expression said: I'll just *bet* you are, sonny boy.

'Forget it,' said Brian.

He would see her in twelve hours, anyway.

He reversed his course again and headed back down Union Street to La Contadina. He needed a glass of wine to steady his nerves. Sometimes a fascist in uniform could screw up your whole day.

When he reached the restaurant, an outlandish figure waved at him from a huge, thronelike chair by the window. It was Mrs Madrigal, decked out in a paisley turban, blue eye shadow and harem pajamas. She beckoned him in.

'Will you join me?'

'Sure,' he said, sitting down across from her. He felt slightly out of sync in his gym shorts and sweat shirt. Mrs Madrigal herself seemed somewhat frayed around the edges.

'Brian . . . you haven't seen Mona, have you?'

'No. Not for a week or so.'

'I'm worried. She left me a note when Mary Ann and Michael left, saying she'd be gone for a while, but I haven't heard a word since. I thought maybe you . . . Nothing, huh?'

Brian shook his head. 'Sorry.'

The landlady fidgeted with her turban. 'She can be . . . quite foolish sometimes.'

'I don't know her that well. How long has she been at the house?'

'Oh . . . well over three years. Brian, has she ever . . . talked to you about me?'

He thought for a moment. 'Never. Why?'

'I'm afraid I've been a little foolish myself. I just hope it's not too late.'

'I don't . . .'

'Mona is my daughter, Brian.'

Her tenants, thought Brian, are always her 'children.' He smiled understandingly. 'You must be very close to her.'

'No, Brian. I mean she's my *real* daughter.'

His jaw went slack. 'Your . . . Does Mona know that?'

'No.'

'I thought she said her mother lived in—'

'I'm not her mother, Brian. I'm her father.'

Before he could utter a word, she pressed a finger against her lips, signaling him to remain silent. 'We can talk about it back at the house,' she whispered.

Company's coming

There was something eerie about the sudden change of mood at the Blue Moon Lodge. Mona sensed it immediately, watching the tension mount as Mother Mucca mobilized her girls for the arrival of the big customer from Sacramento.

'Bobbi, you get the 409 outa the kitchen and clean the crapper in Charlene's room. It looks like a god-damn truck stop! Marnie, you straighten up the parlor. Get rid o' those movie magazines. Bonnie, you and Debby take the Ranchero into town and pick up that costume at the Chinaman's. Wouldn't ya know it! He shows up here the only goddamn week of the year we sent the costume to the cleaners!'

Mona kept clear of the eye of the storm, wanting to help but certain she'd only be in the way. Observing her discomfort, Charlene winked and handed her a dustcloth. 'Crazy, huh?'

Mona nodded. 'Who is this guy, anyway?'

'I . . . You better talk to Mother Mucca first.'

'Where do you want me to dust?' *Well, Mona, you stumped the panel! Arlene, Bennett, I think you'll be surprised to learn that the lovely Miss Ramsey . . . dusts whorehouses for a living!*

'Over behind the bar. And that Kennedy statue on the TV.'

'OK Charlene?'

'Yeah?'

'Mother Mucca said he wanted a new girl. Is she gonna trade with another house or something?'

Charlene continued to dust. 'Yeah. I guess she could.'

'You mean . . . she's never done that before?'

'He's never asked for a new girl before.'

'Oh. Well, then, how come she's not—'

'Don't talk so much. We're wastin' time.'

Moments later, Mother Mucca charged into the parlor, saw Mona at work, and snapped at the head girl. 'Charlene! What's Judy doin' cleanin' for?'

'Well, you said for everybody to—'

'Judy is my receptionist, Charlene! She ain't got no business dustin'—'

Mona interrupted. 'Really, Mother Mucca, I don't mind helping out a—'

'Course you don't, Judy. But it just ain't fittin' for you to be doin' housework, when I hired you as a receptionist.'

Mona shrugged at this breach of protocol and smiled her apologies to Charlene, who frowned and skulked off.

'C'mon,' said Mother Mucca, taking Mona's arm. 'We'll have a nice big glass of milk in the kitchen.'

The old woman's request hit like a sledge hammer.

'What?' gasped Mona, almost choking on her milk.

'He's a piece o' cake,' said Mother Mucca.

'Well, let *them* eat cake! I'm a receptionist, remember?'

'I'll pay you extra, Judy.'

'You've gotta be . . . Oh, no . . . Ohhh, no. Got that? *No!*'

Mother Mucca reached across the table and grasped

Mona's hand. 'He wants somebody with class, Judy. Nobody in Winnemucca's got your kind of class.'

'Thanks a lot.'

'You don't have to fuck him.'

That threw her. 'Well, what the hell does he . . . ? Never mind. Spare me the gory details.'

'Judy, do you think ol' Mother Mucca would . . . ? Judy, you're like my own flesh and blood. I wouldn't do nothin' to make you think less o' yourself. I swear, it hurts me a heap to think . . .'

The old woman let go of Mona's hand and fumbled in her grizzled cleavage for a hanky. Turning away, she dabbed at her eyes.

Mona was shaken. 'Mother Mucca, look . . .'

'You *hurt* me, child!'

'I didn't mean to.'

'I'll tell you the God's honest truth. I've been runnin' this place for sixty years, and you're the first girl I've ever felt was . . . Judy, I'd adopt you, if you'd let me.'

This time Mona reached for the madam's hand. 'You've been really good to me, Mother . . .'

'Did you know I used to have a little boy?'

'No.'

'I did. He was the sweetest little thing you ever laid eyes on. He used to sit right here on this floor and jus' laugh and giggle, and me and the girls, we'd do anything for that little tyke, and I never thought . . .'

'Please don't cry.'

'I never thought in a million years that little darlin' would run off an' leave his mama when he was sixteen. I never thought nothin' like that. I trusted him, Judy, jus' like I trust . . .'

She silenced herself when Bonnie and Debby appeared with the important bundle from the laundry.

'Take it away,' ordered Mother Mucca.

Bonnie frowned. 'But didn't you say . . . ?'

'Take the goddamn thing away!'

'Wait a minute,' said Mona. 'I have to see if it fits OK.'

Mother Mucca stared at Mona for several seconds, dabbed her eyes, and grinned. 'You're an angel, dolly.'

'And you're full of shit,' said Mona.

This year's song

'This is nice,' said Mary Ann, sipping a Pina Colada in the Starlight Lounge of the *Pacific Princess*, while a pianist played 'I Write the Songs.' Burke answered with a nod, smiling at her.

'Michael says this song is this year's "What I Did for Love."'

'I don't get it.'

'Well, you know. Like every year there's a song that *everybody* records. Two years ago it was "Send in the Clowns" – or was it three? Anyway, last year it was "What I Did for Love," which I really like, even though they do play it to death. I mean . . . if a song is good, I don't see what's wrong with playing it a lot, do you?'

'No. I guess not.'

'I think "What I Did for Love" is probably my all-time favorite. At least . . . well, it's the only one on the album that you can hum. Not that that's all that important, but . . . well, I mean, who can hum "The Music and the Mirror"?'

'You've got me there. I don't even know what *album* you're talking about.'

'You know. *Chorus Line.*'

He shook his head. 'Sorry.'

'The musical, Burke. It came to San Francisco.'

'I told you I was out of it.'

Mary Ann shrugged, but she was inwardly relieved. He *couldn't* be gay if he'd never heard of *A Chorus*

Line. She decided to change the subject. Burke seemed uncomfortable with popular music.

'How long did you live in San Francisco, Burke?'

'Not long, really. Actually, I consider Nantucket my home.'

'You work there?' She felt that was more tactful than 'What do you do?' Nine months in San Francisco had programmed that question out of her system forever.

'Sort of. My father's in publishing. I help him out sometimes.'

'Oh, what fun!' Was *that* ever gushy! Why was this conversation such a dud?

'Mary Ann, let's get some air, OK?'

Out on the fantail, they leaned against the rail and watched the moon rise above a calm sea. As usual, she was the one to break the silence.

'I talk too much, don't I?'

He slipped his arm around her shoulder. 'Not at all.'

'Yes, I do. I won the Optimist Oratory Contest in high school, and I haven't stopped talking since.'

He laughed. 'I'm afraid you're holding up both ends of the conversation.'

She let that go, turning to face the water again. 'Do you know what blew me away this morning?'

'What?'

'The lifeboat drill . . . what the captain said. I didn't know that women and children don't get to go first anymore.'

'Yeah. Things have changed, I guess.'

'I wish they wouldn't.'

He answered by squeezing her shoulder.

'I mean, it isn't a bit fair. The song says it's still the same old story, but it isn't, is it? Who the hell gets to be Ingrid Bergman anymore?'

'Now *that's* one I know.' He chuckled.

'How old are you, Burke?'

'Twenty-seven.'

'You seem – I don't know – not *older* exactly, but more . . . It's hard to explain. You seem like you're twenty-seven, but someone who was twenty-seven a long time ago.'

'Out of it, in other words.'

'Why do you keep saying that? I *like* it, Burke. I really do.'

He leaned down and kissed her lightly on the mouth. 'I like *you*.'

'Do you?' she asked.

'Yes. Very much, Mary Ann.'

'Ingrid,' she said, and kissed him back.

Family planning

Under the fluorescent lights of the Doggie Diner, the crags and craters of Bruno Koski's face assumed lunar proportions. The corners of his mouth, Beauchamp noticed, were hydrophobic with mayonnaise.

'Now, lemme get this straight, man. You don't want her greased, you just—'

'Keep your voice down, Bruno!'

Bruno shrugged and cast a contemptuous glance around the diner.

'They're all space cadets, man. They ain't listenin'.'

'You don't know that.'

'I know a fuckin' space cadet when I see one.'

This was true. Bruno did know his space cadets. Beauchamp looked down at his hamburger. 'OK. I didn't mean to . . . Look, I'm just jumpy. I've never done this before.'

'So tell me what the fuck you want, man.'

Beauchamp kept his head down, laboriously removing the onions from his hamburger. 'I want you to . . . see to it that she doesn't have the baby – the babies.'

Bruno blinked at him ingenuously. 'You want me to kick her gut in?'

'I don't want you to hurt her, Bruno.'

'OK. You want me to kick her gut in without hurting her.'

'Your tone is shitty, Bruno.'

'Oh, kiss my ass!'

'Look: she's my wife, right? I don't want her – I don't want any permanent harm done. If you can't promise me that, we might as well forget the whole thing.'

'How the fuck do you expect me to guarantee . . . ? What about . . . I mean, there could be – whatchacallit? – complications.'

Beauchamp made his patient-but-piqued face, an expression that never failed to exasperate harried art directors at Halcyon Communications. 'Now, Bruno, she's seven months pregnant. It shouldn't be *that* hard to arrange for . . . an accident of some sort.'

The coke dealer stared at his client. 'Look, man—'

'On the other hand', said Beauchamp dryly, 'this may be totally out of your league.'

'Says who?'

'You seem a little hesitant. Maybe I should check with someone . . . more professional.'

Bruno sulked momentarily, then looked up. 'How much?'

'What's it worth?'

That stopped him for a moment. 'Uh . . . five thousand. Considerin' the hassle.'

'I'll give you seven. But I want it done right.'

'You know I'll subcontract it.'

'I don't care.'

'I want cash. In advance.'

'You'll get it. How soon?'

'Soon as I get somebody.'

'It has to be soon, Bruno.'

'Fuck off!'

'Bruno?'

'Huh?'

'Wipe your mouth, will you?'

Fifteen minutes later, Beauchamp called DeDe at Halcyon Hill. Her voice was expressionless, a telltale defense against the uncertainties of their day-old separation.

'Just checking on you,' he said.

'Thanks.'

'Is your mother there?'

'Yes.'

'Good. If you need anything sent out, let me know, will you?' Silence.

'OK, DeDe?'

She began to cry. 'Why are you being ... so goddamned nice?'

'I don't know. I guess I miss you.'

'Beauchamp ... I want these babies so much. I'm not trying to hurt you, I promise.'

'I know, darling. We'll give it some time, OK?'

'If I weren't so confused, I'd be a better wife. I just need . . . I want to be by myself for a while.'

'I understand.'

She sniffled, then blew her nose. 'There's a chicken pot pie in the freezer and some leftover quiche in—'

'I'll be OK.'

'Beauchamp . . . I do love you.'

'I know,' said her husband. 'I know.'

Mrs Madrigal's confession

For the first time ever, Brian declined a joint.

He wanted to be straight when he heard this.

'Once upon a time', said Mrs Madrigal, 'there was a little boy named Andy Ramsey. Andy was not a particularly extraordinary little boy, but he grew up under extraordinary circumstances: his mother was a madam. She ran a brothel called the Blue Moon Lodge, in Winnemucca, Nevada, and Andy's best friends and nursemaids were the whores who made that house their home. Perhaps for that reason – or perhaps not – Andy made a startling discovery by the time he reached puberty: There was nothing about him that felt like a boy.

'Oh, he *looked* like a boy, all right. All the appropriate plumbing was there. But he never stopped feeling like a girl, a girl locked up inside a boy's body. To his horror, that feeling intensified as Andy grew older. By the time he was sixteen, he was so frightened that he ran away from the whorehouse and hitched a ride to California.

'For a while he held body and soul together by working as a migrant laborer. Then he worked as a soda jerk in a drugstore in Salinas, then as a laborer again, this time in Modesto. Shortly after his twentieth birthday, he left Modesto for Fort Ord, where he enlisted in the Army as a private. He was a good soldier, but he stayed at Fort Ord throughout the war – World War II, that is – mostly typing munitions reports for a drunken colonel. In the long run, however, Andy hated the all-male environment of the Army as much as he had hated the all-female environment of the whorehouse. And the feeling that he was really a woman persisted through it all.

'One night, shortly after the end of the war, Andy met a pretty young woman at a dance in Monterey. She was *very* young, actually, about seventeen at the time; Andy was twenty-five. She was visiting from Minneapolis, staying at her cousin's house in Carmel. Her name was Betty Borg, and Andy was quite taken with her, in his own way. She had a perky, independent spirit that he admired, and he was relieved to discover that he was attracted to her. Even sexually.

'Betty wanted to get married and move back to Minneapolis. It was she who proposed, in fact, and Andy decided that this might be the best cure for his problem. So ... they did just that. Andy fulfilled his responsibilities as a husband by working in a bookstore in Minneapolis. A year later, a little girl was born to the couple. They named her Mona, after Andy's estranged mother back in Winnemucca.

'None of it worked. Not for Andy, anyway. He ended up leaving his wife and child – deserting them – when the child was two years old. For the next fifteen years, he virtually dropped out of sight, drifting from city to city, a miserable, self-pitying creature who had botched his own life and the lives of the people around him. All of that ended, however, when Andy was forty-four. That was when he picked up the pieces and traveled to Denmark and spent his life savings on a sex change.'

'And came back as Anna Madrigal.' It was Brian who supplied this information. More fascinated than shocked, he smiled at the landlady.

She smiled back. 'It's a nice name, don't you think? It's an anagram.'

'But if Mona is your daughter ... ? Well, I thought you said she doesn't know.'

'She doesn't. She moved to San Francisco three or four years ago, and shortly thereafter I read an item in Herb Caen's column about a Mona Ramsey working at Halcyon Communications. I knew there couldn't be *that* many Mona Ramseys in the world, so I did a little checking, and I cornered her one night at the Savoy-Tivoli.'

'And?'

'She *liked* me, if you please. So I invited her to come live at Barbary Lane. She fancies herself a bohemian, and I think she rather relished the idea of having a transsexual as a landlady.'

'She knew that, then?'

'Oh, yes. From the beginning.'

'Does your . . . your wife know where you are? Or your mother?'

Mrs Madrigal shook her head. 'They must think I'm dead.' She smiled faintly. 'Of course, Andy *is*.'

'And now you think Mona's found out you're her father and freaked out over it?'

'It's possible, don't you think?'

He smiled. 'I'm not thinking very clearly right now.'

'You poor boy!'

'I'm . . . I'm very flattered that you told me, Mrs Madrigal.'

'Good. *Now* can we smoke that joint?'

He laughed. 'The sooner the . . . Wait a minute. How can Anna Madrigal be an anagram for Andy Ramsey?'

'It's not.'

'But you said . . .'

'I said it was an anagram. I didn't say what for.'

'Then what is it?'

'My dear boy,' said the landlady, lighting a joint at last, 'you are talking to a Woman of Mystery!'

Once in a blue moon

Bobbi buzzed around Mona like a bridesmaid making last-minute adjustments to a bridal gown. 'I think you've got the headpiece on backward, Judy. Try it . . . no, the other way. There. Look how pretty that is!'

'For Christ's sake, Bobbi. It's not supposed to be *pretty*!'

'Well, you know. Anyway, you *are* pretty. You should be real proud.'

Mona managed a tiny smile. 'Stop trying to cheer me up.'

'You're gonna be the best yet, Judy. He's gonna *love* you!'

'He'd better *not*.'

Bobbi giggled, 'Don't worry. Lots of our customers are like him.'

'Like *this*?' Mona pointed to her costume.

'No, but they . . . well, they don't wanna screw you. They just want . . . like special services they can't get anywhere else. Like I had this one guy from Stockton who wanted me to wear black lace panties and sit on his knee while he dictated his will to me.'

'Sure.'

'I swear, Judy. And it took *forever*. I had to go see Dr Craig that week.'

'Why?'

Bobbi tittered. 'He said I had single-handedly turned writer's cramp into a venereal disease.'

Still wearing the costume, Mona wandered back to the parlor and took a beer out of the refrigerator behind the bar. She longed for a joint.

Charlene appeared and smirked at Mona's outfit. 'Mighty early, aren't you?'

'I don't like to be rushed.'

'He's not comin' for an hour.'

'It's OK.'

'You'll have BO.'

'Lay off, Charlene!'

'Nervous, ain't you?' Her tone was openly bitchy now. She resents me, thought Mona. It pisses her off that Mother Mucca likes me.

'I'm fine,' said Mona blandly.

'Maybe so,' said Charlene, 'but you're spillin' the beer.'

At fifteen minutes and counting, Mona sat alone in the parlor. Mother Mucca entered from the kitchen and took her place quietly at Mona's side.

'You OK?'

Mona nodded.

'It's something you can tell your grandchildren about.'

'Sure.'

The old woman put her arm gently around Mona's shoulders, taking care not to disturb the costume. 'You look . . . real fine.'

'Thanks.'

'The other girls are all in their rooms. They'll stay there till he's gone. You'll use Charlene's room, so I'll tell you when to come in. He'll be there already. You remember what to do?'

'I think so.'

Mother Mucca patted her hand. 'You'll do just fine.'

'Mother Mucca?'

'How can he . . . ? How's he getting here?'

'Oh, in a limousine.'

'A *limousine*?'

'Sure,' said Mother Mucca, tapping her head to signal a clever man. 'That way, nobody'll think it's him, see?'

The rap came on Mona's door.

'He's here,' whispered Mother Mucca.

Mona slipped out into the starry desert night. A warm breeze blew in from the north, flapping the sleeves of her habit. Mother Mucca took one last look at her new girl, readjusted her wimple and scurried back to the parlor. Then Mona opened the door of Charlene's cubicle.

The customer was seated cross-legged on the floor next to the bed. He was wearing the saffron robes of a Buddhist monk.

'Sister . . . I have sinned.'

Mona cleared her throat, 'I know, my child.'

The whip, as arranged, was lying on the bed.

Interrupted idyll

The taxi ride from Manzanillo offered little more than crumbling hamburger stands, palm-thatched shanties, and occasional burros rummaging in the roadside garbage.

Mary Ann's and Burke's destination, however, was not to be believed.

Perched airily above an azure bay, the resort of Las Hadas gleamed like an opium dream from the *Arabian Nights*. Bougainvillaea blazed electrically against white-washed walls, gargoyles peered from minarets into sun-drenched courtyards, birds sang and palms swayed.

And Mary Ann's heart took flight.

'Oh, Burke, just *look* at it!'

She didn't mean that, of course. What she meant was: Look at us.

The beach was a crescent of silvery sand with water so clear that Mary Ann could watch tiny fish darting between her legs. Burke dunked her with infantile glee, holding fast to her waist as they surfaced into the sunshine.

How long had it been since someone had done that?

How long had she waited for this smile, these eyes, this strong, simple spirit that had come to her in a world marred by greed and anxiety and computer dating? And how long, dear God, would it last?

They sunned together on their backs, fingertips touching.

'Where's Michael today?' asked Burke.

'On the ship.'

'He could have come with us, you know.'

'I think he wanted to take it easy.'

96

'I see.'

'Burke?'

'Yeah?'

'Why did you leave California?'

There was a pause, and then: 'I don't know. I guess
. . . my father and all.'

'Your father?'

'The publishing business. He needed help.'

'Were you . . . in the publishing business in San
Francisco?'

'No. I was just . . . bumming around.'

'For three years?'

He rolled onto his side, facing her, smiling slightly.
'Are you asking me how rich I am?'

It *did* sound that way, and she was horrified by her
gaffe. 'No, Burke! Really. I was just . . . Never mind.
I'm flustered, I guess.'

'Why?'

'Oh, it's just so damn typical!'

'What is?'

'You know. You meet somebody nice, and you get
along with them fabulously, so *of course* they live
three thousand miles away! It's a gyp, that's all.'

He slid closer to her and cupped his hand against her
cheek. 'Was last night a gyp?'

'No. You know that.'

He kissed the tip of her nose. 'We've got a week,
Mary Ann. Let's make the best of it, huh?'

They ate lunch overlooking the water in a garden of
manicured tropical foliage. An artificial waterfall
made lush sounds in the swimming pool behind them.

A child approached wearing a sandwich board that
announced the resort's coming events. 'How precious!'
said Mary Ann, noting his blue clown's costume and
pointy-toed court jester shoes.

But as he came closer, she made the discovery that
he wasn't a child at all.

He was a dwarf.

Embarrassed, she turned away, hoping the little man would pass up their table for a group of boisterous tourists seated near the pool. He didn't, though. He approached the young lovers with a toothy, imploring smile, holding a red rose in his outstretched hand.

Now it was unavoidable. 'Burke, have you got a peso or something for him?'

Her companion didn't answer. He was chalk white, and still as a corpse.

'Burke, is something . . . ?'

His voice was scarcely more than a whimper, a pathetic trapped-animal sound. 'Make him go,' he said.

'Burke, he's only a—'

'Please, please . . . make him go!'

The dwarf needed no encouragement. He was three tables away by the time Burke stumbled into the shrubbery and fell to his knees, vomiting. Mary Ann moved to his side and gently stroked the strawberry curls on the back of his neck.

'It's OK,' she said. 'It's OK.'

Seconds later, he straightened up and tried to regain his dignity. 'Forgive me, please. I'm really sorry. I should have . . .'

'It's OK,' she said softly. 'I can see how he might make you . . .'

Burke shook his head. 'It wasn't him, Mary Ann.'

'What?'

'It was the rose.'

Douchebag

Once a Philippine nightclub specializing in bosomy chanteuses, the Mabuhay Gardens had mutated almost overnight into San Francisco's only punk rock show-place. There, amid the dying palms and tattered rattan, Bruno Koski came off like a bona-fide heavy from an early Bogart film.

The punks and punkettes eyed him with ill-disguised envy, lusting silently after his pitted complexion, his garbanzo-bean eyes, his casual air of native degeneracy.

Bruno Koski was the real thing.

Jimmy, the stage manager, recognized him immediately. 'Hey, Bruno, what's . . . ?'

'I'm lookin' for Douchebag.'

'You know *her*?'

'Just tell me where she is, kid.'

'Over there. Next to the amplifier. The one in the garbage bag.'

Bruno glanced sullenly toward the sound equipment, avoiding the eyes of the assembled punks. Three of the punkettes were wearing Hefty bags, modified as ponchos with safety pins.

'Oh,' amended Jimmy, seeing Bruno's irritation. 'The one with the green hair.'

Bruno approached her.

'You Douchebag?'

'Yeah.' She was chewing gum viciously. Her hair, several shades lighter than the Hefty bag, was chopped off close to her scalp. She was wearing a button that said PUNK POWER.

'My name's Bruno.'

She chewed even harder. 'So?'

'So I wanna talk to you.'

'Nope. Crime is comin' on.' She nodded toward the stage, where a gang of black-leather musicians was slithering into position for its next assault on the audience.

Bruno glowered at Douchebag, but decided to humor her. He *needed* the little bitch, after all. He could put up with her for a few minutes longer.

Crime was so loud he felt his brain was bleeding.

99

The punks and punkettes turned spastic under the spell of the music, quivering like convicts in a hundred different electric chairs. The song was called 'You're So Repulsive.'

At the first break, she turned back to him. 'Outasight, huh?'

'Yeah,' he lied.

'You shoulda seen it when they had Mary Monday and the Bitches.'

'Yeah?'

'Shit, man. They thrashed the microphones and tore up the tables and the stage manager freaked out . . . and, man, it was just deee-praved!'

'Sounds like it.'

'Course, that's nothin' – I mean *nothin'* – compared to The Damned or The Nuns. I mean, that's heavy metal . . . really scuzzy stuff. Some o' that stuff makes you wanna really *puke*!'

The cud-chewing mouth became too much for him. 'Hey . . . get rid o' that stuff, will ya?'

She stared at him, unblinking, for several seconds, then removed the gum from her mouth, rolled it into a neat little ball and stuffed it up her nostril.

She didn't flinch when he outlined his proposal.

'I just . . . trash her a little bit, huh?'

'Yeah. She don't live far from here.'

'You'll gimme her schedule and all? I mean, I don't have to bust in, do I?'

'Nope. We'll arrange a time. You leave that to me, punk.'

She beamed at that. She *was* a punk now. She was earning her punk credentials for real. 'Hey, Bruno . . . like what do I get out of this?'

'What d'ya want?'

She thought for a moment. 'I wanna start my own group. We need three hundred bucks.'

'It's yours.'

'You know The Scorpions?'

'Sure.'

'It's gonna be a group like that. Only it's gonna be all chicks, and we're only gonna sing during our periods, so that we can *really* gross people out when we—'

'Hey, punk . . . OK, OK!'

Douchebag's mouth curled. 'Shit, man! I can't *wait* till I'm thirteen!'

A changed man

Brian was on his way out the door when the phone rang in the little house on the roof.

'Yeah?'

'Hey! What's happenin'?'

It had to be Chip Hardesty. Chip Hardesty would ask 'What's happenin'?' at his grandmother's funeral. He lived in Larkspur, but his home was barely distinguishable from his Northpoint office. Both had Boston ferns, Watney's Ale mirrors and basket chairs suspended from chains. He didn't particularly get off on being a dentist.

'Not much,' answered Brian. For the first time in years, he was lying through his teeth.

'Bitchin'! I've got a plan.'

'Yeah,' said Brian noncommittally. Chip's last plan had involved a case of Cold Duck, a rental cabin at Tahoe and two sure-thing dental receptionist students from the Bryman School. One of these women – Chip's, of course – had been a dead ringer for Olivia Newton-John.

Brian's date had been uncomfortably suggestive of Amy Carter and had loped along at a strange angle in an effort to compensate for a left breast she felt to be smaller than her right.

101

'Are you working tonight?' asked Chip.

'Afraid so.'

'What time you get off?'

'Eleven.'

'OK. Listen. You remember Jennifer Rabinowitz?'

'Nope.'

'OK. Huge knockers, right? Works at The Cannery. Pierced nose—'

'Barfed at the Tarr and Feathers sing-along.'

'Says who?'

'Says me. The barfee.'

'You never told me that.'

'Sorry. I should have mentioned it on my Christmas card.'

A hurt silence followed. Then: 'I'm doin' you a favor, man. You can take it or leave it.'

'Go ahead. I'm listening.'

'OK. Jennifer's got this friend—'

'Makes her own clothes. Great personality. All the girls in the dorm just love—'

'What the hell's wrong with you, man?'

'I'll be out of it, Chip. Better count me out.'

'What's that mean? Out of it.'

'Beat. Exhausted. Eleven o'clock's a little late for—'

'Christ! You haven't crashed before two in five years!'

'Well, maybe I'm getting old, then.'

'Yeah. Maybe you are.'

'Chip?'

'Yeah?'

'Go spray your hair, will ya?'

As a matter of fact, he wasn't a bit tired when he finished with his last customer at Perry's. He felt vigorous, exhilarated, as spirited as a fourteen-year-old about to lock himself in the bathroom with a copy of *Fanny Hill*. Lady Eleven was the best thing that had happened to him in years.

Later, as he climbed out of the shower, he acknowledged the fact that he felt a strong sense of fidelity toward the siren in the Superman Building. She *belonged* to him, in the purest, most satisfying sense of the word. And he belonged to her. If only for half an hour.

He had met an equal, at last.

Love on a rooftop

The Hampton-Giddes were the first to arrive from the ballet. 'Fabulous latticework,' gushed Archibald Anson Gidde, appraising his host's new rooftop deck.

Peter Cipriani nodded. 'I found this *gorgeous* twink carpenter in the Mission. Dirt cheap and pecs that won't quit. Jason something-or-other.'

'They're *all* called Jason, aren't they?'

Peter snickered. 'Or Jonathan.'

'Was his ear pierced?'

'Nope. But he wore cut-offs to *die*. And knee socks with Lands End come-fuck-me boots. He was hot.'

'How is he with kitchens?'

'Who knows? I can only speak for bedrooms, my dear.'

'Ooooh,' said Archibald Anson Gidde.

Minutes before midnight, the deck was crowded with A-Gays, tastefully atwitter over glissades and pirouettes. Charles Hillary Lord lifted a spade of cocaine to Archibald Anson Gidde's nostril.

'I talked to Nicky today.'

Arch inhaled the powder noisily. 'And?'

'I think he's going in on it.'

'Good,' said Arch indifferently. 'That should help you a lot.'

'We don't need *help*, Arch. It's a sure thing. I just want you in on the ground floor.'

'Then you won't be hurt if I say no.'

Chuck Lord sighed dramatically and swept his arm over the rooftops of Russian Hill. 'Arch . . . do you have any idea at all how many faggots are out there?'

'Just a sec. I'll check my address book.'

'There are – and this is conservatively speaking – one hundred and twenty thousand practicing homosexuals within the city limits of San Francisco.'

'And practice *does* make perfect.'

'Those one hundred and twenty thousand homosexuals are going to grow old together, Arch. Some of them may go back to Kansas or wherever the hell they ran away from, but most of them are gonna stay right here in Shangri-la, cruising each other until it's pacemaker time.'

'I need a Valium.'

'Goddammit, Arch, don't you see? *We're* OK. We've got houses and cars and trust funds and enough . . . assets to pay for Dial-a-Model until we're a hundred and two, if we want to. It's those fuckers on food stamps and ATD, selling crap at the flea market and painting houses in the Haight, who're gonna need this when the time comes.'

Arch's face grew serious. 'Doesn't that smack of exploitation to you, Chuck?'

'Oh, for God's sake! *Somebody's* gonna do it! You know that, Arch. Why shouldn't we be the first?'

'I don't know. It just seems . . . risky.'

'Risky? Arch, it's social history! It's *Wall Street Journal* stuff! Think of it! The first gay nursing home in the history of the world!'

Arch Gidde turned and looked at the city. 'Gimme some time, OK?'

Chuck flung an arm over his shoulder and adopted a more affectionate tone. 'Nicky's even thought of a name.'

'What?'

'The Last Roundup.'

'Oh, for God's . . .'

'Don't you see? A tasteful butch Western motif, with barn siding in the rooms and little chuckwagons for the food—'

'Let's not forget the denim colostomy bags.'

Chuck glared at him. 'You joke, but I *know* you see the profit in this!'

Silence.

'Look, Arch: it's very civilized, in a way. I mean, we could have a steam room and everything. The orderlies could be Colt Models!'

'That's always nice to know when they're carrying you to the toilet. Look, Chuck, everybody's different. This is *your* fantasy. What are you gonna do with, like, the drag queens?'

'We could – I don't know – we could have a separate wing.'

'And Helen Hayes look-alike contests?'

'Well, I don't see any reason why—'

He was cut short by Peter Cipriani, shouting excitedly to his guests.

'OK, don't crowd. One at a time, gentlemen, one at a time.' He handed a pair of binoculars to Rick Hampton, who aimed them in a northerly direction.

'Which building?' asked Rick.

'The shingled one. On Barbary Lane. That little house on the roof, see?'

'Yeah, but I don't—'

'The right window.'

'Jesus Christ!'

'What?' asked Arch, as the others crowded around.

'Oh, Jesus, look what he's—'

'What's he doing?' shrieked Arch.

'Wait your turn, Mary. Oh, Jesus, I can't *buhleeve* . . . How long has this been going on, Peter?'

'A couple of weeks, at least. There's a woman he's watching in that white building.'

'He's *straight*?'

'Apparently.'

'He *can't* be! Straight people don't have bodies like that!'

'Lemme see!' said Arch.

The slumber party

Back in her own cubicle, Mona sat perfectly still on the bed and performed the only rite of exorcism she knew:

She recited her mantra.

It wasn't that she felt guilty, really. Or even embarrassed. She had kept her agreement and she could live with that. She had pleased the client. She had pleased Mother Mucca. She had been flawlessly seventies about the whole fucking thing.

It wasn't shame, then, that consumed her. It was . . . nothing. She felt nothing at all, and it scared the hell out of her. The yawning Black Hole of her existence had reached seismic proportions, and she was perilously near the abyss. If she did not keep running, if she did not keep changing, the random and monstrous irrationality of the universe would swallow her alive.

'Knock, knock.'

Silence.

'Knock, knock.'

'Yeah, Bobbi?'

The child-whore peered in, cautiously. She waved a cellophane package through the door, like a vampire-killer brandishing a crucifix. 'I've got some Oreos. Wanna help me eat 'em?'

'I don't think so, Bobbi.'

A pause, and then: 'You feelin' OK, Judy?'

'Why shouldn't I? *He's* the one who's smarting.'

106

Bobbi giggled and shook the package again. 'Don't you want just a *few*?'

'You don't lick the centers, do you?'

'No. I hate that.'

'Me too.'

'My mother wouldn't let me have 'em if I licked the centers.'

Mona smiled. Mothers were good for something, anyway. So what if we ended up turning S & M tricks in a Winnemucca whorehouse? We *always* remembered not to lick the centers out of Oreos, not to sit with our legs apart, not to point at people or scratch ourselves when we itched.

'How 'bout it?' Bobbi persisted.

'Sure,' said Mona. 'Why not?'

Hopping onto the bed with unsuppressed glee, Bobbi tore into the package of cookies. 'So', she said, offering one to Mona, 'what did you think of him?'

Mona deadpanned. 'Beats me.'

Bobbi missed it. 'I think he's real handsome.'

'Bobbi . . . I don't wanna talk about it, OK?'

'Sure. Sorry.'

Bobbi drew her knees up under her chin, hugging them. She munched meditatively on an Oreo as if she were checking its vintage. Then she studied Mona soulfully.

'You know what, Judy?'

'What?'

'You're my best friend.'

Silence.

'Cross my heart, Judy.'

'Well, that's . . . Thank you.'

'Could I stay tonight?'

'Here?'

Bobbi nodded. 'It would be like a slumber party or something.'

'Bobbi, I don't think . . .'

'I'm not a lesbo, Judy.'

Mona smiled. 'What if *I* am?'

Bobbi looked startled at first, then amused. 'No way,' she laughed. 'Not you.'

Mona laughed with her, despite the implicit deception involved. D'orothea, after all, was long gone from her life. In Mona's eyes, lesbianism had simply been the logical follow-up to macrobiotics and primal screaming. She had gotten into it, but seldom off on it, and *never* behind it.

She took an Oreo from Bobbi and split it apart. 'How can we have a slumber party without a stack of 45's and a record player?'

'I know some ghost stories.'

Mona grinned. 'We could do our toenails.'

'I did mine yesterday.'

'Oh, well, then we could—'

'Lick the centers out of Oreos!' They squealed in unison as Mona held up a cookie with the creamy filling exposed. Bobbi held her tongue out expectantly. 'We need milk,' Mona blurted, dropping the Oreo in Bobbi's hand and springing from the bed.

She avoided the parlor, where she could hear Mother Mucca lining up four of the girls for a pair of drunken truckers. She entered the kitchen from the back door, fumbled for the light switch and made her way to the refrigerator. There was half a quart of milk on the top shelf.

A pitcher would be nice, she decided. They could pour each other milk from a pitcher. Bobbi would like that.

She found one on the shelf over the stove, a pale green Depression-ware piece that would fetch a small fortune in a San Francisco antique shop.

As she reached for it, her hand brushed past a row of tattered cookbooks, knocking one to the floor. She bent over to pick it up. The name on the flyleaf filled her with instant terror.

Mona Ramsey.

Temper, temper

Two days before the *Pacific Princess* was scheduled to arrive in Acapulco, Michael awoke to find himself alone in his stateroom. Mary Ann's bed was still made. Eager for a play-by-play, he showered hurriedly and raced down to breakfast on the Aloha Deck.

Mary Ann was already seated, as were Arnold and Melba Littlefield, resplendent in matching denim pantsuits. Arnold's outfit was embroidered with rainbows; Melba's had butterflies. God help us, thought Michael. The Summer of Love is alive and well in Dublin.

'Well,' thundered Arnold, as Michael sat down, 'don't you two *ever* make it to chow at the same time?'

Mary Ann flushed, casting a nervous glance at her lapsed roommate.

Michael turned elfin. 'The little woman's probably worked up one hell of an appetite.'

Mary Ann kicked him under the table.

Arnold chuckled knowingly and winked at Michael.

Melba, as usual, looked puzzled. 'Out boogying all night?' Melba was abnormally fond of words like 'boogy,' 'rap' and 'rip-off,' a vocabulary Michael was certain she had picked up from *People* magazine.

'Boogying?' He might as well have fun with it.

'You know. Dancing. Didn't they set up a disco in the Skaal Bar?'

'Oh, yeah. I forgot. I hit the sack early. With Christopher Isherwood.'

Mary Ann was squirming. 'Mouse, you haven't ordered yet.'

'Wait a minute,' said Arnold, addressing Michael. 'Run that one by me again.'

'It's a book,' said Mary Ann.

Michael nodded. '*Christopher and His Kind.*'

'Mouse . . . I think the steward . . .'

'What's it about?' asked Arnold.

'He wrote *Cabaret*,' said Mary Ann.

'About krauts, huh?'

'You bet,' said Michael.

'They have blueberry pancakes today, Mouse.'

Melba sighed. 'Isn't Liza Minnelli just *darling*!'

'OK,' said Michael, as soon as they had left the dining room. 'Gimme the dirt.'

Mary Ann sulked.

'C'mon. Did he ravish you on the poop deck?'

Silence.

'Brutalize you in the bilge? Suck your toes? Buy you a cup of coffee?'

'Mouse, you *ruined* breakfast for me!'

'You could have asked Burke to join you.'

'Right. And play footsy with him while you're telling Arnold and Melba snappy stories about the little woman?'

'Hey, look: the young marrieds routine was your idea, remember?'

'Lower your voice.'

'Lower your own goddamn voice! What the hell do you think I am, anyway? Rent-a-Hubby?'

Mary Ann glared at him for a split second, groaned in exasperation, and strode past him down the passageway. Michael cooled off on the Promenade Deck, walking laps under the lifeboats until his thoughts were clear. Fifteen minutes later he returned to the stateroom.

Mary Ann was seated at the desk, writing postcards. She didn't turn around.

'Guess what?' said Michael.

'What?' She had drained her voice of expression.

'I'm jealous.'

'Mouse, don't—'

'I am. I'm one jealous little queen. I'm jealous of Burke because he's taken away my playmate, and I'm jealous of you because you've found a lover.'

Mary Ann turned around with tears in her eyes.

'You'll find somebody, Mouse. I know you will. Maybe even in Acapulco.'

'Maybe this time, huh?'

She smiled and hugged him, holding him tight. 'I love you for that, Michael Mouse.'

'What?'

'Turning everything into song lyrics.'

'Yeah,' said Michael. 'Isn't Liza Minnelli just *darling*?'

Later, it was her turn to apologize. 'I've been crabby too, Mouse. I mean . . . well, I'm a little edgy, I guess.'

'About what?'

She hesitated, then said: 'Burke.'

'He wasn't . . . ?'

'He's perfect, Mouse. He's sensitive, strong, considerate. We're – you know – sexually whatever. He's protective, yet he treats me like an equal. He doesn't crack his knuckles. He's perfect.'

'But not perfect?'

'He's afraid of roses, Mouse.'

'Uh . . . pardon me?'

'This dwarf at Las Hadas tried to give us a rose and Burke took one look at it, turned white and threw up in the bushes.'

'Maybe he's from Pasadena.'

'It worries me, Mouse. That's not normal, is it?'

'You're asking *me*?'

'I tried to talk to him about it, and he changed the subject. I don't think he has the slightest idea why he reacted that way.'

111

Everything about Helena Parrish was smart but safe. She wore a navy blue fedora, a navy blue Mollie Parnis suit, and navy blue, medium-height, T-strap calf shoes from Magnin's. She looked, to Frannie, like the kind of woman who would *never* miss a Wednesday night travelogue at the Century Club.

'More tea?' asked Frannie, wondering where her guest had her hair streaked so beautifully.

'No thanks,' smiled Helena Parrish, dabbing her lips with a linen napkin.

'Bourbon balls?'

'No. They're lovely, though. May I call you Frannie, by the way?'

'Of course.'

'How much do you know about Pinus, Frannie?'

The hostess flushed, startled by this abrupt approach to the subject. 'Oh . . . well, most of it's just hearsay, I suppose.' Discretion seemed wise at this point. Helena could do the talking.

The visitor nodded solemnly. 'Word-of-mouth, we find, is our best safeguard.' She smiled thinly. 'Discrimination seems to be a nasty word these days, doesn't it?'

'Isn't it dreadful?'

'We prefer to think of it as quality control. And of course, the less publicity we receive, the more we're able to . . . cater to the needs of our members.'

'I understand.'

'Aside from the social criteria, the only other requirement for membership is the attainment of one's sixtieth birthday.' She spoke the last two words in a stage whisper, as if to apologize for an embarrassing, if necessary, invasion of privacy.

Frannie's smile was sheepish. 'Your timing is close to perfect.'

'I know,' said Helena.

'Vita?'

Helena nodded and continued. 'Our philosophy is that women of our mature station in life are entitled to carve out any lifestyle we can afford. We have, after all, played by the rules for forty years. Raising children, tolerating husbands, joining the right clubs, supporting the correct charities.' She leaned forward and looked Frannie straight in the eye. 'We have paid our dues, Frannie, and we will *not* piddle away the rest of our days as long-suffering Mary Worths!'

Frannie was mesmerized. Helena Parrish had begun to assume the aura of a guru.

'There *are* alternatives, of course. Pinus is not the only solution. It's simply the only *fulfilling* one. And if we have the money for it, why on earth should we squander it on face-lifts and body tucks and youth injections?

'Fortunately,' continued Helena, 'people like us can afford to indulge in this sort of . . . luxury. And what's wrong with that? What's wrong with demanding our piece of the pleasure pie?'

She handed Frannie a brochure. It was printed in brown ink on heavy cream stock with hand-torn edges. There were, of course, no pictures.

PINUS
For gentlewomen who are 60. And Ready.

Nestled snugly in the rolling hills of
Sonoma, Pinus is unquestionably the most
remarkable resort of its kind in the
world. Resort, perhaps, is an ill-
chosen word, for Pinus is a Way of Life.
Pinus is a Flight of Fancy, a mature
woman's idyll, a Dream of Wild Abandon.
Once you have experienced Pinus, nothing
is quite the same again.

'I'll leave it with you,' Helena said quietly. 'I'm sure you'd like to mull over it alone.'

'Yes. Thank you.'

'As you may know, Frannie, admission depends ultimately on our board of directors. In your case, however, I'm sure there won't be any . . .' She finished the sentence with a little wave of her hand. Frannie's social acceptability had never been at issue.

'The decision is yours to make, Frannie. If you feel you're ready, please give me a call at Pinus. The number's on the brochure.'

'Thank you. Uh . . . Helena, when would I . . . how soon?'

'On your birthday, if you like.' The visitor smiled cordially. 'We even provide a *very* interesting cake.'

'What fun.'

'Yes,' said Helena. 'It's about time, isn't it?'

Mona times two

In a house with ten bedrooms, Mona had never expected to encounter the biggest shocker in the kitchen. But there she stood – immobilized by fear – *reading her own name on the flyleaf of a cookbook.*

Her own name! Why? Why?

She dropped the book and lunged at the others, already certain of what she would find. *Mona Ramsey . . . Mona Ramsey . . . Mona Ramsey!* All of them the same, all of them inscribed in the halting, primitive hand of a child – or perhaps a semi-literate adult.

A flashback. That was it. This was the LSD flashback they had warned her about. She sank into a chair, moaning softly, waiting with patient resignation for large purple caterpillars to crawl up out of the sink drains.

114

Minutes passed. No caterpillars. Only the distant, pervasive whine of the desert wind and the insistent drip of the faucet. Out in the parlor, a trucker was laughing raucously with Marnie, who kept saying, 'Gross me out! Gross me out!' in her tinny Modesto accent.

Rising on wobbly legs, Mona went to the sink and doused herself with water. Then she blotted her face with a JFK-Bobby Kennedy-Martin Luther King dish towel and lurched through the back door into the blackness.

She counted the doors from the end of the building until she found the one that was hers.

The light was still on.

Bobbi looked up with a smile. 'No milk, huh?'

'No.'

'I think there're some Dr Peppers in the bar, if you . . . Judy, what's the matter?'

'I don't know.' Mona sank to the edge of the bed and stared glassily at the Autograph Hound the room's former occupant had left on the vanity.

'Bobbi . . . what's my name?'

'Huh?'

'What's my name?'

'Are you . . . ?'

'Please, answer.'

'It's Judy.'

'Judy what?'

'I don't know. You never told me.'

'If I . . . if I had another name, and you knew about it, would you tell me so? Or would you tease me about it, Bobbi? Do you think Charlene would . . . ?' She couldn't finish. It was all so paranoid. If Charlene wanted to torment her about her real name, why the hell would she write it in a goddamn cookbook?

Bobbi smiled forgivingly. 'Lots of us have fake names, Judy. Marnie's real name is Esther. I don't give a hoot if your name isn't—'

115

'How long have you worked here, Bobbi?'

'Off and on?'

Was there any other way to work at a whorehouse?

'Yeah.'

'Oh, I guess . . . three years.'

'You've known a lot of the girls who've been through here, then?'

'Sure.' Bobbi popped a stick of Dentyne into her mouth and chewed it soberly, suddenly aware that she was being interrogated.

'Do you remember one called Mona?'

The chewing continued. If the name had jolted Bobbi, the expression on her face didn't betray it. 'Mona, huh?'

'Yeah.'

Bobbi shook her head languidly. 'No. Not right offhand.'

'Think, Bobbi. Please.'

'You know her last name?'

'Ramsey. Mona Ramsey.'

The light dawned. Bobbi giggled at her own stupidity. 'Oh, gee,' she said. 'We *never* call her that!'

'*Who*, Bobbi?'

'Mother Mucca.'

'*Mother Mucca?*'

'Sure. Mona Ramsey is Mother Mucca's real name.'

Minutes later, when Bobbi had left, Mona sat alone and pondered her mounting paranoia. She hadn't felt so confused and frightened – so utterly abandoned – since Rennie Davis, the foremost deity of her youth, had been discovered selling John Hancock insurance in Colorado.

Why was Buddha doing this to her?

Two Mona Ramseys in the same whorehouse! One grizzled and ancient and weathered by debauchery. The other jaded but youngish and teetering on the brink of lunacy.

Past and future? Yin and Yang? Donny and Marie?

Mother Mucca had been right from the beginning: 'That angel dust'll fuck you up every time!'

It will and it did, thought Mona. It will and it did.

I am twisted beyond recognition, beyond redemption. There are no longer laws that apply to me. Only a miracle could save me now.

She walked back to the empty parlor in a glazed stupor and placed a phone call to 28 Barbary Lane.

'Madrigal.'

'Thank God!'

'Who is this, please?'

'It's me, Mrs Madrigal. Mona.'

'Child! Where are you?'

'Oh, God! Winnemucca!'

Silence.

'Mrs Madrigal?'

'Are you all right, dear?'

'Well, I'm . . . No, I feel like shit.'

'Are you . . . are you at the Blue Moon?'

Mona began to whimper. 'How did you know?'

'Mona, I—'

'How did you know?'

'The question, dear, is how did *you* know?'

'How did I know *what*?'

'About . . . Winnemucca?'

'I'm cracking up, Mrs Madrigal.'

'Please, Mona. I would have told you earlier—'

'Told me *what*?'

'I was *so* afraid you'd hate me for it, for running off and leaving—'

'I didn't *run off*! I needed space. I told you that in the—'

'Not *you*, dear. Me.'

'What? You haven't run off. What in the world are you talking about?'

Silence.

117

'Mrs Madrigal?'

'It looks like we'd better take this from the top, dear. Are you alone?'

'Yes.'

'Well, sit down, then. I've got a little story to tell you.'

Acapulco blues

It was dusk on board the *Pacific Princess*. Michael sat in a deck chair, smoking a joint and watching the gentle, seductive curve of the beach at Acapulco. The air was warm, and the sky was exactly the color it should have been.

Even before he got stoned.

'Mouse?' It was Mary Ann. Dressed for a date.

'Hi,' said Michael.

'I've looked all over for you.'

'I'se heah, Miz Scahlett.'

She pulled up a deck chair and sat on the edge of it. 'Are you all right, Mouse?'

He nodded. 'I'm always all right.'

'You weren't at dinner.'

He patted his stomach. 'Chubbette.'

'Burke and I thought you might . . . We'd really like it if you came into town with us tonight. Somebody told us about this place called BabyO's.'

'Thanks. I don't think I'm up for that tonight.'

'It's a disco.'

'Maybe tomorrow, OK?'

She brushed a lock of hair off his forehead. 'Are you sure?'

He nodded as her hand slid down the side of his face. His cheek was wet. She sat with him for almost a minute, holding his hand, saying nothing.

'You better go,' he said finally. 'I'm OK.'

'You're too hard on yourself, Mouse.'

He shrugged. 'If I don't do it, who will?'

'Mouse, you're the most wonderful—'

'I know, Mary Ann. I know I'm a nice guy. I really do. I know that you love me. I know that old ladies love me and my mother and dogs and cats . . . and every goddamn person I meet except someone who'll commit himself to . . . Please, don't get me started.'

'Mouse, I wish you could—'

'The hell of it is, I know the answer. The answer is that you never, ever, rely on another person for your peace of mind. If you do, you're screwed but good. Not right away, maybe, but sooner or later. You have to – I don't know – you have to learn to live with yourself. You have to learn to turn back your own sheets and set a table for one without feeling pathetic. You have to be strong and confident and pleased with yourself and never give the slightest impression that you can't hack it without that certain goddamn someone. You have to fake the hell out of it.'

'You aren't faking it, Mouse. You *are* strong.'

'I'm tired of it. I'm sick of picking up the pieces and marching bravely onward. I want things to work out just *once*.' He rubbed the corner of his eye, smiled suddenly, and shrugged. 'I wanna do a Salem commercial with a Marlboro Man.'

Mary Ann squeezed his hand. 'We're all that way, Mouse.'

'I know, but it works out for some people.'

'It'll work out for you.'

'No it won't.'

'Mouse . . .'

'I want it too badly, Mary Ann. Any idiot can see that. When you want it too badly, no one wants you. No one is attracted to that . . . desperation.'

He turned away from her, wiping his eyes.

119

'Christ!' he said softly, reaching for her hand again. 'Look at that sky, will you?'

After Mary Ann and Burke had left, Michael spent half an hour in his stateroom reading another chapter of the Isherwood book, then wandered out onto the deck again.

The lights of the city blinked at him beguilingly.

But why should I? he wondered. Why should I put my heart through the wringer again? Who could I find that would possibly matter on a two-day stay in an unfamiliar foreign city?

And should I wear the pink or the green Lacoste?

The taxi driver had a huge white mustache and a jovial, grandfatherly face. Michael hated to ask him.

'Uh . . . do you know any gay places?'

The driver blinked, puzzled. 'Red light?'

'No, not red light. Men.'

'Men?'

'*Sí.*'

'Ah, homosex!'

'*Sí.*'

The driver peered over the seat and studied his passenger for several seconds. 'Homosex,' he repeated, then turned his eyes back to the road.

The man in white

The road up the mountain was poorly lit. Michael caught only rough impressions of dusty foliage and black palms, shabby stucco houses that cowered under the headlights like illicit lovers trapped in the flash of a detective's camera.

The cab stopped at a blocky white building with a

central archway. Iron grillwork over the entrance spelled out SANS SOUCI.

Without care, Michael translated. Without care in Acapulco in a gay bar with a French name on a night when nothing in the world made any goddamn sense at all. He realized now, with some embarrassment, that he had laid the heaviest of trips on Mary Ann. She had glimpsed his soul at its blackest, devoid of humor, poisonous with self-pity. She had seen beyond the brave Disney elf, and the sight couldn't have been pretty.

He paid the driver and walked through the archway, nodding to an old woman sweeping the floor. She returned the greeting without expression. Michael wondered if she had a word for gringo fag.

The archway led to a rear terrace overlooking another hillside and a chunk of the bay. There was a thatched bar at one end of the terrace where an old man seemed to serve as both sentinel and bartender. The whole scene was so shadowy that Michael tripped on a chair while making his entrance.

Recovering his cool, he looked around the terrace for witnesses to his clumsiness. There were none. The place was empty. The only sounds were the skeletal rattle of palms along the hillside and the sepulchral wail of Donna Summer singing 'Winter Melody.'

Something was gravely wrong.

Or maybe not. Maybe this was *exactly* the way a gay bar in Mexico was supposed to look. Or there might have been a language problem with the cabby? No. What else could 'homosex' mean? A joke, then? A macho prank on a simple American pervert?

It was half-past nine when Michael ordered a Dos Equis from the old man and sat down at a table on the edge of the terrace. He lost himself for several minutes in the onyx shine of the bay, the huge illuminated cross at the Capilla de la Paz. A neon Pepsi sign glowed obscenely on a distant hillside.

Several people straggled onto the terrace. Women. Lesbians? A man appeared. He was decked out in spray-on white pants, several dozen gold chains and a patent-leather Latin Lover hairdo right out of *GQ*. In LA, he would have been straight. But here . . . ?

The man began to boogie by himself, rolling his eyes back like a corpse that had died in copulation. His movements were the tip-off for Michael. He didn't stop at limp wrists; he had limp *ankles*.

By eleven o'clock the dance floor was packed. The crowd, for the most part, was nellie, though Michael spotted a coterie of pseudo-lumberjack numbers watching the proceedings with ill-concealed amusement. He made a point of avoiding them. If they were San Franciscans, he didn't want to know about it. He didn't want to meet on a mountainside in Mexico someone he might have gone down on in the back room of the Jaguar Book Store.

A man asked him to dance. Michael accepted, feeling awkward and insincere. He didn't want to dance, really; he wanted to be held.

'First time?' asked his partner, shimmying half-heartedly. He was Mexican.

'Yes,' said Michael, making a conscious effort not to speak in broken English. He usually did that when confronted with foreigners.

'You unhappy, I think?'

Michael tried to smile. 'I'm sorry. I—'

'It's OK. Sometimes . . . me too.'

Damn, thought Michael. Don't be nice. If you're nice, I'll cry all over you. 'I'm happy most of the time, really, but sometimes . . .' He gave up trying to explain it and fell back on a bar cliché he never would have used in California. 'Do you come here often?'

When the answer came, Michael was only half listening.

His eyes were glued to the archway, where a tall

122

blond man in a white linen suit was watching the dance floor. Out of ancient habit, Michael cruised him for a fraction of a second, then he stopped with all the abruptness of a dog that had caught its own tail.

It was Jon Fielding.

Playing games

There were times when Brian was sure she was following him.

His imagination conjured her up in the oddest of places: in laundromats on Saturday mornings, on crowded cable cars and empty escalators, in darkened movie houses when he was ripped on Colombian.

It usually started with a look. A heavy-lidded glance. A private wink. A slow, sardonic smile that devoured him from head to foot. He was used to that, of course, but before, it had meant something different.

Before, it had meant a conquest, *his* conquest, a simple, uncomplicated adventure that remained under his control from beginning to end.

But now . . .

Now it could be someone who knew full well his dependence on her.

Now it could be Lady Eleven.

And *she* could be the one in control.

The question that plagued him remained the same: If she knew who he was, if she knew where to find him . . . why wouldn't she want to get it on with him?

Maybe, of course, she had tried to do exactly that. Maybe she had checked out 28 Barbary Lane in the same way he had searched for her at the Superman Building. His name, he reminded himself, had never been displayed on the mailbox.

Even so, she could have *asked*. Mrs Madrigal would

123

have told her, for Christ's sake! Maybe Mrs Madrigal *had* told her and had forgotten to tell *him* that . . .

On the other hand, there could be something terribly wrong with her. Maybe she was afraid for him to meet her and thereby discover that she was . . . what? Crippled? Insane? Blind? Right, Brian. Blind people always keep a pair of binoculars handy.

Then again, she *could* be somebody famous, a local celebrity who couldn't afford the notoriety of an overt sexual liaison. Or a Hite Report volunteer doing free-lance research? Or a lesbian trying to reform, one step at a time? Or a porno star practicing for her big scene?

Or an All-American cunt trying to drive Brian Hawkins right up the wall.

That night, as they undressed in front of their windows, Brian decided to try a new approach. He stripped to his boxer shorts, but kept his cock out of sight. Leaving the binoculars on the window sill, he folded his arms across his chest and waited.

Lady Eleven watched him through the binoculars, then mimicked his stance.

Brian counted to twenty and lifted his binoculars.

Lady Eleven did the same.

It's a chickenshit *game*, he thought. We're a couple of bratty kids playing copycat. All right, bitch! Let's see if you can handle this one!

He left the window and ran to the kitchen, returning with a large brown paper bag. He tore open the bag and flattened it. Using a Magic Marker, he wrote seven digits on the poster-size banner.

928–3117

Then he held it up to the window, watching Lady Eleven's reaction through the binoculars. She stood frozen for several seconds, finally lifting the bincoulars

124

to study the inscription. She held that position for a long time.

Suddenly – God almighty! – she walked away from the window, and came back moments later holding a telephone. Brian lunged for his own phone, instantly grateful he had ordered the model with an extension cord.

They were both in position now, once again duplicates of each other.

Brian watched her through the binoculars. In the conch-shell pinkness of her room, her robed body seemed to pulse with warmth. He *knew* what she smelled like – the sweet, grassy scent of her wet hair, the smoldering musk of her breasts . . .

Oh, Jesus, she was dialing!

One . . . two . . . three . . . four . . . five . . . six . . . seven.

Brian's phone rang.

He lifted the receiver gently, fearful of frightening her. 'Hello,' he said, in a calm, well-modulated voice.

Silence.

'Look, if you'd just give me your phone number, we could . . . I would call you sometime . . . that's all.' He could hear her breathing now. He could watch her standing mute by the phone.

'Hey . . . tell me your name, then . . . just your first name, if you want. I'm a nice guy . . . I swear. Christ! Don't you think this is a little weird?'

The breathing grew louder. At first, he thought she was toying with him, taunting him with sexy noises. Then he realized she was crying.

'Hey . . . I'm sorry, really. I didn't mean it to sound like—'

She hung up on him. He watched her sink into a chair and crumple into a tight little knot of despair. Half a minute later she stood and closed the curtains.

Brian pulled up a chair and sat watching her window until he fell asleep.

125

Mona's conversation with Mrs Madrigal took forty-five minutes. When it was over, she left her cubicle and wandered out into the desert. About a hundred yards from the house a discarded truck seat offered her a sheltered refuge.

She sat down and watched the midnight sky for several minutes, halfway believing that a flying saucer would appear there to take her away from this hideous, surreal landscape.

In San Francisco now the hills would be green – a delicate shade of celadon – and soft as the fuzz on a deer's antlers. There would be daffodils in Washington Square and purple pleroma trees on Barbary Lane and dozens and dozens of calla lillies stoically bracing themselves for Michael's annual impression of Katharine Hepburn.

And her *father* would be there! Her father, her mother, her best friend and her landlady, all rolled into one joyful and loving human being!

She sprang from the truck seat and ran back to the lodge, her heart pounding with anticipation, her brain almost short-circuiting on hope. Who needed a flying saucer? Like Dorothy of Oz, she had only to click her heels three times to find her way back to Auntie Em.

Without a moment's pause, she flung open the door of Mother Mucca's room, completely unintimidated by the old woman's crabbiness.

The madam was brushing her hair. 'Can't you knock?'

'Mother Mucca ... Oh, I'm sorry, but I ...' She leaned against the wall, trying to catch her breath. 'There's something I ...'

A look of concern furrowed the old woman's brow. 'Are you OK, Judy?'

'No. Not Judy. Mona.'

'Don't you call me that, dolly.'

'I'm *not*, Mother Mucca. I'm saying my name's not Judy. It's Mona. Mona Ramsey . . . the same as yours.'

Mother Mucca glared at her briefly, then turned her gaze back to the mirror and resumed brushing. 'I told you about that angel dust, dolly.'

'Mother Mucca, I haven't—'

'If I catch you smokin' in the house, you're out on your ass, Judy!'

Mona regained her composure and tried to reason with her. 'Look, I *know* you can't believe it. I can hardly believe it myself. It's like a . . . well, it's like a miracle, Mother Mucca. Some invisible cosmic force brought us together because we need each other, because we—'

'Look, dolly, if ya don't mind—'

'I'll get my bag! I'll show you my . . . well, I can't show you any ID's, come to think of it. I *promise* you that's my name. I told you my name was Judy because I . . . I was a little embarrassed about working here and all . . . Please, just answer one question for me.'

'Go on . . . git!'

'Not until you answer this.'

'I *said*—'

'What was your little boy's name?'

'What the hell do you think you're . . . ?'

'*What was his name?*'

Mother Mucca picked up the house phone on her vanity. 'I'm callin' Charlene, Judy.'

'Mona!'

'You're so plumb pitiful I don't even—'

Mona jerked the phone out of her hand. 'Listen to me! I love you, goddammit! It was Andy wasn't it? Your son's name was Andy!'

A stunned silence, then: 'Who told you that?'

127

'Who do you think? Charlene? Marnie? Bobbi, maybe? You never told *anyone*, did you? It must've hurt too much to talk about him.' Mona caught her breath, then sank to her knees, taking the old lady's hands in hers. 'Mother Mucca . . . *he* told me. *Andy* told me. I live with him in San Francisco . . . and he's my father.'

The madam's eyes were full of tears. 'I'm an old lady, dolly. A lie can hurt mighty bad.'

'I would never hurt you, Mother Mucca.'

'Why . . . why did you come here?'

Mona smiled at her. 'You picked *me* up, remember?'

'It don't make no sense.'

'I *told* you. It's a miracle! I'm your granddaughter, Mother Mucca. I've found my goddamn roots!'

The old woman's eyes narrowed. 'Who taught you to talk like that, Mona?'

Falling in love again

The man dancing with Michael could tell that something was wrong. 'Excuse, please . . . you know that man?'

Michael's condition was almost trancelike. 'I . . . yes. I hope you don't mind. He's somebody I used to . . . I'm sorry, OK?'

The man nodded, apparently more puzzled than offended, and boogied off the dance floor toward the bar. Michael stood frozen in his tracks, composing opening lines. Jon hadn't seen him yet.

A scratchy phonograph blared out 'Cherchez la Femme.' The same tune they had played at The Endup when Michael won the jockey shorts dance contest . . . and Dr Jon Fielding walked out of his life forever.

Michael's forevers never lasted for long.

128

'Hey, greengo! You wan buy my seester? She virgin!'

'Michael! Christ!'

'Please, just Michael.'

Jon hugged him heartily. The kind of hug, Michael noted, that Danny Thomas might have given George Burns on Johnny Carson. 'What the hell are you doing here?'

Michael shrugged. 'It's the only queer joint in Acapulco.'

Jon laughed. 'I mean, in Acapulco?'

'I'm on a cruise. Ship-type, that is.'

'The *Pacific Princess*?'

'Yep. What brings *you* here?'

'Oh . . . vaginal infections.'

'You don't *look* sick.'

The gynecologist grinned. 'A convention, turkey.'

'A million laughs, huh?'

'It is, actually. We get a lot of free time.'

That bothered Michael. People he'd been hot for were not supposed to enjoy themselves in his absence. But the doctor was having a ball, so why torture himself? 'It's good seeing you, Jon.'

'You're leaving?'

'Yeah. This place looks like The Kokpit on a bad night. I've had enough.'

Jon gave the terrace another once-over. 'I see what you mean.'

'Yeah. Well, I'm sure you'll find something.'

'I thought I had.'

Michael ignored that. 'I guess it gets better as the evening wears on.'

'I've got a car, Michael. We could go for a ride or something.'

Michael looked at him for a moment, then shook his head. 'I don't think so, Jon. Thanks, though.'

The doctor smiled faintly. 'You're punishing me, aren't you?'

'For what?'

'For . . . that night at The Endup.'

Michael managed a blithe shrug. 'It was a tacky scene. I don't blame you for—'

'No. I was the tacky one. I was . . . embarrassed, Michael. I was out with some pissy queens from Seacliff, and I couldn't handle it. That was my failing, not yours.'

Michael smiled. 'I won, you know.'

'You should have.'

'Gracias.'

They drove to the Capilla de la Paz in Jon's rented Volkswagen Thing. Like strangers in a foreign city, they chatted breezily about night spots in Acapulco, the boredom of sea cruises and the perils of smoking grass in Mexico.

The mountaintop chapel was deserted. Above it loomed the leviathan cross, white as bleached bones against the starry sky. They walked to its base in silence.

'Somebody told me,' said Jon, 'that this is a shrine to two brothers who were killed in a plane crash.'

'That's nice. I mean . . . a nice story.'

'I may have it wrong.'

'I like the story, anyway.'

'You can see the ship, see?' Jon pointed to the toy boat twinkling below in the harbor. Michael could feel the doctor's breath against his cheek.

'And over there,' continued Jon, 'behind that row of hotels . . . Michael?'

'Sorry. I was thinking.'

'About what?'

'Shrines. Funerals, actually.'

'Charming.'

Michael looked at him. 'Don't tell me you've never planned your own funeral?'

Jon shook his head, smiling.

'Well, take this down, please. I'd like a big party at

130

the Paramount theater in Oakland, with lots of dope and munchies and all my friends ripped to the tits in the midst of all that Deco decadence. And when it's over I'd like them to prop me up in a front-row seat, leave the theater . . . and bury the whole goddamn thing.'

Jon laughed and squeezed the back of his head. 'Couldn't you do that without dying?'

'Mmm. I often do.'

Jon laughed, then cupped Michael's face in his hands and kissed him. 'Don't die, OK? Not until I'm through with you.'

The trouble with Burke

Seated in a pink-and-orange booth at the Acapulco Denny's, Mary Ann inspected her french fries and found them suspiciously grayish. 'Ick,' she said, holding one up for Burke's examination.

He smiled uncomplainingly. 'Ditto on the milk shake.'

'I'm sorry, Burke.'

'Why?'

'I shouldn't have dragged you here. I just felt like a hamburger, I guess.'

'That's OK. So did I.'

'We should have eaten at Colonel Sanders'.'

He shrugged. 'We can eat on the ship tonight.'

'I'm not . . . being a drag, am I?'

'I can't tell,' he grinned. 'I'm too much in love with you.'

They rented a horse-drawn carriage and clopped through the city, trailing balloons behind them. It's a Harlequin Romance, thought Mary Ann. Too corny, too perfect to be true. If I think about it too long or plan on *anything*, it'll go away forever. So she nestled against Burke's shoulder and slipped her mind into neutral.

'How's Michael?' asked Burke, as they passed the Ritz.

'Much better. He had company last night. This morning too. I found out the hard way.'

'What d'ya mean?'

'I walked in on them.'

Burke smiled. 'That blond guy he had breakfast with?'

'Uh huh. God, I can't *imagine* what Melba and Arnold thought about that.'

'Who's Melba and Arnold?'

'Mr and Mrs Matching. The couple at our table. They think Michael and I are married.'

'How did that happen?'

'Well . . . I told them. I mean, I didn't want it to look like we were . . . shacked up or something. Plus, if I'd told them he was gay, they'd have freaked out and thought I was a fag hag.'

'A *what*?'

Mary Ann kissed him on the ear. 'I love you. You don't know *anything*.'

Back on the beach, they basted themselves in turtle lotion and stretched out on the sand. The simple, unspoiled beauty of the scene made Mary Ann painfully conscious of her dwindling days with Burke.

But you mustn't push, she ordered herself. You mustn't frighten him.

'Burke?'

'Mmmm?'

'This is really nice.'

'You bet.'

'I mean . . . I never thought I'd meet anybody like you on this trip.'

'C'mon! With *your* looks?'

132

'That's sweet, but I mean it. Most of the guys I meet in San Francisco wanna talk about their dumb Porsches or their tape decks or getting their head together or something. I don't hang around with Michael because I'm . . . desperate or anything. It's just that . . . well, Michael makes me feel like I'm worth something. I was beginning to think that a straight man couldn't do that for me.'

Silence.

She reddened instantly. 'I embarrassed you, didn't I?'

'No, really . . .' He reached over and squeezed her hand. 'I haven't felt very communicative, Mary Ann.'

'It isn't what you *say*, Burke. It's – I don't know – how you look at me, how you react to things. I know that you see me as a person. I'll always be grateful for that. I want you to know that.'

He rolled over on his side and pulled her against his chest, prompting giggles from two passing urchins. Mary Ann couldn't have cared less. For one single, delirious moment she was *certain* they looked like Burt Lancaster and Deborah Kerr in *From Here to Eternity*.

'Burke?'

'Yeah?'

'Have you ever thought about moving back to San Francisco?'

Silence.

You blew it, you dink. He's on to you now. 'I'm sorry, Burke. I shouldn't have said that.'

'That's OK.'

'No it's not. We'll change the subject. I won't get heavy, I promise.'

'No. We should talk. There's something I should have told you a long time ago.'

Somehow, she had known this moment would come. Her whole body tensed as she waited for the truth to fall like an executioner's ax. 'Please,' she said feebly. 'I'd rather not hear it.'

133

'Mary Ann, I lived in San Francisco for three years
. . . three whole years out of my life!'

Oh, God! Had Michael been right all along?

'Do you know why I'm out of it, Mary Ann? Do you
know where my goddamn boyish naïveté comes
from?'

Please no! Please don't let him be . . .

'I can't remember *anything*, Mary Ann. Not a single
goddamn thing about those three years in San Francisco.'

She pulled away from him. 'You've got . . . *amnesia*?'
He nodded.

Thank God, she thought, hugging him. Thank God!

Try to remember

'I'm sorry,' said Burke, sitting up in the sand and
rubbing his forehead with his fingertips. 'I should have
told you a long time ago.'

Mary Ann flailed for the right words. 'You . . . can't
remember anything at all?'

He shook his head. 'Nothing about my time in San
Francisco. I'm clear on the rest. I mean, everything up
to 1973. When I was in Nantucket. There are some . . .
images or whatever that come to me from time to time.
They don't mean anything, really.'

'Like what?'

'Mary Ann, there's no point—'

'I want to help, Burke.'

He traced a line in the sand. 'Everybody wants to
help.' Then, seeing her expression, he added, 'I didn't
mean it like that. You're not everyone. It's just that . . .
well, everything's been done that can be done. My
parents even sent me on this cruise, so I could – you
know—'

'It doesn't matter to me, Burke.'

'It's a form of insanity.'

'I don't believe that.'

'I can't be honest in a relationship, Mary Ann. I don't know what there is to be honest about. I don't even know *why* I—'

Mary Ann gasped, anticipating him. 'God, Burke! The thing about the roses!'

He nodded. 'That's part of it. Cute, huh? I also freak out on walkways with railings.'

'Where?'

'Anywhere. Any walkways with railings. Haven't you noticed me on the ship? That's why I hang around the fantail all day long. I'm scared shitless, Mary Ann.'

Mary Ann moved closer to him, placing a reassuring hand on his knee. 'Well, look: if you can't remember what happened to you in San Francisco . . . I mean, how did you get back to Nantucket?'

'I didn't, exactly . . . Are you sure you want to hear all this?'

'Positive.'

'Well, they found me.'

'They?'

'Some cops in Golden Gate Park. Mounted policemen. I had . . . passed out or whatever in the woods. It took them three days to figure out who I was.'

'And then you went home?'

He nodded. 'I was lucky, I guess. The Nantucket part came back almost immediately – along with my name and all that. I just don't know what I was doing in San Francisco.'

Mary Ann smiled ruefully. 'Welcome to the club,' she said.

They walked for a long time on the beach, watching the sky turn the color of a ripe nectarine. Mary Ann continued to probe gently, certain he would shut her out completely if she ever stopped talking.

'You haven't told me why you went to San Francisco in the first place.'

'Oh, I was a reporter. For the AP.'

'Grocery stores have reporters?'

He touched the tip of her nose. 'The Associated Press.'

She flushed. 'I just did that to make you feel good.'

'Of course.'

'So what did you do before that? Before the AP.'

'I didn't. I left my father's publishing house and interviewed with the head AP bureau in New York. They stuck me in a little glass booth with a lot of disjointed facts about Lucille Ball's wedding in ... whenever, and I wrote a typical AP story and ... they assigned me to the San Francisco bureau.'

'And you don't remember anything after that.'

He chuckled. 'Oh, yeah. That part's gruesomely clear. The boredom, the shitwork, perpetual deadlines. I quit five weeks later. That's where the blackout comes.'

'What about your parents? You couldn't just disappear for three years. You must've written them or something.'

'Not enough to really let them know what was going on. Just I-am-fine-don't-worry-about-me stuff. I lived on Nob Hill for a while, I know that. I did temporary shitwork – clerical stuff. Sometimes I attended services at Grace Cathedral.'

'Well, at least you remember *that* much.'

He shook his head. 'I told them that in the letters. I don't remember a bit of it.'

'You mean there's no record whatsoever ... no evidence of where you were or what you were doing for—'

'Wait!' He stopped suddenly and dug in his pockets. 'Hold out your hand,' he instructed her. Somewhat reluctantly, she complied. He pressed something small and metal into her palm.

'A key,' she said flatly. 'What's that mean?'

'You tell me. It's all that's left of me.'

'What?'

'It was in my pocket, my shirt pocket, when they found me in the park.'

She examined it more closely. 'It's . . . smaller than a door key, or a car key. I guess it could . . .' Finally, she shrugged, giving up.

He shrugged back at her, smiling. It was his collie look again. Gentle and golden and vulnerable beyond her wildest dreams. She knew instantly why she had loved him from the beginning. He was a clean slate, a virgin . . .

And she could show him the way.

Back to Babylon

There they were again, back where they had met, back at the seedy old Greyhound bus station on Seventh Street in San Francisco.

Mona surveyed the snack bar, feeling an unexpected flash of nostalgia, while Mother Mucca slurped coffee noisily out of her spoon. The old lady was still being ornery, but at least she had consented to this visit.

Mona had told her everything about Andy/Anna only three days before.

And the mother-and-child reunion was only an hour away.

Mother Mucca belched. 'I don't feel so good,' she grumbled.

'Now don't start on that again.'

'I *don't*, Mona. My stomach feels a tetch—'

'Your stomach's perfectly fine. You're just nervous, Mother Mucca. That's OK. It's OK to experience a—'

'It ain't OK with *me* girl. This just ain't the right time to—'

'Please, Mother Mucca! I *know* you can handle this. We've been through this before, and we both agreed that . . . well, it's the best thing, that's all.'

The old lady ducked her head moodily. 'Maybe for *you.*'

'For *all* of us.'

'I ain't seen my son for forty goddamn years!'

Mona winced. 'Daughter.'

'Huh?'

'She's your *daughter* now. I know that's hard to deal with, but it would mean so much to Mrs Madrigal . . . I mean, to Anna. Try to remember that, will you?'

Mother Mucca wouldn't look up. 'Whatever.'

'No. Not whatever. Your daughter. Anna.'

'I called him Andy for sixteen years!'

'I know, but a lot's changed. You must've changed yourself.'

'Says who?'

'Please don't be difficult.'

'What does he look like?'

'I *told* you that already.'

'Well, tell me another goddamn time!'

Mona sought for another description. 'She's very . . . majestic.'

Her grandmother snorted. 'Sounds like a fuckin' race horse.'

'See for yourself, then.'

'Does he . . . look like me?'

'You'll just have to wait.'

Mother Mucca glared at her granddaughter, then at a pimply teenager in glitter wedgies eating a doughnut at the next table. 'Nothin' but weirdos in this town,' she growled.

Mona's first glimpse of Barbary Lane brought her heart into her throat. Nothing had changed in the sylvan city canyon. The cats were still there, the miniature cottages and the eucalyptus trees and Mrs Madrigal's courtyard beckoning in the moonlight.

'You tell him we're comin'?' asked Mother Mucca, surveying the cozy old house.

'No. She knows we're coming, of course, but I didn't tell her exactly when.'

'Stupid!'

Mona snapped back, 'I didn't want to put her in a negative space before we got here.'

The old lady blinked uncomprehendingly.

Mona smiled and translated. 'I didn't want her to feel uncomfortable about our arrival.'

'You didn't mind makin' *me* pretty damn uncomfortable.'

'C'mon now. Behave yourself.'

Mona stepped into the alcove next to the door buzzers. Mother Mucca lagged behind, pacing nervously in the courtyard. 'C'mon,' coaxed Mona. 'It's gonna be just fine.'

'I can't, Mona.'

Mona turned and saw the piteous expression on the old woman's face. Mother Mucca took several steps toward her. 'Mona, darlin' . . . I don't look like an ol' witch, do I?'

'Oh, Mother Mucca . . . you're beautiful! Don't worry, please. Anna's gonna love you.'

'We ain't brought her nothin'.'

Mona hugged her. 'We're all she needs.'

'Yeah?'

Mona smiled. 'Yeah.'

'Well, ring the doorbell, girl!'

Key to her heart

Up in the Starlight Lounge, Mary Ann and Burke hoisted Pina Coladas and proposed a toast. 'To new memories,' said Burke.

'Right, and to—' She frowned suddenly, realizing with a little shiver that the pianist had begun to belt out 'Everything's Coming Up Roses.'

'Burke . . . if that bothers you, I don't mind asking him to stop.'

He smiled weakly. 'I hadn't noticed it.'

'Until I mentioned it, huh?'

'It's OK.'

'I'm sorry, Burke.'

He downed his drink. 'I can't bury my head in the sand, Mary Ann.'

'I wish there was something I could—'

'It's just something I have to deal with, that's all. I mean, you can't avoid roses, can you?' His mouth curled in a rueful smile. 'Try it sometime.'

'I know. It must be . . . Burke, couldn't a psychiatrist do something? It seems like . . . well, if you could cure your amnesia, wouldn't that take care of your fear of roses and . . . walkways with railings or whatever?'

'I've seen a shrink already.'

'Oh.'

'He hypnotized me and interrogated me and did everything but stick pins in a voodoo doll . . . and not a goddamn thing happened. Except his bill at the end of the month.'

Mary Ann stared down at her drink for a moment, wondering how she could phrase the next question. 'Burke, what if you . . . ?'

'Yeah?'

'Oh . . . nothing.'

'It didn't sound like nothing.'

'Well, I was wondering if . . . Wouldn't it jog your memory or something if you . . . came back to San Francisco?'

An interminable silence followed. She had risked this question not once but twice. Her face flushed instantly, and Burke seemed to sense her embarrassment. 'It would almost be worth it,' he said at last, 'to be around you.'

Mary Ann tore the edge off her cocktail napkin. 'It just seems like . . . well, if you were exposed to some of the old places and . . . experiences and all, your memory might come back and you could sort of . . . exorcise your phobias.' She looked up at him imploringly. Her eyes were full of tears. 'Oh, who the hell am I fooling!'

He dabbed at her eyes with a cocktail napkin. 'Not me,' he smiled.

'I *hate* goodbyes. I always lose it. *Always.*'

'I know. Me too.'

'Nothing's ever been quite as nice as this.'

'I know. I agree.'

'You do?'

He nodded.

'Well, then, why don't we . . . ? Oh, God, do I look like I'm begging?'

He held both her hands in his. 'Do I look like I'm saying no, dummy?'

They snuggled under a blanket on the fantail, watching the lights along the shore.

'You won't be sorry,' she said.

'You don't have to promise that. You *can't.*'

'What about your parents?'

'I'll phone and tell them. They'll understand.'

'Won't they be a little . . . freaked. I mean, about San Francisco?'

'No more than I am.'

'Don't be. I'll be there this time.' She paused, then said as offhandedly as possible: 'In fact, if you'd like, I think there's a vacancy in my building.'

'Good. Where's that?'

'Russian Hill. Barbary Lane. It's a darling little walkway, like something out of a fairy tale, and the landlady's so neat. Michael lives downstairs.'

'Where's the vacancy, then?'

'Just across the hall.'

'Handy.'

She giggled. 'The guy who lived there moved up to this little house on the roof.' Never mind what had happened to the guy who'd lived *there*.

Sitting up, Burke reached in the pocket of his windbreaker and handed Mary Ann a small package wrapped in tissue paper. She peeled it away, layer by layer, scarcely taking her eyes off Burke's embarrassed face.

Inside, suspended from a twenty-four-karat gold necklace, was the curious little key he had shown her on the beach.

'For what it's worth,' he said almost apologetically, 'I love you.'

DeDe on the town

DeDe knew she made a ludicrous sight. An eight-months-pregnant woman dining alone at the counter at Vanessi's, her battered Gucci tote bag propped against the stool.

Well, screw it, she thought. North Beach had seen weirder things. A lot *weirder*. Like that freaky teeny-bopper hanging out in front of Enrico's. Green hair and a garbage bag. Yecch!

Besides, she loved this restaurant. She delighted in its unaffected sophistication and burly Italian chefs who wielded skillets with all the grace and precision of tennis players.

Beauchamp, she realized, was probably home at the penthouse, and that was only four blocks up the hill. While she dreaded the prospect of a confrontation with her husband, she also drew a kind of perverse pleasure from the knowledge that she was stalking the old neighborhood on her own.

What puzzled her now was why her mother hadn't protested this unorthodox trek into town. She had barely looked up from the suitcase she was packing for the trip to Napa. She had seemed curiously distracted.

But by what?

'Wouldn't you be more comfortable in one of the booths?'

DeDe looked up from her sweetbreads at the kind brown eyes that had posed the question. The woman was very pretty, with dark curly hair and cheekbones that Veruschka would have killed for.

'Thanks. I like watching the show,' she replied, motioning to the chefs behind the counter.

'Oh, God, isn't it *marvelous*? I think it's the best therapy there is, watching them fling that zucchini in the air. You expect all hell to break loose, but it never does.'

'Unlike life.'

The woman laughed. 'Unlike life.'

A waiter set a huge plate of pasta in front of the woman. 'Well,' she sighed, with a grin, 'oink, oink, oink.'

'You look fine,' said DeDe. 'I'm the one who ought to be watching it.'

'Well, you're eating for *two*, honey!'

'Three.'

The woman whistled. 'You get dessert, then.'

They both laughed. The woman was quite fair-skinned, DeDe observed, but there was something almost negroid about the warmth and earthiness of her mannerisms. DeDe liked her immediately.

Setting her fork down, the woman smiled at her. 'You're not married, are you?'

Silence.

'Oh, God,' said the woman. 'If you're a tourist, forgive me. We're a little too liberated for our own good in this town.'

'No . . . I mean, yes, I'm married, but I'm separated . . . I mean, *we're* separated. I live here, though. I'm a native.'

'Mmm. Me too. If you count Oakland, that is.'

'I have lots of friends in Piedmont.'

'That's *not* what I meant.' She appeared to understand the East Bay caste system all too well.

'Why did you think I wasn't married?'

The woman turned and scrutinized DeDe's face, as if to reconfirm something. 'I don't know. You just look . . . independent.'

'I do?'

The woman smiled. 'No. But I thought you'd like to hear it.'

DeDe looked down at her food, fascinated by this stranger's insight, and a little afraid of it. 'Do you think it's too late for me to . . . do something about it?'

An elfin grin spread over the woman's face. 'What would you *like* to do – I mean, right this very minute – if you could do anything you wanted and . . . you didn't have friends in Piedmont who might not approve of it?'

DeDe smiled uneasily. 'Oh . . . you mean, in the neighborhood?'

'If you like.'

'I'd like to see that topless dancer across the street who turns into a gorilla.'

'Why?'

'Just to see how they do it. With mirrors, I guess.'

The woman shook her head soberly. 'It's actually a gorilla in a girl mask with a flesh-colored body stocking.'

'You mean they . . . ?' When the light dawned, DeDe laughed. 'You *see* how gullible I am?'

'There's only one way to find out for sure.'

'You're joking!'

'There's *nothing* I'd rather do than take a pregnant friend to a topless lady gorilla act.'

DeDe thought for a moment, then extended her hand. 'It's a deal. I'm DeDe Day . . . or DeDe Halcyon. Take your pick.'

A flicker of recognition seemed to pass over the woman's face. 'Have we met before?' asked DeDe.

'I . . . read the social columns.'

'Oh, God!'

'It's OK. I like you anyway. I'm D'orothea.'

'That's a pretty name,' said DeDe.

Mama's boy

When she opened the door, Mrs Madrigal was wearing a red satin cloche with her plum-colored kimono. Her makeup was better than Mona had ever seen it.

The landlady smiled at her daughter. 'Do I get a hug or don't I?'

Mona flushed. 'Oh, yes . . . oh, yes, you do!' She stepped gracelessly into the apartment, dropped her Persian saddlebag on the floor and threw herself into Mrs Madrigal's arms. The landlady patted Mona's head for a moment, then gently removed herself.

'Isn't there someone you'd like me to meet, dear?'

'Oh . . . God, I'm sorry.' She turned and confronted Mother Mucca, still standing in the doorway. The old woman glowered, shook her head at Mona, and addressed Mrs Madrigal.

'She ain't got the manners God gave a mule!'

Mrs Madrigal smiled evenly, holding out her hand to Mother Mucca. 'I'm so glad you came.'

The madam took her hand and grunted. 'It was *her* idea.'

'Well, then I should thank you, Mona. It's good to see you both.'

'I can't stay long,' said Mother Mucca.

'I know,' said the landlady, taking Mona's arm. 'We'll have a little sherry and a nice chat.' Her eyes linked only briefly with Mother Mucca. It was the same cordial, but distant, expression Mrs Madrigal used on Jehovah's Witnesses.

The hostess ducked into the kitchen, leaving Mona and her grandmother in the living room. Mother Mucca was rouged granite, sullen and unreadable.

'Well,' said Mona, 'isn't she nice?'

'It ain't natural.'

'I thought we'd gotten past that.'

'Speak for yourself. That's my son out there.'

'Well, she's *my* father!'

'That's different.'

'Oh, please!'

'I raised that child, girl! That's my own flesh and blood!'

'You raised her in a goddamn whorehouse! What did you expect, anyway? John Wayne?'

'I'm gonna slap you right—'

The old woman stiffened again as Mrs Madrigal re-entered the room. She was carrying a tray containing three glasses of sherry and a bowl of chocolate-covered cherries.

'I thought I had some butter cookies, but I think Brian or one of the other children may have polished them off.'

Mother Mucca frowned. 'You got children?'

146

'He's a tenant,' snapped Mona.

'Yes,' said Mrs Madrigal calmly. 'I call them my children. It's a little silly, I suppose, but they don't seem to mind.' She smiled at Mona. 'At least, if they do, they don't tell me.'

Mother Mucca reached for a chocolate and popped it into her mouth. She wouldn't look at her hostess. Mona sensed that disaster was imminent.

'So,' said Mrs Madrigal, curling her legs up under her on the sofa, 'you've had *lots* of adventures, I suppose?'

Mona nodded. 'Winnemucca's a trip.'

'I can imagine.' The landlady turned to Mother Mucca, who had just finished sucking the chocolate off her teeth. 'I hope this young lady didn't get in the way.'

The old woman snorted, forgoing comment by swilling her glass of sherry in one motion. Mrs Madrigal held her ground, keeping her eyes on Mother Mucca. 'Mona's a lot like both of us, isn't she?'

Silence.

'She's got your looks, though,' added Mrs Madrigal.

Mother Mucca stared into her glass. 'Ain't no wonder,' she said finally.

'What?'

'You call that a hat?'

'I don't see what that—'

'Damnation, girl! Ain't ya got no hair?'

'Of course I've got—'

'Well, why the hell do ya keep it all crammed up under that bonnet like you was bald or somethin? Look, girl . . . you and me gotta talk!'

'I *assumed* that was the purpose of this little—'

'Where's your bedroom?'

'What does that have to do—'

'Where's your goddamn bedroom?'

The two women had been gone for at least ten minutes.

147

Mona sat terror-stricken in the living room, listening to their muffled voices. Then she heard Mrs Madrigal say, 'Mama, Mama,' and begin to cry.

She waited until the sound died down again, then moved quietly to the bedroom door and opened it. Mrs Madrigal was seated at her vanity. Her back was to the door. Mother Mucca was standing beside her, brushing her daughter's shoulder-length hair. She looked up and saw Mona.

'Git,' she said softly.

Table for five

As the *Pacific Princess* pulled out of Acapulco, Michael's eyes stayed glued on the ever-diminishing figure on the dock. 'Look at him,' he said. 'That asshole would look gorgeous in an aerial photograph!'

Mary Ann slipped her arm around his waist. 'Didn't I tell you things would work out?'

'Yeah. I guess you did.'

'When's he flying back to San Francisco?'

'Friday. I'm meeting him at the airport.'

'He's awfully nice, Mouse.'

'I know. It scares the hell out of me.'

'Why?'

'Don't make me analyze it. When I analyze things they . . . stop happening.' He turned and looked in her eyes. 'You know what I mean, don't you?'

She nodded grimly. 'God, yes.'

'It seems like every time I start up with somebody new . . . I don't know . . . I see the beginning and the end all at once. I *know* how it'll die. I can play those scenes in my sleep. This time, though . . . well, I don't wanna know the end. Not for a while, anyway.'

'Maybe there won't be an end.'

He smiled at her indulgently. 'Everything ends, Babycakes.'

'Now, Mouse, that's not ... What about us, then? You and I haven't ended.'

He laughed. 'We'll be cruising the old folks' home together.'

'Then what's the difference?'

'The difference, dearheart, is that you don't need me and I don't need you. It's these *other* turkeys we need ... these one-and-onlys. Or at least, we *think* we do. Our poor little psyches have been marred forever by Rock Hudson and Doris Day.'

Mary Ann was composing a retort when Burke suddenly appeared behind her. 'Well, we're off, huh?'

She turned and took his hand. 'We wondered where you were. We were just waving goodbye to Jon.'

'I did a little dickering with the maître d'.'

'About what?'

'I'm at your table now. That's OK, I hope?'

'Of course! That's wonderful!'

Michael grinned wickedly. 'Arnold and Melba will just adore you.'

'Oh, hell,' said Mary Ann. 'What in the world are we gonna tell them?'

'Well ...' Michael tapped his forefinger on his chin. 'I think we should say that you and I are mature, freethinking adults. Our marriage simply isn't working, so ... we're planning an amicable divorce, after which Burke and I will have a simple Episcopal wedding at Grace Cathedral.'

'Very funny.'

Burke laughed, winking at Michael. Then, turning to Mary Ann: 'He's got a point, you know. I *could* be gay. I mean, if I don't remember ...'

'You are *not* gay. That's an order.'

'I don't know,' said Michael ominously. 'I'm sure I've seen him wearing green on Thursdays. And look

149

at that body, girl. Straight dudes don't have washboard stomachs.'

Mary Ann patted Burke's waist. 'This one does.'

Burke reddened visibly.

Michael took both their hands. 'C'mon, you sickos. I'm so hungry I could eat a steward.'

The trio shared a joint in Mary Ann and Michael's stateroom before heading to the dining room. When they sat down at the table, the matched pair from Dublin was conspicuously absent.

'What?' mugged Michael. 'How can I eat without Arnold and Melba?'

Mary Ann giggled. 'Maybe they ran out of clothes.'

'Or', suggested Burke, 'the maître d' tipped them off, and they're busy reporting us to the—'

He cut himself short when the couple appeared, pink as cooked shrimp and obviously delighted with their latest ensemble: matching Mexican cotton shirts, each embroidered with a single red rose.

Melba's voice was pure white sugar. 'Hi, Young Marrieds! Who's your friend?'

Mary Ann began to stammer, seeing the Littlefields, seeing the rose, seeing Burke.

'Oh, hi. This is . . . Oh, Burke, why don't you . . . ?' She jerked to her feet, knocking over her water glass. Burke had his head between his knees, gagging. She snatched a linen napkin off the table and pressed it to his mouth.

'Burke . . . here, I'll help you. Melba, I'm sorry. Give me your arm, Burke. It's OK . . . There, it's OK.' She led him away from the table without further explanation. Michael and the Littlefields watched their exit in silence.

'*Goddamn!*' thundered Arnold. 'What the hell was that about?'

'Seasick,' said Michael quietly, still watching his friends.

Arnold grunted. 'He sure doesn't seem like that kind of a fellow.'

'No,' said Michael under his breath. 'Great legs, though.'

'Huh?'

'Uh . . . it's great to have sea legs.'

'Right on!' concurred Melba.

Eccentric Old Bachelors

Somewhere in the nighttime sky above the Monterey peninsula, Michael loosened his seat belt and turned to check on his traveling companions.

Burke was asleep, sprawled obliviously against the window like a Raggedy Andy doll.

Mary Ann was still awake, trying her damnedest to get engrossed in PSA's in-flight magazine. When she saw Michael watching her, she managed a tired smile.

'I'm reading about Swinging Singles in San Francisco.'

'Arrgh.'

'It's so depressing. Do you think I'm a Swinging Single?'

Michael shook his head. 'Not a bit.'

'Thank God!' She leaned closer, whispering. 'I don't think you're a faggot, either.'

'Much obliged.'

'I've come a long way on that, Michael.'

'I know. I've noticed.'

'No. You don't know how bad I was about it.'

'It doesn't matter.' He paused, massaging his brow with his fingertips. 'I just hope my parents can hack it.'

'You've told them.'

'No, but I think I'm going to.'

'Mouse . . . do you think they're ready?'

151

'No. They'll never be ready. They're past changing now. They just get more the same.'

'Then why?'

'I love them, Mary Ann. They don't even know who I am.'

'Yes they do. They know that you're kind and gentle and . . . funny. They know that you love them. Why is it necessary for you to . . . ?'

'They know a twelve-year-old.'

'Mouse . . . lots of men never marry. Your parents are three thousand miles away. Why shouldn't they just keep assuming that you're . . .' She sought for a word, making a little circle with her hand.

'An Eccentric Old Bachelor,' smiled Michael. 'That's what they used to call them in Orlando. My Uncle Roger was an Eccentric Old Bachelor. He taught English and raised day lilies, and we never saw much of him, except at weddings and funerals. My cousins and I liked him because he could make puppets out of knotted handkerchiefs. Most of the time, though, he kept to himself, because he knew what the rules were: Shut up about it, if you want us to love you. Don't make us think about the disgusting thing you are.

'He did what they said, too. I don't know . . . maybe he'd never *heard* about the queers in New Orleans and San Francisco. Maybe he didn't even know what queer was. Maybe he thought he was the only one . . . or maybe he just loved living in Orlando. At any rate, he stayed, and when he died – I was a junior in high school – they gave him a decent eunuch's funeral. Mary Ann . . . I had never seen him touch another human being. Not one.'

Michel hesitated, then shook his head. 'I hope to God he got laid.'

Mary Ann reached over and put her hand on his arm. 'Things have changed, Mouse. The world has grown up a lot.'

'Has it?' He handed her the third section of the

Chronicle and pointed to Charles McCabe's column. 'This enlightened literal says there's gonna be a big backlash against homosexuals, because the decent folks out there are sick and tired of the "abnormal."'

'Maybe he—'

'I've got news for him. Guess who else is sick of it? Guess who else has tried like hell *not* to be abnormal, by joking and apologizing and camping our way through a hell of a lot of crap?

'*Abnormal?* Anita Bryant would be a nonentity today if she hadn't put on a bathing suit and strutted her stuff in that cattle call in Atlantic City. If you know how that differs from a jockey shorts dance contest, I wish the hell you'd tell me.'

His voice had grown strident. Mary Ann glanced nervously at the other passengers, then said in a placating tone: 'Mouse, it's not *me* you have to convince.'

He smiled and kissed her on the cheek. 'I'm sorry. I sound like Carry Nation, don't I?'

They slept for the rest of the flight. Michael woke during the descent into San Francisco, feeling the comforting hand of the city on his shoulder again.

'Well,' quipped Mary Ann as the trio deplaned, 'it's all over but the Hare Krishna in the airport.'

Michael winked at Burke. 'No sweat. If they try to sell us a rose, we've got the perfect secret weapon.'

The pilot emerged from the cockpit. As Michael disembarked, the ancient, unwritten but unmistakable eye signal passed between the two men.

'Welcome home,' said the pilot.

'Really!' said Michael.

Mary Ann ribbed him in the terminal. 'I saw that, you know.'

'You're right about one thing,' grinned Michael. 'They don't make Eccentric Old Bachelors like they used to.'

Tonight, because it was a special occasion, Mrs Madrigal had piled her hair into a Gibson Girl do and adorned it with a large silk iris.

Thank God it wasn't a rose, thought Mary Ann instantly, watching the landlady turn almost coquettish in the company of her newest tenant.

'Well, Burke, I asked Mary Ann to pick up something nice for me in Mexico, but I didn't expect it to be *this* nice.' She appraised the young man long enough to see his embarrassment, then shifted her focus to Michael. 'What about you, child? Didn't you bring me anything?'

Mary Ann giggled. 'He's arriving on Friday.' Michael shot her a reproving glance, so she covered her mouth in mock penitence.

'What's that all about?' asked Mrs Madrigal.

'Mouse doesn't like to talk about it.'

The landlady's eyes widened. 'Ah hah!'

'C'mon,' said Michael. 'Lay off.'

Mrs Madrigal passed a joint to him. 'I understand, dear. You're . . . superstitious about him.' She touched his arm suddenly. 'It *is* a him, isn't it?'

Michael took a toke off the joint and nodded.

'Thank heavens,' sighed Mrs Madrigal. 'There are *so* few things you can count on these days.'

Michael laughed. 'Speaking of which . . . where's Mona? I haven't seen her since we got back.'

'She's down at the Searchlight, picking up some munchies for us.'

'No, I mean . . . the apartment's just like I left it. It doesn't look like she's even been home.'

The landlady patted her hair nervously. 'No. She's

been away. And lately she's been staying here, in my spare room.'

Michael hesitated, certain now that something was amiss. 'Where . . . where did she go?'

'Nevada.'

'Tahoe?'

Mrs Madrigal shook her head. 'Winnemucca.'

'Winnemucca?' Michael frowned. 'Why in the world did she pick that tacky place?'

The landlady shrugged. 'To get it together. In her words.'

'Did she?'

'She says she did.'

Michael smiled. 'She's lying.'

'Maybe,' said Mrs Madrigal, clearly relishing the enigma she had begun to spin, 'but she brought me a present.'

Baffled silence.

'She's down at the store with Mona now, so I've got some quick explaining to do, if we're going to be one big happy family again.' Mrs Madrigal excused herself and hurried to the phone. Mary Ann heard her ask Brian to come down.

He appeared minutes later, barefoot, in Levi's and a shrimp-colored T-shirt. He nodded greetings to Mary Ann and Michael ('Hey, long time no see!') and shook hands with Burke. Mrs Madrigal took his arm in a gesture that struck Mary Ann as surprisingly intimate.

'Brian's heard all this before,' said the landlady calmly, 'but I want the whole family here while I clear the air.'

It took her fifteen minutes to do just that.

She told her story without stopping. When she had come to the end, she fussed distractedly with her hair again and glanced apologetically at Burke. 'So, dear boy . . . it's not too late to back out.'

Dazed and touched, Mary Ann looked first at Mrs

155

Madrigal, then at a red-faced Burke, then back at Mrs Madrigal again. Brian stood by awkwardly, hands in pockets. Michael's eye caught Mary Ann's briefly, just as Mary Ann stepped forward.

'Mrs Madrigal, please don't . . .' She took the landlady's hand and squeezed it. 'I'm so . . . proud of you. I think Mona's the luckiest person in town.' She flung her arms around the landlady's neck and held on tight.

When she let go, Michael was standing there, smiling at Mrs Madrigal. 'I don't believe you,' he said admiringly.

She smiled back at him, cupping her hand against his cheek. 'You'll manage,' she said softly.

When Mona arrived with Mother Mucca, there were more introductions and hugs, more hasty explanations and heartfelt apologies and clumsy declarations of love.

Burke found a natural ally in Brian, Mary Ann noted.

Brian, however, excused himself from the gathering just before midnight.

'Late date?' Burke asked discreetly.

Brian nodded.

Mary Ann couldn't resist kidding him. 'Look what can happen in two weeks,' she said coyly. 'Are you seeing somebody now, Brian?'

'Yeah,' he replied. 'You could say that.'

The road to ruin

Pinus-bound at last, Frannie Halcyon made herself comfortable in Helena Parrish's Fawn Mist Mercedes and smiled out at the golden Sonoma countryside.

Helena took a long drag on her Du Maurier. 'What did you tell your daughter?' she asked.

'The truth. At least, part of it. I said I was going to the

house in Napa. She wasn't really listening. She's been so *distracted* lately.'

'Didn't I read somewhere that she's pregnant?'

'Uh huh. Eight months. Eight and a half, actually.'

'You aren't nervous about leaving her?'

Frannie looked at Helena. 'How long will this *take*?'

'It depends.'

'On what?'

Helena smiled. 'On how much you like it.'

Frannie giggled. 'A few days can't hurt. DeDe's been – you know – irritable lately, and I think she'd probably like a little time to herself. Besides, she's got a divine young gynecologist, and I'm a little tired of playing doting grandmother before the fact.'

Helena chuckled. 'You won't have to worry about that at Pinus. Most of us are grandmothers, but you're shot at dawn if you talk about it.'

They rode in silence for several minutes. It was almost as if Helena knew instinctively not to disrupt the fantasies that had begun to take shape in Frannie's mind.

'Well,' said Helena finally, 'it's almost time to go like sixty!'

'I'm not sure if this road is safe enough to—'

Helena smiled. 'I meant your birthday.'

'Oh, yes.' Frannie looked at her watch. 'In only one day, four hours, twenty-three minutes and thirteen *wonderful* little seconds.'

'You're a new woman already!'

'I can hardly believe it. Do you realize that a month ago I was seriously considering face-lifts and rejuvenation shots!'

'Oh, Frrrannie . . . no! You *must* have known that Pinus was just around the corner.'

Frannie thought for a moment. 'I'm not sure I actually believed in it. I'd heard stories, of course, but that was all hearsay. Oh, Helena . . . I feel so privileged!'

The Pinus hostess beamed proudly. 'We are *all*

157

privileged, Frannie.' Keeping one hand on the wheel, she pointed to the glove compartment. 'Open it, darling.'

'Why?'

'Go on, open it.'

Frannie did as she was told. 'And . . .'

'The little silver pillbox.'

'This?'

'Mmmm. Now . . . there's a thermos on the back seat. Pour yourself a nice cup of apple juice and take a vitamin Q tablet.'

'Vitamin Q?'

'Don't ask questions. It's good for what ails you. You're in our hands now, Frannie.' Her smile was warm but authoritative.

The initiate removed a tablet and studied its inscription. It said: Rorer 714.

'Down the hatch,' said Helena.

And down it went.

Driving through Glen Ellen, Helena motioned toward a sign marking the mental hospital. 'If Pinus gets too much for you,' she smiled, 'we can shift you with no problem at all.'

Frannie giggled, feeling sort of comfy-groggy. 'This is such a sleepy little town. I used to think this was all there was to it.'

'You'd never guess, would you?'

'Is it near here?'

'The turnoff's just up the road. You'll see.' Helena sucked on her cigarette, then winked. 'We haven't blindfolded initiates since the early forties.'

Frannie grew reflective. 'There's something about all this that reminds me of Edgar.'

'We're *all* widows, Frannie. The past is behind us.'

'I didn't mean it . . . sentimentally. Edgar was so damned mysterious about his two weeks at the Bohemian Grove. All that hocus-pocus about owls and

158

goblins and muses in the forest. He *used* it, Helena. He used it to keep me at arm's length.'

Helena sniffed. 'Compared to Pinus, darling, the Bohemian Grove is a Boy Scout jamboree.'

After leaving the highway, they bumped down a dirt road for several miles, passing the grove of towering pines that presumably gave the resort its name. When the Mercedes rounded the last bend, Frannie drew in her breath and clutched the dashboard.

'My *God*, Helena!'

'Yes,' beamed the hostess. 'Isn't it grand?'

Before them, marking the entrance, loomed a sixty-foot fieldstone tower, rounded at the top. As they passed it, Frannie peered out the window at the discreet brass plaque affixed at eye level.

PINUS

Established August 23, 1912

Too Much of a Good Thing is Wonderful

Mona's Law

Jon had no trouble spotting Michael in the crowd at the American Airlines terminal. He was wearing Levi's, a clean white T-shirt, and a black and silver satin Jefferson Starship baseball jacket.

And roller skates.

The doctor brushed past him, striding toward the baggage claim area in his Blue Brioni blazer. 'I don't know you,' he muttered.

'Aw, c'mon, big boy . . . you remember. We bumped into each other at the roller rink in South City. Nineteen forty-eight I believe it was.'

'You're an asshole, you know that?'

'How was your flight?'

'Michael, that gray-haired man over there is the most distinguished gynecologist on the West Coast.'

The skater slowed down and shifted his gaze. 'He has dandruff,' he said.

'He knows me,' said Jon.

'I would *never* hire a gynecologist with dandruff.'

'Would you at least slow down?'

'Why? You wanna smooch?'

'I'll punch you out. So help me.'

'I love it when you're butch.'

'Somebody's gotta do it.'

'You're a stuffy bastard, you know that?'

Jon glared daggers at Michael and grabbed the back of his belt, bringing him to a standstill. Then, in full view of the most distinguished gynecologist on the West Coast, he spun him around and kissed him on the mouth.

'Satisfied?'

'Satiated,' beamed Michael.

They picked up Jon's car in the airport garage and drove to his apartment in Pacific Heights. On the way, Michael rattled on about Barbary Lane and Mrs Madrigal's recent revelation to her 'family.'

Jon shook his head incredulously. 'That is . . . a mind-fucker.'

'Don't you love it?'

'You mean Mona didn't *know*?'

Michael shook his head. 'She knew that Mrs Madrigal was a transsexual – she was the *only* one who knew that – but she didn't know that Mrs Madrigal was her father.'

'What about Mona's mother?'

'What about her?'

'Does *she* know?'

Michael shrugged. 'She called Mona just before Mona left for Winnemucca. She was acting pretty freaky, Mona said – about Mrs Madrigal, that is – but Mona isn't sure how much she knows.'

Jon whistled. 'Bizarre!'

'And I haven't even gotten to Mary Ann yet. She's turned into Nancy Drew under our very noses.'

'Jesus. How's Burke taking all this?'

'Not badly, everything considered. He and Mary Ann are too obsessed with that damn key to notice much of anything else.'

'Any leads?'

'Zilch. I think it's a locker key myself.'

'Like at a bus station or something?'

'Or a bathhouse.'

Jon scolded him. 'The whole world isn't gay, Michael.'

'I know, I know.'

'Well, is that it?'

'What d'ya mean?'

'That's *all* the news? No earthquakes to report? No Mongolian hordes barricading the bridge?'

Michael smiled mysteriously. 'You're close.'

'What?'

'I got a job today.'

'Great! Where?'

'Halcyon Communications. Mary Ann got me the interview. The mailboy Xeroxed his cock one too many times, and Beauchamp Whatshisname canned him. I take his place starting Monday.'

'That's wonderful, Michael.'

'Yeah, I guess.'

'Sure it is. You can advance from there, Michael.'

'I know. I know it's a good job. That's the problem. It got me to thinking about Mona's Law.'

'Huh?'

'Mona's Law. That's what she calls it. She says you can have a hot job, a hot lover and a hot apartment, but you can't have all three at the same time.'

Jon laughed, then winked at Michael. 'What makes you think you've got a lover?'

161

Heroic couplets

Burke's first week back in San Francisco offered no new clues to the cause of his amnesia. One night, after a particularly nasty red rose scene at the Washington Square Bar & Grill, Mary Ann made up her mind to propose a new plan of attack.

'You know,' she said casually, as she crawled into bed with Burke, 'maybe we've been handling this whole business in the wrong way.'

He grinned at her. 'You wanna start carrying barf bags?'

'Burke, be serious!'

'Right.'

'The thing is, we've been *avoiding* roses and walkways – at least, we've been *trying* to – and as long as we do that, we're gonna keep avoiding the cause of your amnesia.'

'That's fine with me.'

She frowned. 'You don't mean that. I know you don't.'

He shrugged. 'Go on. Finish.'

'Well, I just think we should be . . . dealing with it, that's all.'

'What shall I do? Camp out in a rose garden?'

'Well, yes . . . something like that.'

'Forget it.'

'Look, Burke: there's a place down south of Market called the San Francisco Flower Mart. It's where the retailers get their flowers.'

'At five o'clock in the morning, no doubt.'

'Three.'

'Ouch.'

'We could stay up all night and find a place with

onion soup, like they used to do at that flower market in Paris. We could make it into a real adven—'

'Now *you've* flipped out.'

'Don't you see, Burke? If we exposed you to a *lot* of roses, thousands of them, we might be able to – I don't know – short-circuit whatever it is that's freaking you.'

'Terrific.'

'It wouldn't be like a surprise or anything. You'd know about it in advance. You could prepare yourself. And I'd be with you the whole time. Doesn't that sound reasonable?'

He stared at her in disbelief. 'And just when do you propose we pull off this caper?'

'Well . . .'

'Tonight, right?'

She nodded.

He flung back the covers and leaped out of bed.

'Where are you going?'

'Back to my apartment.'

'Burke, I didn't mean—'

'I have to change, don't I? Will jeans do . . . or do I need a tuxedo for Les Halles?'

'Come back here.'

'Why?'

'Because', she grinned, 'if I'm going to deflower *you*, you can at least return the favor.'

It was midnight now. Downstairs, on the second floor of 28 Barbary Lane, Michael and Jon were in bed watching a rerun of *The Honeymooners*.

'I love the tube,' sighed Michael, passing Jon their communal dish of Rocky Road ice cream. 'I loved this program almost as much as I loved *Little Lulu* comics.'

Jon smiled. 'Remember Little Itch?'

'Sure. And Tubby! My father built me a playhouse just like Tubby's, complete with a No Girls Allowed sign.'

'Maybe *that's* what turned you queer.'

'Nah. I know who did that. That guy on ice in LA.'
'Who?'
'Walt Disney. The Mickey Mouse Club.'
'The Mickey Mouse Club turned you queer?'
'Well . . .' Michael took a long drag on the hash pipe and handed it to Jon. 'You either got off on Annette's tits or you didn't. If you did, you were straight. If you didn't, you had only one alternative.'
'I'm waiting.'
'*Spin and Marty*. God, I used to agonize over that show!'
Jon smiled wistfully. 'I'd almost forgotten about that.'
'That's because you identified with Spin. Those of us who identified with Marty will never, ever, forget it.'
'What makes you think I identified with Spin?'
'Because you were cool even when you were eight years old. You've *never* known what it feels like to be a wimp. You won all the prizes at summer camp, and the other kids were electing you to some-fucking-thing-or-another every time you turned around. Am I right?'
Jon ignored the question. 'You ate all the ice cream,' he said.
'I *knew* I was right.'
The doctor simply smiled at him.

To market, to market

A blue and yellow armada of *Chronicle* delivery trucks was the only sign of life on Fifth Street when Mary Ann checked her wristwatch just after 3 A.M.
'It's eerie,' she said, settling back in the cab again, 'but kind of glamorous at the same time. I feel like Audrey Hepburn in *Charade*.'
Burke nodded in silence.

'You aren't nervous, are you?'

'I think the word is numb.'

'We can turn back, Burke, if you really think—'

'No. I wanna do it.' His eyes were glazed with steely determination, but Mary Ann could sense the terror beneath. 'Burke, you have nothing to fear but—'

He put his hand to her lips. 'Don't say it.'

Just then, the cab stopped at Brannan Street, where a row of pastel florist vans marked the entrance to the San Francisco Flower Mart. Burke paid the driver, while Mary Ann waited anxiously on the curb.

The market was a series of interlocking buildings, fragrant white caverns ablaze with fluorescent light. The pungent odor of cut stems tingled in Mary Anne's nose even before they entered the largest building.

'Burke . . . do you want me to go in first?'

'No. I'm ready.'

'Remember, we can leave whenever—'

'I know. Let's go.'

The mammoth floral hangar was bustling with tired-eyed retailers. Nodding to each other in the intimate language of night people, they pawed through mountains of blooms to find exactly the right gladiola, the right cyclamen, the right tinted daisy or potted palm.

Mary Ann felt awkward and conspicuous, like a space traveler on another planet. She took Burke's arm. 'Do you think they can tell the Flower People from the Non-Flower People?'

'Beats me.'

'I haven't seen any roses yet.'

'Who's looking?'

They moved from table to table, chatting briefly with the pleasant, Norman Rockwell-looking people who stood wrapping flowers in newspapers.

'Do you have roses?' Mary Ann asked at last.

'Over there,' smiled a dumpling-shaped woman in a green smock. 'The table against the wall. This is wholesale, though.'

Burke grinned uneasily as they walked away. 'They *can* tell, can't they?'

'Burke . . . I want you to let me know if—'

'It's OK, sweetheart. I promise.'

The roses were crammed by the thousands into large green metal cans. Seeing them, Mary Ann unconsciously tightened her grip on Burke's arm.

Burke seemed to grow paler. 'It's all right,' he assured her. 'Let's go closer.'

Next to the table, half a dozen retailers were surveying the selection of roses. Mary Ann tried to concentrate on the people, suddenly realizing that Burke's discomfort had brought her to the brink of sympathetic nausea.

The customer closest to them was a hawk-faced man in his early forties. He was wearing a pale blue leisure suit, and the flesh above his brow was covered with neat rows of tufted scabs. Mary Ann flinched and turned away.

Burke, she suddenly realized, was white as chalk.

'C'mon,' she said forcefully. 'This isn't fair to you.'

'No . . . wait . . .'

'We can't, Burke!'

'But . . .'

'C'mon!'

Out in the parking lot, he threw up behind a coral-colored van that said ROSE-O-RAMA. Mary Ann stood by silently in the shadows, racked with guilt.

When Burke returned, he managed a smile. 'Well, it seemed like a good idea at the time.'

'It was a *crummy* idea. And we should have left earlier.'

'I would have, but . . . Did you see that guy next to us?'

'With the hair transplant?'

He nodded. 'Maybe I'm wrong, but I could have sworn he recognized me.'

'Burke, are you *sure*?'

'No, but . . . it was like I startled him, like he knew me from somewhere. I thought if I waited around long enough, he might—'

'Wait here!'

Her heart pounding, Mary Ann ignored the puzzled gazes of the flower sellers and raced back into the building, back to the table with the roses.

But the man with the transplant was gone.

It was 3.35 when they left the market. At that moment, back at Barbary Lane, Jon stirred in his sleep, then woke to the sound of Michael's voice.

'Jon . . . help me . . . something's wrong.'

'You're dreaming, sport. It's OK.'

'No . . . it's not. I can't move, Jon.'

The doctor propped himself up on his elbow and looked into Michael's face. His eyes were open, blinking. 'Sure you can,' said Jon. 'You just reached for me.'

'No . . . it's my legs. I can't move my goddamn legs!'

The emergency room

When Mary Ann and Burke returned to 28 Barbary Lane, Jon heard their footsteps on the stairway and motioned them into Michael's apartment. 'Michael's sick,' he explained tersely, leading them into the bedroom, where an illuminated plastic goose cast a yellow glow on the motionless figure in bed. Then the doctor knelt down next to his patient.

'Mary Ann and Burke are here.'

'They're . . . you woke them up?'

Mary Ann took a step forward from the doorway. 'We've been out at the . . . Mouse, what's the matter?'

Michael hiked himself up on his elbows. 'We're working on that. My leg's . . . gone to sleep.'

167

Jon tapped on his leg with a hemostat – the hemostat that Michael used as a roach clip. 'Feel that?'

'Nope,' said Michael, as the clamp moved up his calf. 'Nope . . . nope . . .' Finally, when it reached midthigh, he said, 'There.'

'Good.'

'Good, my ass! What's the matter with me?'

'I think it's only temporary, Michael. I'm gonna take you to the hospital.'

'I'm in labor, right? C'mon, you can tell me.'

Jon smiled. 'Don't talk, babe. We'll have you out of here soon.'

'Will you stop playing Chad Everett and tell me what the fuck—'

'I don't know, Michael. I don't know what it is.'

Jon arranged for an ambulance, which arrived fifteen minutes later. He and Burke and Mary Ann rode in the back with Michael, making small talk most of the way to St Sebastian's Hospital. It was anything but natural, and Mary Ann felt painfully inadequate in the crisis.

'Mouse,' she said softly as they passed Lafayette Park, 'if you give me your parents' number, I'll call them when we get to the hospital.'

He hesitated before replying. 'No . . . I'd rather you didn't.'

'Mouse, don't you think they should . . . ?'

'No, I don't.'

Jon leaned over and stroked Michael's hair. 'Michael, I think your family deserves to—'

'This is my family,' said Michael.

Mary Ann and Burke sat mute in the waiting room while Jon accompanied Michael into the emergency room. Twenty minutes later, he reported back to them.

'They're going to do a spinal,' he said.

Mary Ann fidgeted with the *McCall's* in her lap. 'Jon . . . I don't know what that means.'

'A lumbar puncture. They check for elevation of the protein level and . . . diminishment of the white cells in the . . .' The doctor was barely looking at his friends. 'They think it's Guillain-Barré.'

This time Burke stepped in. 'Jon . . . a translation?'

'Sorry. Remember those people who were paralyzed by the swine flu shots?'

Burke shook his head.

'I do,' said Mary Ann.

'Well, that was the Guillain-Barré syndrome. I mean, the syndrome caused the paralysis.'

Mary Ann frowned. 'But . . . I don't think Michael ever had a swine flu shot.'

'That's just one cause. They don't know what causes it, really.'

'But . . . what does it do?'

'It's an ascending paralysis. It starts in the feet and legs usually, and it . . . well, it climbs.' He looked down at his hands, tapping his fingertips gently against each other. 'Lots of times it goes away completely.'

'Jon, he's not . . . ?'

'The only real danger is to the respiratory system. If the paralysis becomes advanced enough to impede breathing, they have to perform a tracheotomy in order to . . .' He brought his hands up to his face and pressed his fingertips against his eyes. For a moment, Mary Ann thought he might cry, but his face retained the same masklike expression. 'That poor little fucker,' he said softly.

Mary Ann resisted the urge to touch him, to stroke him. He looked like a man about to explode. 'Jon, he won't . . . ? Did the doctors . . . ?'

'Fucking doctors!'

'What . . . did they tell you?'

'Nothing! Not a goddamn thing!' The rage in his voice made Mary Ann flinch, so he reached out and squeezed her shoulder apologetically. 'I think he could die, Mary Ann. We've gotta get ready for that.'

Inside Pinus

The long drive up to Pinus came to an abrupt end at an imposing steel security gate. Helena Parrish stopped the Mercedes and spoke into an intercom. 'A cheeseburger, an order of fries and a chocolate shake – and step on it.'

Laughter. A young man's laughter. 'Mrs Parrish . . . you're back!'

'Six whole hours. You miss me, Bluegrass?'

'The Pope Catholic?'

'You're sweet. Open up, Blue. We've got the new girl with us.'

'You bet!'

The gate swung open. Helena smiled at Frannie as she maneuvered the car along yet another tree-lined road. 'You're gonna like Bluegrass,' she winked. 'Under normal circumstances, he's assigned to me, but . . . well, I like you, Frannie. I'd like you to have him.'

'Helena! I couldn't!'

'No . . . please. I'd like you to. Really.'

'You're a dear.'

'Pish.'

'Goodness, I feel just . . . I feel so marvelous.'

The hostess smiled. 'We're inside now. You can jane, if you like.'

'What?'

'Scream. We call it janing here – as in "Me Tarzan, you Jane." It's sort of a Tarzan yell for women – like primal screaming, but a *lot* more fun. Go ahead, give it a whirl.'

Frannie felt inhibited. 'Oh, Helena!'

'Go on! You're at Pinus now.'

'Now? In the car?'

'Now and any other time you please, darling.'

Frannie grinned sheepishly, then stuck her head out the window and made a noise that sounded like: 'Eeeeeiiiiii!'

'Nice,' said Helena unexcitedly, 'but you're not janing, darling.'

'Well, how do you . . . ?'

'Like this.'

The hostess extended her swanlike neck and opened her mouth to the fullest. 'Aaaahhhhaaaahhhheeee-aaaahhhh!'

Somewhere in the depths of the pine forest an identical sound reverberated.

'An echo!' exclaimed Frannie.

'No,' smiled Helena. 'Sybil Manigault. She's into nature.'

The hostess parked the car next to the reception building, a rambling, chalet-style structure with leaded glass windows. Lady Banksia roses trailed along the dark wooden eaves.

Frannie clucked her tongue admiringly. 'Lovely . . . absolutely lovely.'

'The cottages are of the same design. They're all Julia Morgan – perhaps her greatest triumph.'

'Incredible! Edgar was intrigued by Julia Morgan's architecture, but I never heard a *word* about this.'

'Naturally. There was a clause in Morgan's contract with Pinus that forbade publicity. Originally, the founders had hired Bernard Maybeck as architect, but he backed out when he discovered . . . well, you know.'

Helena led Frannie into the spacious lodge, allowing the newcomer to soak up the atmosphere in silence: the parchment-shaded lamps, the dusty-rose velvet upholstery, the copper pots brimming with wild-flowers.

'I feel funny without luggage,' said Frannie.

'Why? Everything you need is here. Two days from now it'll kill you to part with your kaftan.'

171

'Where is everybody?'

Helena chuckled. 'Hiding, probably.'

'Why?'

'Oh, it's silly, really. Technically, you're not sixty until tomorrow at — what? Seven-thirty or so? The other girls are a little wary of talking to initiates until after you're . . . one of us.'

'Then . . . what do I do until then?'

Helena slid a willowy arm across her shoulder. 'First of all, darling, I think you should take another vitamin Q. Then I suggest you ask Birdsong.'

'Who?'

Helena winked. 'Follow me.'

Three minutes later, the hostess flung open the door of Frannie's cottage. A young man sitting on the edge of the bed jumped to his feet. He was about twenty-four, Frannie guessed, with a lean body, curly black hair and astoundingly blue eyes. He was wearing a dusty-rose terry cloth jumpsuit, unzipped to the waist.

And he was clearly flustered. 'Mrs Parrish, I'm sorry. I didn't mean to—'

'That's all right, Birdsong. You didn't know we were coming. This is Mrs Halcyon.'

Birdsong nodded shyly. 'Hello.'

'How do you do?'

'Birdsong is your houseboy,' explained Helena. 'He can fill you in on everything. Meanwhile, I must get ready for your little do tomorrow, so . . . ta-ta!' She made a lightning-quick exit. Frannie was left standing there, smiling nervously at Birdsong.

'Well,' said the houseboy, suddenly more sure of himself. 'It's time for our bath, I suppose.'

Outside in the toasty Sonoma sunshine, Helena Parrish was janing at the top of her lungs.

Bedside manner

When Michael woke at St Sebastian's Hospital, Jon was at his side, armed with a pot of mums, three back issues of *Playgirl* and something in a brown paper bag.

'Look at you,' smiled Michael. 'A queen's wet dream.'

Jon winked at him. 'How ya feeling?'

'Less and less. But that's normal, isn't it?'

'Sure. It usually . . . ascends. Michael . . . it gets worse before it gets better.'

'Gotcha.'

'Are you . . . can you feel it moving?'

'Yeah, I guess. Kind of a tingling, right?' He placed his hand on his leg just below the groin. 'Won't be long now, kiddo. Better get it while the gettin' is good!'

Jon laughed. 'Speaking of which, I just checked out the orderly. I'm a lot more worried about *him* than I am about . . . this.'

'Right. So what's in the bag, liar?'

Jon dropped the bag in his lap. 'Guess.'

'My very own Accu-Jac?'

'Open it, turkey.'

Michael picked up the bag. A *Little Lulu* comic book fell out. 'God Jon! It's . . . vintage! It must be late fifties at least! Where did you find it?'

'That comics store on Columbus.'

'Christ!' he flipped excitedly through the comic book. 'Look! There's that clubhouse with the No Girls Allowed sign! And the ads must be . . . Oh, God I *gotta* see the ads!'

'Whatdya mean?'

'You know . . . joy buzzers and whoopee cushions and that goddamn little metal thing that was supposed

173

to turn you into a ventriloquist when you stuck it under your tongue. Christ! Didn't you ever send off for one of those?'

The doctor shook his head, smiling.

'No,' sighed Michael, 'of course you didn't. And you never read the Charles Atlas ads either. You were *never* a ninety-eight-pound weakling. Or was it ninety-seven?'

'You got me. And listen, asshole, if you were ever a whatever-pound weakling, you got over it pretty quick.' He reached over and felt Michael's bicep, then kept his hand cupped gently against the muscle.

Michael looked down at his arm. 'That'll go.'

'Michael . . .'

'*And* the pecs. The pecs'll go down like a preacher's daughter.'

Jon chuckled. 'Where the hell did you pick *that* one up?'

'Where else? Florida. Land of the Free and Home of the Butch. When will this be over, Jon?'

Jon let go of his arm. 'Well . . . sometimes the syndrome can run its course in a matter of weeks.'

'Sometimes.'

'A high percentage of cases have—'

'Jon, what the fuck. I'm gonna be paralyzed, aren't I? Completely.'

The doctor nodded. 'I think so.'

'How am I gonna breathe?'

'It may not spread that far.'

'What if it does?'

'If it does, a tracheotomy may be necessary. It's not as awful as it sounds, Michael. In most cases, the condition is only—'

'You poor bastard!' Michael laughed sardonically.

'What?'

'You thought you had a fruit, but you ended up with a vegetable!'

'Just shut up, will you?'

174

'I thought that was pretty good.'

'Well, don't think, then.'

'Hold my hand, will you?'

Jon took his hand. 'That better?'

'It's tingling.'

'Your hand?'

'Uh huh. Act Two, right?'

Silence.

'I don't wanna die, Jon.'

'Michael, shut up!'

'I'm sorry. That was terribly Jane Wyman of me.'

'There's nothing to worry about. I'm gonna be with you the whole time.'

'You won't let me get zits, will you? I'm twenty-six years old . . . I don't need zits.'

'Such vanity.'

'I love you, Dr Fielding.'

The answer was a squeeze of his hand.

The last straw

Mary Ann's anxiety over Michael severely hampered her efficiency at Halcyon Communications. Beauchamp Day found three typos in his letter to the chairman of the board of Adorable Pantyhose.

'Mary Ann, for God's sake!'

'What?'

'Look at this shit! I know the Old Man didn't put up with this kind of sloppiness! Christ! I could do better with a Kelly Girl!'

'I'm sorry. I . . . Beauchamp, I can't seem to concentrate on—' She spun her chair away from him, buried her face in her hands and began to sob.

Beauchamp watched her, unflinching. 'Cheap shot, Mary Ann. Cheap shot.'

175

Her sobs grew louder. 'I'm not . . . Oh, God, I . . .'

'All right. Do your little Gidget number or whatever. I'll get Mildred's secretary to retype it.'

She straightened up. 'No. I'll do it.'

'You aren't being very professional, you know that?'

'I'm sorry. I have a friend who's sick. He . . . may die.'

'A boyfriend?'

'No. I mean, he's a good friend.' She had decided earlier not to tell Beauchamp about Michael in the faint hope that Michael would recover in time to take over the mailboy job.

Beauchamp studied her for several seconds, then said, 'I'm sorry about that, but you'll just have to cope with it, Mary Ann. I can't afford to give you any time off right now.'

'I didn't ask for that.'

'You were crying. I've seen that routine before.'

'It's not a *routine*.'

He shrugged blithely. 'Whatever. I've seen you do it before, that's all.'

'Gimme the letter.'

'Look, I said I was sorry about your friend. You don't need to get sullen with me.'

'Gimme the letter, goddammit!'

Beauchamp glared at her murderously, then held out the letter and dropped it, allowing it to float to her desktop. Mary Ann looked at the letter, then back to Beauchamp again. She picked up the letter and crumpled it into a ball.

Beauchamp shook his head and smiled. 'You're pushing it, girl.'

'No. You are.'

'Tsk tsk. Is that right?'

'Leave me alone.'

Beauchamp folded his arms, staying put. 'You think you're a fucking *fixture* around here, don't you? You think I won't shitcan you because you worked for the

176

Old Man. Or better yet, because I screwed you a couple of times!'

Mary Ann pushed back her chair and stood up. 'Actually I think about you as little as possible.'

'Oh, that's clever! Farrah Fawcett-Dumbshit made a funny! Yuck yuck!'

Mary Ann looked him in the eye. 'Get out of my way.'

Beauchamp didn't budge. 'God, you're a laugh!'

'I'm leaving.'

'You're goddam right you're leaving! Jesus H. Christ! How long did you really think I could stomach you and your cutesy-pie *Snoopy* cartoons on the filing cabinets? And that precious goddam bug-eyed frog planter with the—'

'Decorate it yourself, then. Maybe one of your chic closet-case friends can help out.'

Beauchamp's eyes were ice blue. 'You're as common as they come.'

'Maybe.'

'*Maybe?* Hah! Why the hell do you think you're a secretary, sweetie pie? You're a dumb little bourgeois bitch! Christ, look at you! You're the same bland little thing you were at fifteen, and you'll stay that way until somebody gives you a set of Tupperware for twenty years of faithful service – only it won't be me, thank God!'

She stared at him, blinking back the tears. 'I've never met anyone as . . . horrible . . .' She pushed past him and headed for the door.

'By the way,' Beauchamp added, 'if you plan to keep pushing paper, you might as well forget about the other agencies. There won't be any glowing references from Halcyon.'

Mary Ann stopped in the doorway, composed herself as much as possible, then turned and raised her middle finger to the president of Halcyon Communications.

'Go fuck yourself,' she said.

Bruno comes through

Five minutes after Mary Ann stormed out of his office, Beauchamp used his private line to call Bruno Koski.

'It's me, Bruno.'

'I know a lotta me's.'

'Yeah. Well . . . the one at Jackson Square. Look, I haven't heard from you.'

'The first move is yours, remember?'

'OK, OK. You got the man?'

'Yeah. I got the . . . person.'

'Is he reliable, and discreet?'

'Nah. He's a fucked-up junkie, man. Don't know his ass from a hole in the ground. What the fuck you think, man? My ass is on the line more than yours is!'

'Does he know about me? Does he know I'm the one who . . . ?'

'Look, numbnuts! If you don't trust me, why don't you get another patsy to do you—'

'All right. OK. When is he . . . available?'

'I told ya. Soon as ya get me the money.'

'How do I know you won't—'

'Ya don't. Tough shit.'

'OK. Look. She's going to a League fashion show tomorrow night—'

'League?'

Beauchamp sighed. 'Junior League, Bruno. That doesn't matter. It's out at the Palace of the Legion of Honor. It starts around eight, so you can tell your man . . . well, you can figure out when it'll be over. She'll be driving her mother's Mercedes, I'm sure. The license plate says FRANNI.'

'Her old lady's gonna be with her?'

'Nope. She's in Napa, I think. I'm sure she'll be alone.'

'I thought you two was separated.'

'We *are*, Bruno.' Beauchamp's patience was growing short.

'Well, if you guys are separated, how the fuck do you know all this, anyway?'

'I read it.'

'You *read* it.'

'In the social columns, Bruno.'

'Oh.'

'Don't worry. She'll be there. If there's a photographer around, she'll be there.' His tone became more businesslike. 'How do you want the money?'

'Tens and twenties.'

'Just like the movies, huh?'

'This ain't no fuckin' movie.'

'You want to meet the same place we did before?'

'Yeah. Eight o'clock. Tomorrow night.'

'Isn't that pushing it?'

'You gimme the money. I'll call the contact. Ain't no big deal.'

'You sure he knows how to . . . ?'

'It'll happen. You gimme the money and it'll happen.'

'I don't want her . . .'

'I know.'

'I won't accept responsibility if she's . . . if it's permanent. I want to make that perfectly clear.'

'Right. Gotcha. You're a fuckin' prince.'

After an hour-long conference with the copywriter for Tidy-Teen Tampettes, Beauchamp paced his office for ten minutes, then telephoned an office at 450 Sutter.

'Dr Fielding's office.'

'Is he in?'

'One moment, please.'

A thirty-second wait and then: 'Yes?'

'What's up, Blondie?'

Silence.

179

'Well,' said Beauchamp, 'I didn't expect a trumpet fanfare, but after all this time . . . well, the least you could do is muster a cheery hello.'

'Are you calling about your wife's pregnancy?'

'Actually, I thought you and I might get together and make a few babies. Just for old time's sake, mind you.'

'I'm going to hang up.'

'Oh, come off it!'

'I think I made it clear to you before that I don't want you calling this office – or anywhere else, for that matter.'

'Whatsamatter? You goin' steady or something?'

'You're a slug, Beauchamp.'

'I'll bet you say that to all the boys.'

The doctor hung up. Beauchamp sat at his desk for half a minute, spinning himself around in his chair. Then he got up, went to the refrigerator and made himself a Negroni, downing it in a single gulp.

Life, sometimes, was a pain in the ass.

The girl with green hair

Manuel the gardener was grumpy, so DeDe didn't have the nerve to ask him to clean the yucky things out of the swimming pool at Halcyon Hill. Instead, she sat on the terrace, munching M & M's and reading the copy of *Fear of Flying* she had bought the previous summer.

With mother in Napa and Beauchamp in the city and Daddy only a memory, she felt like an orphan princess in the great house. As usual, her loneliness drove her to the telephone.

Only *this* time it wasn't to call Binky, Muffy, Oona, BoBo or Shugie.

'Hello,' said the honeyed voice on the other end.

'Hi. It's De-De Day.'

'Ape Woman.'

DeDe laughed. 'I promise *never* to drag you to something like that again!'

'As I recall, I dragged *you*, hon.'

'You were right, though. An ape in a girl mask would have been cuter.'

'Whatever. Hey . . . how's the tummy?'

'Bigger.'

'But not better?'

'I don't know, really. I worry a lot.'

'About what?'

'Nothing in particular. I know it's morbid, but sometimes I get the creepiest feeling that something is wrong. My gynecologist says that's typical for a first-timer, so I guess I just shouldn't *think* about it so much.'

'You need to get out more.'

'I don't think I could handle any more Ape Women.'

'Well, don't feel like the Lone Ranger, honey!'

'Actually, I was wondering if you could handle going to a Junior League fashion show tonight?'

Silence.

'I know it's late notice . . .'

D'orothea chuckled throatily. 'You don't know how funny that is.'

'I know it's kind of a bore, but I thought we might get a giggle or two out of—'

'I used to be a model, DeDe. At your father's agency. At Halcyon Communications.'

'What?'

'I was one of the Adorable Pantyhose girls.'

'Why didn't you tell me?'

'For one thing, your husband fired me . . . and I wasn't sure if you find him as big an asshole as I do.'

DeDe laughed, reservedly at first, then with happy abandon. 'Oh, God, D'orothea. We separated, remember?'

'Yeah, but things are so goddamn mellow these days. I mean, you two could be taking est together or going to Incompatibility Rap Sessions or something.'

'How well did you know Beauchamp, anyway?'

'Long enough to merit one of his infamous tirades.'

'Why did he fire you?'

'Oh . . . I didn't show up for a couple of jobs. My skin was . . . I had a skin condition, and I looked like hell. It's a long story.'

'My *precise* words about me and Beauchamp!'

'You still want me to go with you to that fashion show?'

'Of course! Even more now.'

'Sure they won't check my pedigree at the door?'

'Positive. We're on, then?'

'We're on, honey!'

Back in the city, something else was on. Douchebag had made final arrangements with Bruno Koski.

'You got it straight now?' he asked on the phone.

'Yeah, yeah. I got it.'

'You don't move until I call you. When I call, you run like hell up the hill to the Legion of Honor. You sure you know where . . . ?'

'I *told* you, man!'

'It'll be sometime after eight o'clock. I promise, punk – you screw this up and you won't get the dough!'

'OK, OK.'

Bruno hung up.

Fifteen minutes later, the punkette made preparations to leave. Her mother appeared in the bedroom door.

'Do you *have* to wear that garbage bag?'

'What's wrong with it?'

'Heidi, for God's sake, it's disgusting! It's all torn and . . . disgusting.'

'I *told* you to buy some new ones.'

'I'm not going to argue with you. Where are you going, anyway?'

'I . . . to the Mab.'

'The what?'

'The Mabuhay!'

'You'll miss *The Brady Bunch*.'

'Big deal.'

'Heidi . . . promise you won't stick gum up your nose tonight.'

'OK.'

Douchebag smiled at her mother, then retrieved a wad of Dentyne from her left nostril, popped it in her mouth and began to chew rhythmically.

'See ya,' she said, heading out the door.

Thinking out loud

In less than twenty-four hours Michael's paralysis was complete. He could blink his eyes and move his lips, but the rest of him was horribly still. He looked at his visitor using a mirror angled over his bed.

'Hi, lover,' he said.

'Hi.'

'Shouldn't you be at the office?'

'It's OK. Slow day.'

Michael grinned. 'Me too.'

'I talked to Mary Ann. She and Burke are coming over later.'

'God, I'm popular today! Miss Congeniality. Brian and the Three Graces just left.'

'Who?'

'That's what I call 'em now. Mona and Mrs Madrigal and Mother Mucca.'

Jon laughed. 'They're quite a trio.'

'Yeah. And it's good for Mona, too. I'm glad.'

'Are you . . . doin' OK, Michael?'

'Well . . . I remembered something funny today.'

183

'Yeah?'

'When I was a kid, fourteen or so, I used to worry about what would happen when I didn't get married. My father was married when he was twenty-three, so I figured I had nine or ten years before people would figure out that I was gay. After that . . . well, there weren't a whole lot of good excuses. So you know what I used to hope for?'

Jon shook his head.

'That I'd be paralyzed.'

'Michael, for Christ's sake!'

'Not like this. Just from the waist down. That way, I could be in a wheelchair, and people would like me, and I wouldn't have to worry about what they'd say when I didn't get married. It seemed like a pretty good solution at the time. I was a *dumb* little kid.'

'You're also a maudlin grownup. You can't dwell on this stuff, Michael. It's not healthy for you to . . . Hey, I almost forgot. *Chorus Line* is coming back. I sent for our tickets today.'

'Nice fake.'

'Goddammit, Michael! Will you stop being so . . . melodramatic! I hate to disappoint you, but you're not gonna . . .'

'The word is die, Babycakes.'

'You're *not*, Michael. I'm a doctor. I know.'

'You're a gynecologist, turkey.'

'You *like* playing this scene, don't you? You're getting off on this whole goddamn Camille—'

'Hey, hey.' Michael's voice was gentle, consoling. The flippancy was gone. 'Don't take me seriously, Jon. I've just gotta talk, that's all. Don't listen to what I'm saying. OK?'

'You got a deal.'

'You know what? They've got me on The Pill. I mean, they call it steroids or something, but it's still The Pill. I've been tripping on that all morning. I'm on The Pill, and my gynecologist spends more time with me than my doctor does. Isn't that a hoot?'

Jon smiled. 'That's pretty good, all right.'

'Maybe there's a lot to be said for all this. I mean, for one thing, I can go for hours at a time without looking nellie. If they could prop me up or something, I'd be *dynamite* in a dark corner at The Bolt!'

Mary Ann arrived half an hour later. Michael winked at her in the mirror.

'Hi gorgeous. Where'd ya get that Acapulco tan?'

'Hi, Mouse. Burke's here too.'

'I see. Hello, Hunky.'

'Hi, Michael.'

'The coast is clear, kiddo. Not a rose in sight.'

The couple laughed nervously. 'Mouse,' said Mary Ann, 'I picked up your mail for you. Do you . . . want me to read it to you?'

'What is it? A pink slip from the Clap Clinic?'

Mary Ann giggled. 'I think it's from your parents.'

Michael said nothing. Jon cast a warning glance at Mary Ann, who instantly tried to backtrack. 'I can leave it, Mouse . . . and maybe later Jon can—'

'No. Go ahead.'

Mary Ann looked at Jon, then back to Michael. 'Are you sure?'

'What the hell.'

So she opened the letter.

Saving the children

Mary Ann began to read:

Dear Mikey,

How are you? I guess you're back from Mexico by now. Please write us. Your Papa and I are real anxious

*to hear all about it. Also, how is Mary Ann and when
will we get a chance to meet her?*

*Everything is fine in Orlando. It looks like we'll do
fine with this year's crop, even with the frost and all.
The homosexual boycott may make orange juice sales
drop off a little, but Papa says it won't make any
difference in the long run, and besides it won't . . .*

Mary Ann looked up, 'Mouse . . . I think we should
save this for some other time.'

'No. It's OK. Go on.'

Mary Ann looked at Jon, who shrugged.

'I've handled it for half my life,' said Michael.
'Another day won't make a difference.'

So Mary Ann continued:

*. . . besides it won't do anything but show Jesus
whose side we're on.*

*You remember in my last letter I said we didn't say
anything in our resolution about renting to homosexuals, because Lucy McNeil rents her garage to that
sissy man who sells carpets at Dixie Dell Mall? I
thought that was OK, because Lucy is a quiet sort who
has stomach trouble, and I didn't think it would be
Christian to upset her unduly.*

*I guess the man was right when he said the road to
Hell is paved with good intentions, because Lucy has
all of a sudden become real militant about the
homosexuals. She said she wouldn't sign our Save Our
Children resolution, and she called us all heathens
and hypocrites and said that Jesus wouldn't even let us
kiss His feet if He came back to earth today. Can you
imagine such a thing?*

*I was real upset about it after the meeting until your
Papa cleared it up for me. You know, I never thought
about it much, but Lucy never did marry, and she was
really pretty when her and me used to go to Orlando
High. She could of gotten a real good husband, if she*

had set her mind to it. Anyway, your Papa pointed out that Lucy takes modern art classes at the YWCA now and wears Indian blouses and hippie clothes, so I guess it's possible that the lesbians have recruited her. It's mighty hard to believe, though. She was always so pretty.

Etta Norris had a Save Our Children get-together at her house last Saturday night. It was real nice. Lolly Newton even brought a Red Devil's Food Cake she made using Mrs Oral Roberts' recipe from Anita Bryant's cookbook. That gave us the idea of making lots of food from the cookbook and selling it at the VFW bazaar to raise money for Save Our Children.

We are all praying that the referendum in Miami will pass. If the homosexuals are allowed to teach in Miami, then it might happen in Orlando. Reverend Harker says that things have gotten so bad in Miami that the homosexuals are kissing each other in public. Your Papa doesn't believe that, but I say that the devil is a lot more powerful than we think he is.

Mikey, we had to put Blackie to sleep. I hate to tell you that, but he was mighty old. I know the Lord will look after him, like he does with all His creatures. Bubba says hi.

Love,
Mama

Mary Ann moved to Michael's bedside, addressing him directly without using the mirror. 'Mouse . . . I'm really sorry.'

'Forget it. I think it's a riot.'

'No. It's awful. She doesn't know what she's saying, Mouse.'

Michael smiled. 'Yes she does. She's a capital-C Christian. They *always* know what they're saying.

'But she wouldn't say that, Mouse. Not if she knew. Not her own son.'

'She'd say it about somebody else's son. What the hell's the difference?'

Mary Ann looked back at Jon and Burke, tears streaming down her face. Then she reached out and touched the immobile figure in the bed.

'Mouse . . . if I could change your life for you, so help me I'd—'

'You can, Babycakes.'

'What? How?'

'Got your Bic handy?'

'Sure.'

'Then take a letter, Miss Singleton.'

Letter to Mama

Dear Mama,

I'm sorry it's taken me so long to write. Every time I try to write to you and Papa I realize I'm not saying the things that are in my heart. That would be OK, if I loved you any less than I do, but you are still my parents and I am still your child.

I have friends who think I'm foolish to write this letter. I hope they're wrong. I hope their doubts are based on parents who loved and trusted them less than mine do. I hope especially that you'll see this as an act of love on my part, a sign of my continuing need to share my life with you.

I wouldn't have written, I guess, if you hadn't told me about your involvement in the Save Our Children campaign. That, more than anything, made it clear that my responsibility was to tell you the truth, that your own child is homosexual, and that I never needed saving from anything except the cruel and ignorant piety of people like Anita Bryant.

I'm sorry, Mama. Not for what I am, but for how you must feel at this moment. I know what that feeling is, for I felt it for most of my life. Revulsion, shame,

*disbelief – rejection through fear of something I knew,
even as a child, was as basic to my nature as the color
of my eyes.*

*No, Mama, I wasn't 'recruited.' No seasoned homo-
sexual ever served as my mentor. But you know what?
I wish someone had. I wish someone older than me
and wiser than the people in Orlando had taken
me aside and said, 'You're all right, kid. You can grow
up to be a doctor or a teacher just like anyone else.
You're not crazy or sick or evil. You can succeed and
be happy and find peace with friends – all kinds of
friends – who don't give a damn who you go to bed
with. Most of all though, you can love and be loved,
without hating yourself for it.'*

*But no one ever said that to me, Mama. I had to find
it out on my own, with the help of the city that has
become my home. I know this may be hard for you to
believe, but San Francisco is full of men and women,
both straight and gay, who don't consider sexuality in
measuring the worth of another human being.*

*These aren't radicals or weirdos, Mama. They are
shop clerks and bankers and little old ladies and people
who nod and smile to you when you meet them on the
bus. Their attitude is neither patronizing nor pitying.
And their message is so simple: Yes, you are a person.
Yes, I like you. Yes it's all right for you to like me too.*

*I know what you are thinking now. You're asking
yourself: What did we do wrong? How did we let this
happen? Which one of us made him that way?*

*I can't answer that, Mama. In the long run, I guess I
really don't care. All I know is this: If you and Papa
are responsible for the way I am, then I thank you with
all my heart, for it's the light and the joy of my life.*

*I know I can't tell you what it is to be gay. But I can
tell you what it's not.*

*It's not hiding behind words, Mama. Like family and
decency and Christianity. It's not fearing your body, or
the pleasures that God made for it. It's not judging*

your neighbor, except when he's crass or unkind.

Being gay has taught me tolerance, compassion and humility. It has shown me the limitless possibilities of living. It has given me people whose passion and kindness and sensitivity have provided a constant source of strength.

It has brought me into the family of man, Mama, and I like it here. I like it.

There's not much else I can say, except that I'm the same Michael you've always known. You just know me better now. I have never consciously done anything to hurt you. I never will.

Please don't feel you have to answer this right away. It's enough for me to know that I no longer have to lie to the people who taught me to value the truth.

Mary Ann sends her love.

Everything is fine at 28 Barbary Lane.

Your loving son,
Michael

The end

Mary Ann was severely shaken when she and Burke left St Sebastian's. She had planned on staying most of the evening, but her tears had proved uncontrollable. Jon had promised, however, he would call her 'if anything changes.'

Back on Barbary Lane, she tried to thaw a strip steak under the hot-water tap.

'Don't do that on my account,' said Burke.

'I thought you liked steak.'

'I'm not hungry. Really.'

She sighed and tossed the meat onto her Rubbermaid dish rack. 'Neither am I.' She turned to face Burke, forcing a smile. 'Do you know how I met Michael?'

'In a supermarket, right?'

'I told you already?'

Burke nodded. 'In Puerto Vallarta.'

Mary Ann dried her hands with a dish towel and sat down opposite Burke at the kitchen table. 'He was so cute, Burke . . . but I was *furious* with him, because he was with this guy I really liked, and all night long I just kept saying to myself, "What a waste . . . what a waste." I believed that, too. I really believed he was wasted, that he had gone wrong somehow. Of course, I *told* myself I felt sorry for him, but I was really just feeling sorry for myself. I found out all the Mr Rights weren't made for me, and I couldn't handle it.'

'That's OK. People change.'

'I didn't. Not for a long time. I used to feel . . . I don't know. I guess I thought I could change him, become his friend and make him relax around women or something. I didn't count on finding out that *I* was the one who needed to relax.'

'Don't be so hard on yourself.'

'It's the truth, Burke.'

'Michael loves you, Mary Ann. You must've done *something* right.'

'I hope.'

'Hope? Dammit, Mary Ann, there were times in Mexico when I was almost eaten up with jealousy.'

'Jealousy? Of Michael?'

'Michael and you together. Michael and you laughing and conspiring together. Michael and you playing tricks on Arnold and Melba. Michael and you pretending – hell, you weren't pretending – you *were* married. You were as married as two people could ever be.'

She blinked at him in amazement, unconsciously fingering the funny little key around her neck. 'Burke . . . I love you. I never meant to—'

'I'm not accusing you. I just don't want you to chastise yourself. Not about Michael. You two have had something great together.'

She let go of the key and reached for his hand. 'Could we go to the bedroom?' she asked.

There, on the bed, she lay in his arms and cried.

Later, they watched television, each pretending for the sake of the other to be interested. Then Burke rose and switched off the set.

'Do you want to call the hospital?'

'No . . . I . . . no.'

'You might feel better.'

'Jon's there. I don't think I should . . .'

'I think Michael would like it.'

'Well, what could I . . . ?'

The phone rang. They both jumped.

'Do you want me to get it?' asked Burke.

She hesitated. 'No . . . I'll get it.'

She turned her back as she spoke. She didn't want Burke to see her face.

'Hi, Jon . . . All right, I guess . . . Yes . . . God! Oh, my God! . . . No, I'm all right. What time did he . . . ? Thanks . . . Yeah, I will . . . I will, Jon. I love you, Jon.'

She hung up.

Burke put his arm around her.

'Thank God,' she said softly. 'It wasn't Michael, Burke. It was Beauchamp Day. Jon and Michael just heard it on the radio. Beauchamp's car hit the side of the Broadway tunnel and blew up. They couldn't get to him, Burke. He burned alive.'

Sixty at last

The delectable herbal scent of Vitabath tingled in Frannie's nose as she lay back in the huge marble tub and enjoyed the effects of vitamin Q.

'Oooh, goodness! This thing is big enough for two.'

Birdsong stopped massaging her feet. 'Do you want me to come in, Mrs Halcyon?'

'Oh, no.' She giggled. 'No, that wasn't a hint, Birdsong.'

'It's no problem.'

'No. I'm sure it isn't . . . Birdsong?'

'Yes, ma'am?'

'How long have you worked at Pinus?'

'About two years.'

'Since you were how old?'

'Uh . . . twenty.'

'You like it here, then?'

'Yes, ma'am.'

'All these old ladies. You like . . . waiting on them?'

'I don't think of them as old.'

Frannie smiled forgivingly. 'I know they tell you to say that, but surely . . . well, I mean, we're all over sixty, aren't we? A young man like you must feel a little . . . strange . . . you know.'

'No, ma'am. I like mature women.'

She grinned at him under heavy-lidded eyes. 'You're a diplomat, young man.'

Birdsong winked and wiggled her big toe.

'What's your real name?' she asked.

'We're not allowed to tell that.'

'You're not, huh?'

'No, ma'am.'

'Are you going to rub my back?'

'If you like.'

'I like,' smiled Frannie, rolling over in the suds.

The matriarch slept soundly until 6 P.M., when Helena Parrish rapped on her door. 'The hour is nigh,' she said cheerily, peering into the cottage. She had changed from her street clothes into the dusty-pink kaftan of the resort. Her hair was down now, flowing triumphantly into a single reckless braid.

Frannie rubbed her eyes and swung her feet off the bed. 'I'm not especially nervous. Should I be?'

'Darling . . . this is going to be the most extraordinary night of your life.'

'*Now* I'm nervous.'

'You'll do fine.'

'I'm beginning to feel like a silly old fool.'

'Nonsense. You'll be the youngest girl there.'

Frannie giggled. 'I hadn't thought of it that way.'

'Don't *think*, darling . . . *feel*. That's the secret to Pinus. Let yourself feel.'

'I'll try.'

'Good. Now . . . one more vitamin Q and we'll be on our way.'

The amphitheater took Frannie's breath away. Against the darkening hillside a hundred women lounged in dusty-pink deck chairs, gazing languidly at the open-air stage before them.

In the center of the stage, a bonfire was blazing, casting a mystical light on the giant golden P that dangled overhead. When Helena made her entrance, the audience began janing.

'Aaaahhhhaaaahhhheeeeeaaaahhhhh!'

The sound was thunderous, almost deafening. It sent little shivers down Frannie's spine. She readjusted her kaftan and fidgeted with her hair, awaiting the signal from Helena.

'Ladies,' boomed Helena, without a microphone, 'we all know why we're here tonight, so let's get on with it. Without further ado, may I present to you . . . the newest recipient of the mysteries of Pinus . . . Frannie Halcyon!'

This time the janing nearly shook the trees. Frannie walked onto the stage with her head held high, taking her place beside Helena at the bonfire. Then simultaneously, the women rose to their feet and a gargantuan cake was wheeled onto the stage. The women janed again and broke into a jubilant chorus of 'Happy Birthday.'

The top of the cake exploded in a flurry of flesh and firelight.

The naked figure that emerged sent gasps of delight and recognition through the audience. 'Bluegrass,' squealed a woman near the stage. '*She got Blue-grass!*'

Frannie looked up to see an enormous golden-haired man who looked for all the world like Joe Palooka. He smiled down at the Birthday Girl and leaped enthusiastically out of the cake.

In a single effortless motion, he scooped Frannie into his arms and ran off with her into the forest.

And the janing began again.

The last of Beauchamp

When Bruno finally phoned, Douchebag was livid.

'Jesus Christ, man! You said eight o'clock!'

'Yeah? Well, I lied. Go home, punk.'

'Watcha mean, go home? I been freezin' my ass off out here for—'

'I said go home!'

'What about my money?'

'There ain't gonna be no money, 'cause there ain't gonna be no job. The client just got barbecued in the Broadway tunnel.'

'Huh?'

'I'll explain it to you when you grow up.'

'Wait just a fuckin'—'

'Look, kid, if you want a blue face to go with that green hair, just keep messin' with me, hear?'

Douchebag composed a hardass reply, then decided against it and hung up. Readjusting the safety pin on

195

her garbage bag, she slammed out of the phone booth and set off in the direction of home.

There might be a cat she could kick on the way.

Leaving the Palace of the Legion of Honor, DeDe paused for a moment to watch the Golden Gate Bridge twinkling in the darkness.

'It never fails, does it?'

'What?' asked D'orothea.

'That. I mean . . . it never gets old. I was born here, and I've never stopped catching my breath whenever I see it. Sometimes I think there's a huge magnet in it that keeps me from leaving.'

'Do you want to leave?'

'I think about it. *Everybody* thinks about leaving home, don't they? The problem is, when you're born at the end of the rainbow, there's no place to go.' She turned and smiled at her new friend. 'It's not really fair, is it?'

'Maybe there's a city you haven't seen.'

'There are lots of cities I haven't seen. Athens . . . Vienna . . .'

'No. I mean here.' D'orothea smiled, arching an eyebrow. 'Those Junior Leaguers back there are as alien to me as . . . Mars. DeDe, there are a surprising number of people in this town whose shoes don't match their handbags.'

DeDe thought about that in silence all the way back to D'orothea's house in Pacific Heights. When they reached the cinnamon-and-buff Victorian, D'orothea thanked her for 'an edifying evening.'

DeDe smiled apologetically. 'Pretty dull, huh?'

'Not with you, hon.' She leaned over suddenly and kissed DeDe on the cheek. 'Where are we having the babies, by the way?'

'St Sebastian's,' said DeDe. 'And thanks for that *we*.'

D'orothea shrugged. 'You can't do it alone, can you?'

'I thought I might have to.'

'Bullshit.' She bounded out of the car, slammed the door authoritatively and blew a kiss to DeDe from her front steps. 'I'll call you soon,' she yelled.

Forty minutes later, DeDe arrived at Halcyon Hill alone. A police car was parked in the circular driveway. As she locked the Mercedes, she spotted a chunky officer standing next to the cast-iron negro lawn jockey that Mother had painted white after the Watts riots.

'Mrs Day?' The officer approached her.

'God! Not another burglary?'

'No, ma'am. I'm sorry. We couldn't find any other members of your family, so they asked me to . . . There's been an accident, Mrs Day.'

'Mother! Is it Mother?'

The officer took her arm. 'No, ma'am. It's gonna be OK. Why don't we go sit down?'

Inside, she took the news more stoically than the officer might have expected.

'When did it happen?' she asked.

'Several hours ago. His car apparently skidded in the Broadway tunnel. There was . . . a fire.'

'God.'

'Mrs Day . . . I'm really sorry. If there's somewhere you'd like to go, I'd be more than happy to take you.'

'No. Thank you. I'm OK.'

'Would you like me to stay for a while?'

'I don't think that'll be necessary, thank you.'

With obvious discomfort, the officer handed her an envelope. 'I'm supposed to give you this. It's his – your husband's – personal effects.'

Two Scotches and several hundred M & M's later, DeDe retreated to her bedroom and worked up the nerve to open the envelope.

All that was left of her husband landed with an ugly clatter on her mirror-topped vanity.

A golden belt buckle, composed of interlocking G's.

Burke's bad dream

For different reasons, Mary Ann and Burke both slept fitfully on the night of Beauchamp's death. When she awoke, Mary Ann called St Sebastian's and checked on Michael's condition. Nothing had changed, Jon told her. Mona and Mrs Madrigal were expected at the hospital later that morning.

Then the secretary called Halcyon Communications and asked for Mildred in Production. It was not yet eight-thirty; the spinster's voice sounded tired and far away.

'When did you hear?' she asked.

'Last night,' said Mary Ann, consciously injecting a funereal note into her voice. 'A friend called me.'

'It's awful. The media is eating it up. I'm *dreading* Van Amburg and his Happy Talk news tonight.'

'Should I come in, Mildred?' The *real* question, of course, was whether Beauchamp had told Mildred – or anyone else in power – that he had fired Mary Ann.

'No,' replied Mildred. 'We've shut down, actually. I'm just handling the calls . . . and the press. Oh, one thing?'

'Uh huh?'

'I talked to DeDe Day this morning. She's holding up just fine, all things considered. It must be *terrible* for her, with the babies due any day now, and – worst of all – her mother missing.'

'Mrs Halcyon is missing?'

'Well, not exactly missing. They just haven't been able to locate her. She told DeDe she was going up to their house in Napa, but so far she hasn't turned up there. I suspect – this is just *my* theory, mind you – you know, she's a deeply religious woman, and she may just be touring the missions like Angelina Alioto.'

'Does the press know she's—'

'Heavens, no! DeDe told me in strictest confidence! She's making a few discreet inquiries with her mother's friends. I think she expects her to turn up any minute now. Keep it under your hat, will you, Mary Ann?'

'Of course. Mildred . . . have there been any arrangements made about the funeral?'

'Oh . . .' Mildred's voice faltered. 'That's the sad part, I'm afraid. Beauchamp had a provision in his will for cremation. But considering the . . . nature of the accident, the family felt that cremation might be in bad taste.'

'I see.'

'I think there'll be a memorial service of some kind. DeDe talked to Beauchamp's parents in Boston this morning.'

'Thanks, Mildred. I won't keep you.'

'I know you must be wondering about your job at this point . . . so don't worry about that, dear. I'm sure there'll be a place for you when the dust settles. In the meantime, why don't you take a little time off?'

'Thank you, Mildred.'

'Not at all, Mary Ann. I'm sure that's the way Beauchamp would have wanted it.'

If Mary Ann had so much as a moment's speculation about what to do with her leisure time, the question was settled in the middle of breakfast.

'I dreamed about our friend last night,' said Burke.

Mary Ann set down her mug of Orange Cappuccino. 'Michael?'

'No. The man with the transplant . . . at the flower market.'

'Ick.'

'You're right. I shouldn't have brought it up.'

'No. You should talk about it, Burke.'

'It was only a dream.'

'It could have been a *memory*, Burke. Tell me about it.'

He looked at her skeptically. 'I don't want to be . . . your favorite hobby, Mary Ann.'

'Is that what you think?'

He hesitated. 'No. Not really.'

'Then *tell* me.'

'Well, there was a walkway in it, the kind that I've told you about. There was a metal railing on it, and I think I was walking on concrete – only it was really high up.'

'From what?'

'I don't know. People, maybe – but I couldn't see anybody down below. There were people with me on the walkway – people I knew.'

'Who?'

'I don't know. I just know that I knew them.'

'Great.'

'Then the man with the transplant came up – I mean, walked up beside me – and suddenly there was this rose, this *horrible* rose.'

'Why was it horrible?'

'I . . . don't know.'

'Did he give you the rose? The man with the transplant.'

'No, not exactly. It was just there. And then he leaned over and said, "Go ahead, Burke, it's organic" . . . and then I started to run.'

'And?'

'That's it. I woke up.'

Mary Ann took a sip from her mug. 'Well, I suppose we shouldn't make too much of the guy with the transplant. I mean, we've both been talking about him, and you could've, like, superimposed him on your existing memories.'

'Mmm. Except for one thing.'

'What?'

'He didn't have a transplant in my dream. He was bald as an egg.'

The proposal

Michael's night nurse was a fellow Floridian named Thelma. Sometimes she would sit and talk to him after giving him his eight o'clock injection of pentazocine.

'Thelma?'

'What, hon?'

'Is this my fourth day here?'

'Uh . . . your fifth, I think.'

'If I'm completely paralyzed, how come it hurts? I mean . . . I can *feel* it hurt.'

'Where?'

'My legs . . . my thighs . . . and my arms a little bit. It's freaky. I can see my leg lying still down there, but it feels exactly like somebody's bending it towards the ceiling. I almost asked you to push it down for me.'

She stroked his brow. 'It'll go away, hon.'

'Last night I woke up and I was positive I was propped between two pews.'

'Like in a church?'

'Uh huh. I could feel the edge of – you know – the plank behind my ankles and up behind my neck. God, I could almost *see* it.'

'That's normal, believe it or not. Dr Beery says there's almost always some sensory disturbance with Guillain-Barré.'

'Can't I be wacko, Thelma? I'd love to be wacko.'

'Go on!'

'I would. Just a little bit. A mild schizoid, maybe, with traces of melancholia and occasional drooling.'

Thelma smiled. 'You're not crazy, hon. You might as well face it. You're normal.'

'Not in Florida I ain't.'

Thelma reddened. 'I wouldn't know about that.'

'You know what?' said Michael.

'What, hon?'

'You're cute as pie.'

She tucked in his sheet with nervous efficiency. 'I wasn't even cute in Florida.'

'I'll bet you were, Thel. I'll bet you made those good ol' boys horny as hell.'

'You hush up!'

'I'll bet they used to wait outside in their Chevy pickups and bay at the moon like hound dogs and . . . take you downtown for an RC and a Moon Pie . . . and I'll bet you loved every minute of it.'

'I bet you're gonna get another shot in about two seconds.'

'I don't care if you give me a lobotomy. I know cute when I see it.'

'Get some sleep.'

'You won't leave, will you, Thel?'

'No, hon. Not until your friend comes.'

His friend came shortly after nine. Thelma excused herself as soon as she saw Jon in the doorway.

'Hi,' said Michael sleepily.

'Hi. I won't stay long. You sound tired.'

'No, please. I need the company.'

'Good.' Jon pulled up a chair next to the bed. 'I had a great idea today.'

'What?'

'We're gonna paint your apartment!'

'Swell. I'll be the stepladder.'

Jon smiled. 'Look: I brought you some paint samples from Hoot Judkins.' He held one of the cardboard strips in front of Michael's eyes. 'I kind of like this putty color.'

'Mmm. Faggot fawn.'

'Cut it out.'

'Well it *is* the color of the year. Three years ago it was chocolate brown, then forest green. It was handy, anyway. If you woke up in a strange bedroom, at least you knew what year it was . . . Look, Dr Kildare, painting my apartment is definitely above and beyond the—'

'Bullshit. If I'm gonna live there, that cosmic orange of Mona's has gotta go!'

The impact of Jon's words registered in Michael's face instantly. 'Uh . . . isn't this a little premature, Jon?'

'Haven't you always wanted to shack up with a doctor?'

'Jon, I'm so fuckin' flattered I could—'

'I'm not flattering you, asshole. I'm asking you to marry me.'

Silence.

'So?'

'Jon, you can't . . . haul me to the toilet.'

'Says who?'

'This isn't *Magnificent Obsession.* It doesn't work like that. You're gonna take all the mystery out of our unnatural relationship.'

'I'll risk it. What about it?'

Michael hesitated. 'When will . . . I get out of here?'

'I . . . I don't know. It depends on a lot of things, Michael.'

'Ahh.'

'Michael, look . . .'

'You know how to cheer a person up, anyway. I'll give you credit for that, Babycakes.'

Ashes to ashes

The memorial service for Beauchamp Talbot Day was held on a Tuesday at 11 A.M. in St Matthew's Episcopal Church, San Mateo.

The front pew was occupied by members of the immediate family, including Mr and Mrs Richard Hamilton Day of Boston, Massachusetts; Miss Allison Dinsmore Day of New York City; Mrs Edgar Warfield Halcyon (nee Frances Alicia Ligon) and the widow, Mrs Beauchamp Talbot Day (nee Deirdre Ligon Halcyon).

Accompanying the widow and her mother were the family maid, Miss Emma Ravenel; Miss D'orothea Wilson of San Francisco; and a young man of unidentifiable origin who answered to the name of Bluegrass.

Seated four rows behind the family were Miss Mary Ann Singleton, secretary to the deceased; her escort, Mr Burke Christopher Andrew; and Dr Jon Philip Fielding, the widow's gynecologist.

Friends of the deceased in attendance included Mr Archibald Anson Gidde, Mr Richard Evan Hampton and Mr Peter Prescott Cipriani.

The Reverend Lindsey R. McAllister of Boston conducted the service.

At the request of the deceased's family, there were no floral offerings at the ceremony, with the exception of the single red rose that adorned the processional cross.

Shortly after the commencement of the service, Mr Burke Christopher Andrew clutched his stomach suddenly, dropped his hymnal, and vomited onto the pew in front of him.

There was no eulogy.

Voice from the past

After the memorial service, Jon drove Mary Ann and Burke back to 28 Barbary Lane. The couple were unusually quiet, he noticed, presumably because of the mishap involving the rose on the processional cross.

'I wouldn't worry about that,' the doctor said at last.

'I should have brought more Wash'n Dris,' said Mary Ann.

Jon shook his head. 'He was a horse's ass. I thought it was entirely appropriate.'

'Who?' asked Burke.

'Beauchamp. He was a gaper from way back.'

Mary Ann looked puzzled. 'I thought you just knew DeDe.'

'Yeah. Mostly. But I met him once or twice.'

There was no point in telling them about his brief affair with Beauchamp. He had never even told Michael, because he had never been proud of that interlude in his life.

Back at Michael's apartment, he checked the bedroom for closet space. As soon as Mona's stuff could be shifted downstairs – she had already expressed her intention of moving in with Mrs Madrigal – there would be plenty of room for his clothes and furniture. Michael's possessions were minimal.

He stood at Michael's dresser for a moment and examined the items decorating the perimeter of the mirror.

Polaroids of Mona mugging in the nude at Devil's Slide. Others of Mary Ann posing demurely in the courtyard. A gold pendant charm shaped like a pair of jockey shorts – obviously Michael's prize from The Endup's dance contest. A photo, torn from a magazine, of a shirtless Jan-Michael Vincent.

There was nothing of Jon, nothing of the two of them. They had not been together long enough. The only evidence of their relationship was a cocktail napkin from the Sans Souci, tucked jauntily at an angle behind Jan-Michael Vincent.

Suddenly, sinking to the edge of Michael's bed, Jon began to cry.

Michael, as usual, had been right. The fuss over the paint chips *had* been premature. There was no indication – none whatsoever – that Michael's condition was improving. And that flip little romantic perched on the brink of death could not be bullshitted when it came down to the end.

Jon rose, rubbing his eyes, just as the phone rang.

'Hello,' he said, answering the phone in the kitchen.

'Who is this?' A woman's voice. Brassy.

'Jon Fielding. A friend of Michael's.'

'Isn't this Mona Ramsey's apartment?'

'Oh . . . well, sort of. She's—'

'Sort of?' Not brassy, actually. Bronze.

Jon gave up any effort at cordiality. 'She's in the process of moving right now. You can reach her downstairs at her . . . at the landlady's apartment.'

The caller muttered under her breath. 'Bloody idiot.'

'Would you like the number?'

'Yes. Please.'

Jon gave it to her.

The call came while Mrs Madrigal and Mother Mucca were shopping in North Beach. Mona was alone in the apartment.

'Yeah?'

'Mona?'

'Hello, Betty.'

'I thought you were dead.'

'Oh, yeah? Well . . . surprise!'

'That's no bloody way to talk to your mother!'

'I sent you a postcard from Nevada.'

'I was worried sick. What were you doing in Nevada?'

'Just . . . stuff.' Mona thought it best to change the subject. 'How's the weather in Minneapolis?'

'The winter was horrid.'

'Too bad. Hope it didn't hurt your property values. Hey . . . how did you get this number?'

206

'I called your apartment. A young man there told me.'

'That must've been Jon.'

'Mona, listen to me . . . I have to talk to you.'

'Fine. Go ahead.'

'No. In person. You're making a serious mistake, Mona.'

'About what?'

'I can't talk about it over the phone. I'm coming to see you.'

Silence.

'Did you hear me, Mona?'

'It won't work, Betty. There's not enough room.'

'I can stay at a friend's apartment. I've already . . . worked that out. You can give me two hours of your time, Mona. I'm not asking your permission . . . I'm coming. You owe me that, at least.'

'Yeah,' said Mona resignedly. 'I guess I do.'

Minor miracles

Jon returned to St Sebastian's with Michael's mail in hand: a postcard from a friend on Maui, a newsletter from his congressman and a notice from the Reader's Digest Sweepstakes informing him happily that he might already be a winner.

Michael was asleep, so the doctor sat quietly in a chair by the window.

Five minutes later, the night nurse entered.

'Just get here?'

'Yeah.'

The nurse nodded toward her patient. 'He's a nice boy.'

Jon nodded.

'Him and you are . . . good friends, aren't you?'

'Uh huh.'

'He talks about you a lot.'

'I know.'

'Him and me spent a long time talking today. We're both from Florida, ya know. I'm from Clearwater. I mean, my folks used to live there when I was a teen-ager, and I met my husband there and all, but then we moved to Fort Bragg, North Carolina, when he joined the Army.'

'I see.'

'I don't mind admittin' it one bit: we're both real conservative, Dr Fielding. We voted for Goldwater in '64 and Earl always says that socialism is gonna ruin this country, and I guess I agree with him. I don't think that's reactionary, no matter what people say. I was raised to believe in the Constitution and the Bible and Free Enterprise, and I guess I always will.'

The nurse moved closer to Michael's bed. Jon felt vaguely uneasy. What was she getting at?

'Sometimes', she continued, 'I think things are just moving too fast. The world is goin' crazy, and people don't have ... they just don't have standards of *decency*. You can't *depend* on things the way you used to. Families and marriages are falling apart, and the liberals are just destroying everything that ever mat-tered to folks.'

Now she was standing by the head of the bed. She looked down at Michael for a moment. When she looked up again, there were tears in her eyes.

'I know all that's true. I *know* it, Dr Fielding. There's lots of things I'd change about this world, but ... I don't ...' She wiped her eyes, then looked down at Michael again. 'I'd be proud ... I'd be *proud* for this boy to teach my children. I swear to God I would!'

Jon blocked his emotions with a smile. 'Thank you,' he said quietly.

The nurse turned away, blowing her nose. She busied herself with straightening Michael's covers, avoiding Jon's eyes. She didn't confront him again until she was ready to leave.

'Doctor, I hope you didn't . . . take offense?'

'No. Of course not. That was a very nice thing to say.'

'Aren't you mighty tired?'

'A little.'

'Why don't you go home. I'll look after him.'

'I know. I'll go soon.'

'Doctor?'

'Yes?'

'When this is over . . . when he's better . . . I'd be glad to have you . . . I mean, the two of you . . . over for dinner sometime. I make good red beans and rice.' She smiled, nodding toward Michael. 'He says he likes that.'

'Thank you. We'd be happy to.'

'Earl's real nice. You'll like him.'

'I'm sure. Thank you.'

'Good night, Doctor.'

'Good night. God bless you.'

He sat there for another hour, finally dozing off in the chair. An insistent voice awakened him.

'Pssst, turkey.'

'Wha . . . ? Michael?'

'No. Marie Antoinette.'

'What's the matter?'

'Come here.'

Jon went to his bedside. 'Yeah?'

'Look.'

'At what?'

'Down there, dummy. My hand.'

Jon saw Michael's index finger moving ever so slightly.

'Don't just stand there,' grinned Michael. 'Clap your hands if you believe in fairies!'

209

The shop at St Sebastian's

A sudden hint of spring in the air caught Mrs Madrigal off guard as she swept the courtyard at 28 Barbary Lane.

Spring again on the lane! Vagrant daffodils loitering among the garbage cans, the smell of cat fur and lilacs and sun-warmed eucalyptus bark . . . and dear sweet Brian sunning himself on the bricks.

For the first time in weeks, her family seemed intact again. Michael was greatly improved, according to Jon, and would be coming home in a matter of days. Mary Ann and Burke were nesting comfortably in their respective apartments, though they appeared to need only one.

Brian, of course, was still in the little house on the roof.

And Mona – her own precious daughter – had moved in permanently downstairs as soon as Mother Mucca had returned to Winnemucca.

It was springtime, and all was well.

Except for . . . something about Mona's behavior that disturbed her.

'Brian, dear?'

He arched his neck, smiling up at her, greased and graceful in his green Speedo trunks. This boy, thought Anna, is a curious mixture of menace and vulnerability. A coyote begging for scraps. 'Yeah?' he said. 'I'm in your way?'

'No, no. I can sweep around you. I wanted to ask you something.'

'Sure. Shoot.'

'Do you and Mona . . . communicate very often?'

Brian laughed cynically. 'I think "relate" is the word she'd use.'

'Oh, dear. There's been friction?'

He nodded. 'Nothing drastic. I invited her to dinner and she told me that the *energy* was wrong. She couldn't relate to someone who – in her words – spent his Wonder Bread years learning to unhook bra straps.'

'Oh, my! I hope you didn't let her get away with that.'

Brian smiled wickedly. 'I told her she wasn't putting off enough energy to power a dime-store vibrator. Just your basic small talk. She told you about it, huh?'

'No. I just thought you might have some clue as to why . . . She isn't herself, Brian. Something's bothering her a great deal, but I can't get her to talk to me about it, and I thought that maybe you . . . I guess it'll pass.'

Brian sensed her distress. 'She's happy with you – her new home, I mean. I know that much.'

'Oh . . . she told you that?'

'She's told *everybody* that.'

The landlady smiled. 'She's a good person most of the time. Please don't give up on her for dinner.'

So Brian tried again. He called Mona as soon as he got back to the little house on the roof.

'Why do you hate me?'

'Who is this?'

'Is it because I work at Perry's? Or that I'm straight?'

'Brian, I'm in no mood—'

'I'm not a pig, Mona. I'm promiscuous as hell, but I'm *not* a Male Chauvinist Pig. For Christ's sake! I was at Wounded Knee, Mona!'

'Don't expect me to validate your . . . You were?'

'Uh huh.'

'I don't believe you.'

'I cooked a meat loaf.'

'At Wounded Knee?'

'*Yesterday*, you heartless woman! I cooked a god-damn meat loaf for the first time in my life, and you won't even eat it with me!'

She laughed in spite of herself. 'You didn't tell me that.'

'I'm telling you now. Come to dinner, Mona. Tonight.'

She accepted more readily than he expected.

He spent the rest of the afternoon cooking his first meat loaf.

Mona and Mary Ann passed on the stairway at four-thirty. Mona was making a last-minute dash to the laundry. Mary Ann was heading out to meet Jon for a trip to St Sebastian's.

Mona, Mary Ann noted, seemed far less laid back than usual. And she was *smiling*.

'Give Mouse a sloppy kiss for me, OK?'

'I will,' said Mary Ann.

When she and Jon reached St Sebastian's, Mary Ann realized with some guilt that kisses were *all* she had given Michael during his time of crisis. Burke's phobia had ruled out even the quickest visit to the hospital florist.

But Burke was in Jackson Square now, getting a haircut at Alexandre's, so why shouldn't she pick up a nice azalea or something?

She told Jon she would meet him upstairs and headed for the glass-fronted shop in the hospital lobby. When she entered, there was no one in sight, so she rang the bell on the counter.

Presently, a man emerged from the refrigerated chamber in the rear of the shop. 'Brrr,' he said merrily, 'I like it better out here.' If he recognized his customer, he gave no indication of it.

But she knew who he was. Instantly.

The man with the transplant.

212

Meat loaf at Wounded Knee

Brian's dinner was a qualified success. Mona remarked on the tastiness of his meat loaf, but chastened him for being scornful of vegetarian principles.

'Wait a minute,' he countered. 'If you're such a vegetarian, why didn't you tell me so in the . . . ?'

'You said you'd already cooked it, Brian. Besides, I'm not as . . . strict with myself as I used to be.'

'I see.'

'Ground beef isn't nearly as personal as a solid hunk of steak. I mean, it seems much less of a violation of the sanctity of the animal. You don't know which part of the cow it came from.' She grinned suddenly, recognizing the inanity of the remark.

Brian grinned back at her, dropping another chunk of meat loaf onto her plate. 'This isn't *cow*, I'll have you know!'

'Well, steer or whatever.'

He shook his head. 'Dog. Cocker Spaniel, to be specific. Do you think a waiter from Perry's can afford *beef*?'

After dinner, they sat on the edge of his bed and perused a scrapbook opened across their knees. A MAKE LOVE NOT WAR bumper sticker was plastered on the cover.

'Look,' said Brian uneasily, 'if this gets to be a big drag . . .'

'It was my idea wasn't it?'

'OK. Well . . .' He flipped past the first few pages. 'This is just boring stuff.'

'No. Stop. What's that?'

'Law school. The *Law Review* at George Washington.'

'Which one is you?'

213

'The dip with the David Harris glasses.'

'You wear glasses?'

'Not any more. Contacts.'

'Green-tinted, huh?' She smiled teasingly. He pretended to be mildly affronted, but inwardly he was pleased. She had noticed his eyes. That was a start, anyway.

He pointed to a newspaper clipping. 'This one made the AP wires. That's me in Chicago, 1968, on the left.'

'How can you tell? Your head is down.'

'I was going limp for the police.'

'Really? Where else did you go limp?'

'Oh . . . Selma, Washington . . . Are you making fun of me?'

She smiled. 'I went limp in Minneapolis.'

'No shit?'

She nodded, beaming.

'The War?'

'Yeah. Did you know Jerry Rubin?'

'I met him once in Chicago. We talked for about half an hour, I guess.'

'I just read his book. *Growing Up at 37*. I was really blown away.'

'Good, huh?'

She made a face, shaking her head. 'He said he got on this big power trip — militancy and all that — because he was uptight about the size of his penis. I mean, that's a really heavy thing to say.'

He nodded solemnly. She wasn't joking.

'Christ,' she said angrily. 'Is *that* what we did it for? Is that what the sixties were all about? The size of Jerry Rubin's goddamn *dick*?'

There was simply no profound reply for that. Brian ended up laughing. 'It's enough to make you go limp,' he said.

Later, they stood together by the window facing the bay. Brian lit a joint of Maui Zowie and handed it to

Mona. She took a short toke and handed it back. 'That's all I want,' she said. 'I might get bummed out.'

'What's the matter?'

She sighed and stared out at the beacon on Alcatraz. 'My mother's coming to town,' she said finally.

The implication took a while to sink in. Then Brian whistled. 'Does Mrs Madrigal know?'

Mona shook her head glumly. 'I want to try and handle it myself. My mother said something really weird on the phone. She said I was making a terrible mistake.'

'Do you think she knows about Mrs Madrigal?'

'I'm not sure. But if she does know, she must assume that I know and that I know she knows. So what could she possibly tell me? What's all this "terrible mistake" shit?'

Her voice was trembling. Brian slipped his arm around her waist.

'I don't need any more surprises, Brian. I'm frightened.' She was crying now. Pulling away from him, she crossed the room to the other window, where she stood wiping her eyes.

'Mona . . .'

'I'm all right now.' She looked around for a clock. 'It's late. I should go.'

He moved to her side, risking it all. 'You can stay . . . if you'd like.'

'No. But ask me again.' She hugged him awkwardly, laying her head against his chest. 'I like you, Brian. You're a closet Tom Hayden.'

He kissed her forehead. 'Where's my Jane Fonda?' he asked.

They held each other tight, framed against the window like a cliché out of Rod McKuen.

Lady Eleven watched them for less than a minute, then took off her binoculars and closed the curtains.

A poem to ponder

It may have been the palm trees or the oddly tropical night or the swarthy man sipping Campari at the next table, but *something* about the terrace at the Savoy-Tivoli gave Mary Ann a shivery flashback to Mexico.

Burke felt it too. 'Remind you of Las Hadas?'

'I didn't plan it that way, I promise.' She had called him excitedly from the hospital, choosing this as the spot for their rendezvous. She had refused to reveal her discovery over the phone.

'So what's up?' asked Burke, as soon as their coffee and desserts had arrived.

Mary Ann smiled mysteriously and plunged a spoon into her butterscotch trifle. 'I've found our friend,' she replied at last.

'Who?'

'The man at the flower mart. With the hair transplant.'

'Jesus. *Where?*'

'At the hospital. He runs the flower shop there. I went by there this afternoon to pick up an azalea or something for Michael, and there he was behind the—'

'Did you talk to him? Did you ask him about me? Did he recognize you?'

She was surprised at the urgency in his voice. 'I didn't ask him, Burke. I was afraid to.'

'*Why?*'

'Because I think he *did* recognize me. He acted like he didn't, but I just couldn't shake the feeling that he knew who I was.'

'What if he did? Look, Mary Ann, *I* don't mind approaching him, if you're squeamish about it. Anything is better than this constant speculation and anxiety. This man could be the key to it all.'

'I know that, Burke. I'm sure of it. I just don't think we should risk the . . .' She reached across the table and took his hand. 'Something horrible may have been the cause of your amnesia, Burke. This man may have been a part of it.'

'You've seen too many movies. Maybe I worked for him or something.'

She shook her head. 'I asked Jon to check the hospital records for me. You were never on the payroll at St Sebastian's, and you were never a patient there. There's no evidence that you ever set foot in the place before this month.'

He smiled at her affectionately. 'You have been the little sleuth, haven't you?'

'I want to help,' she said quietly.

'Good.' He reached in the breast pocket of his corduroy jacket and produced an index card which he placed in front of her. 'Tell me what *that* means, then.'

She picked up the card. On it Burke had written a verse of four lines:

> High upon the Sacred Rock
> The Rose Incarnate shines,
> Upon the Mountain of the Flood
> At the Meeting of the Lines.

'What is it?' she asked.

'I dreamed it. Pretty nifty, huh?' His tone was much too flip, a defense mechanism that Mary Ann had learned to recognize. He was more frightened now than ever.

'Did you *hear* it in your dream, Burke?'

'Yep. Up on that damned walkway thing with the railing. The rest of the dream is the same. It's dark and the transplant man is there and there are people just beyond me in the darkness and the transplant man says, "Go ahead . . . it's organic." '

'So how did you hear it? The poem.'

217

'They were chanting it. Over and over again.'

'How many people?'

'I don't know. They were whispering, sort of . . . as if someone nearby could hear.'

Mary Ann looked down at the index card, then fingered the little key around her neck. Did any of this fit together? Was she exorcising Burke's demons or simply helping to create new ones?

'You dreamed this last night?'

He nodded. 'So what now, my love?'

'I'm . . . not sure.'

'I think we should talk to the man with the transplant.'

'No. Please. Not yet. Let's give it a little longer, Burke.'

He agreed to that begrudgingly. Mary Ann was about to restate her argument, when a familiar figure moved into her line of vision.

'Burke, we've gotta go.'

'I haven't finished my coffee yet.'

'Please, Burke, leave some money!'

He complied, looking peeved. He pushed his chair back noisily and stood up.

Mary Ann took his arm and propelled him down Grant Avenue, only seconds before Millie the Flower Lady descended upon her regular customers with a basketful of roses.

Penance

On the day after his dinner date with Mona, Brian sailed smoothly through his shift at Perry's. He felt *comfortable* about Mona now, confident he had stumbled onto something more real, more fulfilling – and infinitely more sensual – than he had ever known before.

He also felt guilty as hell about Lady Eleven.

How could he have forgotten her so easily? He had seen her – yes, that *was* the only word for it – for almost a month now. Every night for a month. She had blessed their relationship with predictability, if nothing else. Surely that counted for something?

He had planned, of course, on phasing her out eventually. The fantasy aspects of their liaison had all but vanished, and he had recently found it impossible to achieve orgasm with her without thinking of someone else. Still, he had treated her shabbily; he had broken their unwritten pact on the strength of a little Maui Zowie and a simpatico bird in the hand.

So that night at midnight he sat penitently in his chair by the window and watched the eleventh floor of the Superman Building.

Her window, however, remained dark.

She's punishing me, he thought. She's making me suffer for my transgressions. Or perhaps – just perhaps – she's in torment herself, torturing herself needlessly over her failure to hold my interest.

But then, at 12.07, her light came on, and Brian detected a slight stirring of her curtains. He stood up excitedly, lifting his binoculars to his eyes. The curtains opened.

It was Lady Eleven, all right, but her appearance had changed radically. She was no longer wearing the floppy terry cloth robe. She was dressed in what appeared to be a gray wool suit. Her hair was bound up in a tight little bun, and her features – even at that distance – seemed severe and judgmental.

She raised her own binoculars and studied Brian for a moment.

He suddenly felt silly, wearing only his bathrobe. He wondered if she had planned it that way.

She left her window for several minutes, returning with a large piece of poster paper. She laid it on a table by the window and scribbled something on it. Then she held it up to the window.

It said: DROP HER.

Brian felt the blood rising to his face. Anger, confusion and guilt warred within him. He stared out across the moonlit city at the sign that accused him, then skulked into the kitchen in search of a large paper bag.

He found one, tore it open and scrawled on it with a Magic Marker.

His reply was: SHE'S JUST A FRIEND.

He held the paper up to the window for a half a minute while she studied it with her binoculars. When he finally put it down, Lady Eleven was standing with her arms folded, shaking her head.

Brian muttered 'Goddammit' under his breath and retaliated by writing I SWEAR on the paper bag. He held it up again, shaking the paper for emphasis. Lady Eleven kept her stance for several more seconds, then bent over her poster paper again.

This time she wrote: TAKE OFF YOUR CLOTHES.

Enraged, Brian shook his head emphatically.

Lady Eleven shook the poster.

Brian shook his head.

Lady Eleven scribbled on the poster again and held it up. To TAKE OFF YOUR CLOTHES she had added, IF YOU LOVE ME.

For one angry moment, Brian considered closing the curtains and curling up in bed with his scratch 'n sniff *Hustler* centerfold. He didn't need this kind of bullshit. There were *loads* of girls who loved his ass without such degrading demands.

Why *this* one, then? Why should he demean himself before this anonymous, neurotic, compulsive weirdo?

He knew the answer, of course:

Because she needed him. Because there was something more pathetically humbling about writing 'If you

220

love me' to a stranger than stripping naked before a stranger. Because she was desperate and no one else could save her.

So he unknotted the cord of his bathrobe.

Lady Eleven lifted her binoculars again as Brian let the bathrobe drop. She watched him – smiling? – until his hard-on was visible, then she began to unbutton her suit.

When they both were naked, the ritual began again, more feverish and committed than ever.

From the purple haze of his passion, Brian heard someone knocking on his door.

Then a voice: 'Brian, it's Mona. I just scored some you-know-what. What say we share a few lines?'

Frozen like a satyr on a Pompeian frieze, he waited in silence until the intruder had gone.

Then he turned back to his lover again.

Riddle at dawn

For the third time that week, Mary Ann slept at Burke's apartment. Something – a noise, a bad dream, or the last cry of the trout she'd cooked for dinner – woke her just before dawn. She propped her head on her elbow and willed Burke awake.

He blinked at her. 'What's the matter, sweetheart?'

'It *must* be in the country somewhere.'

'What?'

'The Sacred Rock.'

'For God's sake! Get some sleep, will you?'

'In five minutes. Just say it one more time.'

Burke groaned. Then he recited the verse like a sixth-grader spitting out the Gettysburg Address under duress:

High upon the Sacred Rock
The Rose Incarnate shines,
Upon the Mountain of the Flood
At the Meeting of the Lines.

'See?' said Mary Ann. 'The terrain is hilly.'

'Clever girl.'

She dug her fingers in his side. 'What's the name of that mountain in the Bible?'

'Calvary.'

'No, silly. The one that Noah's ark landed on. The Mountain of the Flood, get it?'

'Ararat.'

She chewed meditatively on her forefinger. 'I wonder if anything is named that. Around here, I mean.'

'You got me.'

Mary Ann threw back the covers and scrambled out of bed.

'What the hell are you doing?' asked Burke.

'Checking the phone book.'

'Come to bed, goddammit!'

'It won't take a second.' She found the directory on the floor and leafed through it hurriedly. 'Arante . . . Araquistain . . . Ararat! Ararat Armenian Restaurant, 1000 Clement Street! Look, Burke!'

'So?'

'There could be some connection.' She wrinkled her nose, piqued by his total lack of enthusiasm. 'Don't you *want* to figure this out, Burke?'

His smile was meant to goad her. 'All right, Angie Dickinson. What's Rose Incarnate, then? A belly dancer at the restaurant?'

'It *could* be, smartass.'

'And the Meeting of the Lines?'

'I don't like your attitude.'

'Then you don't wanna hear *my* theory, I guess?'

'You've got one?'

'Yep.'

'Then let's hear it.'

'It'll cost ya.'

'No *way*.'

He pressed his fingertips to his forehead histrionically. 'Ohhh . . . it's going. I'm afraid I'm losing it. It's only a dim, dim . . .'

'Oh, all riiight!' She grinned at him and crawled back into bed. There was an air of urgency and intrigue to their love-making that made it the best in weeks.

Afterward, Burke heated some milk in the kitchen. They drank from the same steaming mug, sitting up in bed.

'So what's your theory?' asked Mary Ann.

Burke took a sip before answering. 'I think it could have something to do with cocaine.'

'*Cocaine?*' She was still very Cleveland about *that* drug.

'Yeah. A line of coke, see? The Meeting of the Lines.'

'Oh.'

'You don't like that one, huh?'

'But why would anyone be chanting about that?'

He shrugged. 'People chant about *everything* in Northern California. Some cult might have—'

'You think it was a cult?' The thought had already occurred to her, but she'd been terrified of broaching the subject. Burke had grown increasingly sensitive about his veiled past.

'I don't know,' he replied.

'Yes you do. You think it was a cult.'

'I don't *think* anything,' he snapped. 'I'm guessing. I'm guessing about my own goddamn life, which is not the easiest thing in the world to do.'

'I know. I'm sorry.'

He pulled her closer. 'I didn't mean to growl.'

'I know.'

'Let's get some sleep, OK?'

'OK. Burke?'

'Yeah?'

'In the dream . . . do you remember if you . . . Never mind, it doesn't matter.'

'C'mon. What is it?'

'I was wondering . . . do you remember if you were chanting?'

'No.'

'You weren't?'

'No, I mean, I don't remember.'

For the first time ever, she wasn't sure that she believed him.

Michael's theory

Mary Ann left Burke's apartment after breakfast. She was uneasy, she told him, about her status at Halcyon Communications. She had to make a few phone calls to remind the hierarchy of her need for a new position. This unexpected vacation couldn't last forever.

She was telling only half the truth.

After a quick call to Mildred (who assured her that the board would elect a new president next week), she dialed the number of the Ararat Armenian Restaurant and asked if a Burke Andrew had ever worked there.

They had never heard of him, the manager told her.

It had been a dumb idea, of course, but that stupid poem and the man with the transplant and the messy ordeal with Burke and the roses had begun to make her genuinely nervous.

Burke himself seemed on edge these days. His irritability, moreover, seemed to increase as Mary Ann delved deeper into the riddle of his past. Had he remembered enough, she wondered, to be frightened of the final revelation?

Was he telling her all he knew?

She needed an ally, she realized, an impartial third

party who could help her sort out the pieces of the puzzle.

'Anybody home?'

Michael grinned at her from his hospital bed. 'Just me and Merv.'

'Oh . . . yeah.' She went to the bed, kissed Michael on the cheek and feigned interest in the television. 'Eva Gabor still looks so *young*,' she said lamely.

'That's because of the clothespins.'

'What?'

'She's got clothespins.' Using both hands, he pinched the scalp behind his temples. 'Here . . . and here. They fit under her Eva Gabor wigs.'

Mary Ann giggled. 'Oh, Mouse . . . I've *missed* you.' She sat on the edge of the bed and fussed with his hair. 'You're getting all shaggy,' she said.

He turned off the television with a remote switch. 'How's ol' Mystery Meat?' he asked.

Mary Ann groaned softly. 'It's getting more bizarre every day.' She told him about the dream poem, about the subtle shift in Burke's behavior, about her growing fear that Burke had begun to resent her amateur sleuthing.

Michael's eyes were dancing. 'Tell me the poem again.'

She repeated it. 'What do you think?'

'It sure smacks of a cult.'

'I was afraid you'd say that.'

'Well, it would explain a lot. The amnesia, for instance. Maybe they had him deprogrammed or something. Maybe his *parents* had him deprogrammed. Like a Moonie.'

'Oh, Mouse!' *That* possibility had never even occurred to her.

'It's possible.'

'Do you think they would *do* that? Without telling him, I mean?'

He shrugged, smiling. 'My parents would *love* to deprogram me. Hmmm . . . I wonder what that entails? Maybe they lock you in a padded cell full of Muzak and zap your genitals with an electric shock every time you respond positively to a Bette Davis movie.'

'Mouse, have you *heard* from your parents?'

'I guess you could call it that. My mother wrote to say that my "sin against the Lord" was killing my father, and my father wrote to say that it was killing my mother.' He smiled wanly. 'They're terribly worried about each other.'

Later that afternoon, Jon showed up at St Sebastian's.

'Guess who's gonna be checking into the maternity ward pretty soon.'

'Who?' asked Mary Ann and Michael in unison.

'DeDe Day. She's almost a week overdue. With twins, no less.'

Mary Ann frowned. 'That's kind of sad.'

'How so?'

'Well, with no father, I mean.'

Jon shrugged it off. Beauchamp Day had been no loss to the institution of fatherhood. 'I saw that guy in the parking lot,' he said, changing the subject.

'Who?'

'The guy who runs the flower shop. I don't blame you for being spooked.'

'*Why?*' Mary Ann felt the hair on her forearm prickling.

'Well, he looked at me like I'd just caught him raping a nun or something.'

'What was he doing?'

Jon shrugged. 'Nothing that I could see. He was loading a cooler into the trunk of his car.'

'A cooler?'

'You know . . . Styrofoam. Like for beer.'

'Speaking of which,' said Michael, 'didn't my gynecologist promise to get me loaded today?'

Jon laughed, then made sure the door was closed. He handed Michael a joint of Mrs Madrigal's finest Home Grown. 'You two can smoke it,' he said, 'but keep the door shut, and wait till I'm out of the building.'

Mary Ann didn't even hear him.

A Styrofoam cooler?

Father knows best

Mona was washing dishes with a vengeance when Mrs Madrigal walked into the kitchen.

'Are you upset with me, dear?'

Mona frowned. 'No. Of course not.'

'You're upset with *somebody*. Is it Brian?'

Silence.

'I thought you said you had a lovely dinner with him.'

'He is totally fucked up,' Mona said flatly.

Mrs Madrigal picked up a towel and began drying dishes next to her daughter. 'I know,' she deadpanned. 'I thought he'd make a splendid son-in-law – with or without the sacrament of marriage. You need a friend, Mona.'

'I don't need this one.'

'What did he *do*, for heaven's sake?'

Mona turned off the tap, dried her hands and slumped into a chair. 'We did have a nice dinner. It was wonderful, OK? So I went back to see him the next night. It was late, I guess, but not *that* late, and he could've at least shouted through the door or something, if—' She cut herself off.

'If what?' asked Mrs Madrigal.

'If he had somebody with him.'

'Ah.'

Mona turned away, fuming.

227

'How do you know he was even there,' asked Mrs Madrigal.

'He was there. I saw him going up the stairs less than ten minutes before.'

'Was he with someone then?'

'No, but he could've . . . I don't know. Let's just drop it, OK?'

Mrs Madrigal smiled benignly at her daughter, then pulled up a chair and sat down next to her. She laid her hand gently on Mona's knee. 'You know that sign you hate so much, the one outside Abbey Rents?'

'Yeah,' said Mona sullenly. '"Sickroom and Party Supplies."'

'Well, that's it, isn't it?'

'What?'

'*Life*, dear.' She gave Mona's knee a squeeze. 'We have to put up with the sickrooms if we want the parties.'

Mona rolled her eyes. 'That's so simplistic.'

'No, dear,' smiled Mrs Madrigal. 'Just simple.'

Mona's snit subsided. Later that afternoon, she and Mrs Madrigal strolled arm in arm to Molinari's Delicatessen, where they bought salami and cheese and a carton of pickled mushrooms. They picnicked in Washington Square, watching Chinese grandmothers perform martial arts exercises on the grass.

Finally, Mona took the plunge. 'I have something to tell you,' she said blandly.

'Yes, dear?'

'It's kind of . . . sickroom.'

Mrs Madrigal smiled. 'Go ahead.'

'My mother's coming to town.'

Mrs Madrigal's smile faded.

'The lovely Betty Ramsey,' explained Mona. 'I believe you've met her.'

'Mona . . . why?'

'I don't know exactly.' She reached out and took Mrs

Madrigal's hand. 'I'm sorry. Really. I begged her not to come. She said I owed it to her and told me I was making a terrible mistake. I did everything I could to stop her.'

'Did you tell her about me, Mona?'

'No! I swear!'

'Well, what's this "terrible mistake" business?'

'I was hoping you could tell me. I mean, is there anything I should know, besides your operation and all?'

'I can't imagine what . . .' Mrs Madrigal's voice faltered. She fussed distractedly with the loose wisps of hair that framed her angular face. 'Mona, if she doesn't know that you and I are together, I don't see how I could possibly know anything that would be pertinent to her remark.'

'But she *does* know. I mean, I *think* she knows. Oh, Christ – the moon is in ca-ca!'

Mrs Madrigal managed a chuckle. 'So what do we do, daughter?'

Mona smiled weakly. 'Invite her to dinner?'

'Oh, sickroom, sickroom!'

Mona laughed. 'Maybe I should talk to her first. If she doesn't know about you, there's no point in blowing our cover.'

'Splendid idea.'

But less and less splendid as the day wore on. That night, while Mona was visiting Michael at the hospital, Mrs Madrigal broke one of her own rules of life by sitting in her room and agonizing over the future.

She knew that was silly. If a confrontation with Betty was inevitable, what point was there in fretting over it? The important thing now was to direct all her energy toward Mona's happiness.

So she marched upstairs and had a little talk with Brian.

He told her more than she had expected to hear.

Burke explodes

A low-hanging spring fog slid under the bridge toward the city as Mary Ann filled her lungs with air and read the instructions for an isometric squat.

'Ick. This one is the pits.'

Burke grinned and placed his back firmly against an oak piling, easing himself down slowly. 'This was *your* idea, remember.'

She stuck out her tongue at him. He was right, of course. For weeks she'd been promoting this trip to the Marina Green exercise course, spurred on by a semi-flabby tummy and a sexy *Apartment Life* article about couples who work out together.

Burke reveled in her agony. 'It's not too late to quit before you rupture something.'

'Ha! Who beat who at the hop kick *and* the log hop?' She chose the piling facing Burke and lowered herself defiantly into position.

Burke's face was bright red as he held the squatting position. 'That's because you're doing Intermediate stuff. I'm going for Championship.'

'And you'll poop out at the end. Don't you know anything about endurance?'

Burke completed his count of thirty, springing into an upright position again. 'Healthy body, healthy mind!' he exclaimed.

Mary Ann couldn't manage a snappy comeback. They were both thinking the same thing.

'Well,' shrugged Burke, 'some of us can't have both.'

When they had finished their run, they strolled back to a bench on the edge of the bay. Mary Ann smiled into the wind, feeling the blood tingle in her limbs. She slipped her arm through Burke's and leaned her head on his shoulder.

'Do I smell as gross as you do?'

He kissed her damp temple. 'Every bit.'

'Swell.'

'We won't shower when we get back. I wanna screw on the living room floor.'

'Burke!'

'I *like* musky women.' He kissed her again and began to sing a chorus of 'I Remember You.'

Mary Ann ignored the irony. 'I don't think I've ever heard you sing. You have a gorgeous voice.'

'I do, don't I?' He continued singing.

'Did you ever sing . . . like professionally?'

He turned and looked at her, hesitating. 'Not professionally. Only in church, back in Nantucket. The Good Shepherd choir. What are you up to, anyway?'

Her tone was defensive. 'Nothing. Can't I be curious about you?'

'That's what my mother said on the phone last night.'

'She called you?'

He nodded grimly.

'They're freaking, aren't they?'

'What do you expect? They hate this town. Their only child ended up in a bush in Golden Gate Park with amnesia. Now he's back, chasing ghosts.'

'Do you remember that, Burke?'

'What?'

'Waking up under that bush in the park.'

'Not really. I remember being in a hospital for a while, then—'

'*What* hospital, Burke?'

'Presbyterian.' He smiled sympathetically.

'Well, then how do you know it happened? The stuff about the park and all.'

He stared at her uncomprehendingly. 'What?'

'How do you know your parents are telling the truth?'

'What in hell are you . . . ?'

231

'They could've deprogrammed you, Burke.' Mary Ann drew back slightly, bracing herself for the repercussions. Burke blinked at her momentarily, then exploded with a derisive laugh.

'I may be loony, lady, but I'm not *dumb*! Christ, don't you think I know when people are jacking me around? Don't you think I have enough sense to . . . Christ!'

There was nothing to do but placate him. 'Burke, don't take it so personally. I'm sorry, OK?'

He brooded in silence, gazing out at the fog-blurred bay. 'I'm no baby,' he said at last. '*I was in the AP, Mary Ann.*'

That night, at her suggestion, they slept apart for the first time since his arrival in San Francisco.

Mary Ann dreamed about roses.

She was walking along a catwalk with a dozen roses cradled in her arms. Behind her was the man with the transplant, leading an entourage of rose-bearers.

They were all there: the dwarf from Las Hadas, the rose vendor from the flower market, Millie the Flower Lady, and Arnold and Melba Littlefield, brandishing the processional cross from Beauchamp's funeral.

Suddenly, Burke appeared at the end of the catwalk. He grabbed Mary Ann by the shoulders and shook her beseechingly. '*I was in the AP, Mary Ann. I was in the AP.*'

When she woke up, she knew what she had to do next.

The freak beat

The Associated Press, Mary Ann learned, was located on the third floor of the Fox Plaza high-rise, a cold concrete tombstone of a building that marked the grave of the old Fox Theater.

The theater had been demolished about five years before Mary Anne's arrival in San Francisco, but Michael had told her of its loveliness, its rococo majesty which conformed so gracefully to the needs of human beings.

She thought about that now as she stood in the fluorescent-lit office, waiting for a man named Jack to look up from his computer-screen typewriter long enough to acknowledge her presence.

'Uh ... excuse me. The bureau chief said you might...'

His eyes didn't stray from the symbols on the screen in front of him. 'Fuck, shit, piss!'

'I'm sorry, if this is a bad time.'

'Not *you*.' He turned off the machine and spun around to face her, offering a tired smile. 'How many goddamn words can you write about Patty Hearst, anyway?'

Mary Ann smiled back. 'I've never tried.'

'Well, *don't*. For sheer column-inches, that broad's a bigger pain than Angela Davis, Charlie Manson and Zodiac put together!'

'It must be kind of exciting, though.'

The reporter snorted. 'I put in for Buffalo. I *begged* 'em for Buffalo. But oh, no! Those assholes in New York thought ol' Jack Lederer would be fuckin' *perfect* for San Francisco.' He fumbled for a More, lit it and tossed the match on the floor. 'So what can I do for you?'

'The bureau chief said you used to work with—'

'Pull up a chair.'

She obeyed, wedging herself uncomfortably between his desk and a filing cabinet marked 'Mass Murders, Etc.'

'The bureau chief said you used to work with a guy named Burke Andrew.'

233

He thought for a moment. 'Yeah. Two – no – at *least* three years ago. But not for long. Four or five months at the most. He couldn't hack it for shit.'

'They fired him?'

'Nah, he quit. He was slow, that's all. Spent *hours* workin' on a goddamn grabby lead when the world was fallin' apart around him. He was nice enough, I guess. Friend of yours?'

'Yeah.'

'Disappear or something?'

'No, why?'

He shrugged. 'This is the place, right? For droppin' off the face of the earth?'

Mary Ann smiled, inwardly shuddering. She hadn't thought of Norman Neal Williams in ages. 'Burke has amnesia, Mr Lederer. He can't remember anything after the AP. I thought maybe you might—'

The reporter whistled. 'It's a friggin' soap opera!'

'Tell *me*.'

'You want me to fill in the pieces, right?'

She nodded. 'Did he tell you anything about where he was going after the AP? Did he talk about his plans?'

'Are you makin' this up?'

'No! Why in the world should I? Look, the bureau chief says you and Burke worked together a lot.'

'Yeah. We worked nights together. But he never talked about personal stuff.'

'When he was here did he ever do stories about cults?'

Jack Lederer shook his head. 'The freak beat is mine, sweetheart.' He grinned annoyingly. 'You think the Moonies got him, huh?'

She ignored it. 'Do you think there's any possibility he might have—'

'When did this amnesia zap him, anyway?'

'About three months ago the police found him in Golden Gate Park. He was passed out or something.'

The reporter jerked open a desk drawer and removed a spiral notebook. 'I think it must've been – no, earlier than that – right about . . .' He began to flip through the notebook. 'I saw your boyfriend just briefly about five months ago at Lefty O'Doul's one night. He told me he was free-lancing and that I could eat my heart out because he was onto something really bizarre.'

Mary Ann's mind raced wildly. 'You mean he was still a *reporter*?'

The AP man smirked. 'A *free-lancer*. There's a difference. They always talk crazy.' He looked down at the notebook again. 'Yep. There it is. "Transubstantiation."'

'What? I'm afraid I don't . . .'

'Yeah. Well, neither did I. I asked your boyfriend if he had any substantiation for his so-called bizarre story and he laughed and said, "*Trans*ubstantiation is more like it." So I asked him what the hell that was supposed to mean, and he polished off his drink and told me to look it up.'

'And?'

'He walked out of the joint.'

'But what *does* it mean?'

Jack Lederer stubbed out his More, then pointed to a dictionary on top of the 'Mass Murders, Etc.' filing cabinet. 'Look it up, sweetheart.'

Homecoming

With Michael in his arms, Jon took a deep breath and confronted the precipitous wooden stairway leading up to Barbary Lane. 'Are you ready?' he asked.

'Am *I* ready? *You're* the one I'm worried about. What happened to our Sherpa guide, anyway?'

'He died of exposure at eight thousand feet.'

'Well, shit! You just can't get good Sherpas anymore.'

Jon staggered under his weight. 'Don't make me laugh. I'll drop you.'

'The hell you say. If I go, you're goin' too.'

Jon took long, steady strides up the steps. 'I think we'd better pack in provisions. Something tells me we won't be going out too often.' He stopped, panting, on the landing at the entrance to the lane.

'For God's sake,' Michael said melodramatically. 'Whatever you do, *don't look down*. Pretend you're Karen Black in *Airport*.' He smiled bravely up at Jon, crossing his eyes.

'So help me, Michael, if you don't . . .'

'Sorry.'

The doctor lumbered down the leafy walkway, cursing angrily when Boris, the resident cat, emerged from the shrubbery to rub his back ecstatically against Jon's leg. 'Aw,' said Michael. 'A little pussy never hurt anyone.'

Mona was waiting for them in the courtyard. 'Can I run get your wheelchair or something?'

Jon shook his head. 'It's easier to carry him.'

'Across the threshold, please note.' Michael winked at Mona.

'You could've at least thrown me the garter belt,' she said.

'Since when did *you* wanna get married?'

'A *joke*, Mouse.'

Mrs Madrigal scurried into the courtyard and held the door for them. 'Welcome home, dear. It just hasn't been the same.'

Michael blew her a kiss. 'This place never is, is it?'

Jon fixed pot roast for dinner. Afterward, he moved Michael's wheelchair to the window and pulled up a chair next to him.

'I've missed that fish,' said Michael.

'What fish?'

'Down there. The neon one on the wharf. It's always seemed kind of cheerful to me.'

Jon lit a joint and handed it to Michael. 'The fish was an early Christian symbol for hope. They carved it on the walls of the catacombs when they were hiding out.'

'You don't say?' Michael grinned and took a toke. 'I could learn a lot from you.'

Jon kept his eyes fixed on the bay. 'I can stay, then?'

Silence.

'Well . . . say *something*.'

'I love you, Jon—'

'That's good for starters.'

'I don't want it to be a doctor-patient thing, that's all.'

Jon turned and stared at him. 'Is that what you think?'

'You're a doctor, Jon. It would only be natural for you to get off on nursing someone back—'

'I *hate* wiping your butt!'

'Look, I didn't mean to . . . You do?'

'Goddamn right!'

Michael smiled. 'You don't know how much that means to me.'

They laughed until the tears streamed down their faces. Michael lost control of the smoldering roach, letting it fall to the floor. Jon snuffed it with his foot, then leaned over to look directly into Michael's eyes.

'I want you well, sport. I don't care who does it.'

'I know.'

'On the other hand, I *do* get off on sex with paraplegics.'

They sat up in bed together, poring over back issues of *Architectural Digest.*

'Hey', said Jon, 'you wanna have Mona up for brunch tomorrow?'

'She may be in no mood. She's seeing her mother tonight.'

'Her mother's a bitch?'

'According to Mona, it's "hair by L'Oreal, jewels by Cartier and heart by Frigidaire." But who knows?'

'Yeah.' Jon got lost in his magazine.

Michael stopped reading and savored for a moment this rare new form of inactivity. All his adult life he had searched for someone to do *nothing* with in bed. And now he had found him, this bright, generous person whose love was so strong that sex was in perspective again.

Jon held up his magazine. 'Isn't that magnificent?' It was an early photograph of the Pacific Union Club, the palatial stone edifice that still adorned the top of Nob Hill.

Michael shook his head in appreciation. 'Imagine a club with that kind of money!'

'The club didn't build it. The Floods did.'

'The Floods?'

'The Flood family. *Big* bucks in the old days.'

Michael's brow wrinkled. 'You don't suppose . . . ?'

'What?'

'Christ!' yelped Michael. 'That could be it, Jon. *That could be it.*'

The Mountain of the Flood

It was late, but Michael was too excited to wait until morning before calling Mary Ann.

'Ajax Detective Service here.'

'Mouse?'

'You thought you'd screw me up with that damn poem, didn't you?'

'You've got something?'

'*Mais naturellement!* Can you come down?'

'*Can* I!' She hung up without another word.

Jon laid his *Architectural Digest* on the nightstand. 'Shall I get up?'

'Why?' asked Michael.

'Isn't she coming down?'

Michael looked mildly miffed. 'I think she knows we sleep together, Jon.'

'I know, but . . .' The doctor smiled at himself. 'I'll feel like Nora Charles or something.'

Michael tugged at the lapel of Jon's pajamas. 'It's OK. You're wearing your peignoir.'

Seconds later, they heard Mary Ann in the hallway, rapping demurely on the door. 'It's open,' Michael shouted.

When Mary Ann peered cautiously into the bedroom, Michael made sure there would be no embarrassed silences. 'It's OK,' he grinned. 'Just pretend we're Starsky and Hutch.'

Mary Ann giggled. 'You *do* sorta look like them.' She pulled up a chair next to the bed. 'I hope you don't mind this intrusion, Jon.'

Jon smiled. 'I can't wait to hear what this is about myself.'

'In fact,' added Michael, 'he's the one who gave me the clue.'

Mary Ann was practically bounding in the chair. 'Tell me, tell me!'

Michael smiled mysteriously, heightening the suspense. 'I think Burke's little dream poem is about the PU Club.'

'The what?'

'The PU Club, you poor cornfed thing! The Pacific Union Club, up on Nob Hill.'

'That big red brick thing?'

Michael nodded. 'It was built by a man named Flood, which makes Nob Hill the Mountain of the Flood! And the PU Club is not only a *cult*, it's our

239

oldest cult. All those overstuffed old banker farts, sitting around in their overstuffed chairs!'

Mary Ann was slack-jawed. 'Mouse, do you think they recite that poem in one of their rituals or something?'

'Doesn't it make a lot of sense?'

Mary Ann thought for a moment. 'Well, *that* part makes sense. But what about the rest of it? What about the Meeting of the Lines, for instance?'

Jon, who had been listening intently, couldn't resist asking, 'What's the Meeting of the Lines?'

'It's part of the poem,' Michael explained. '"High upon the Sacred Rock/The Rose Incarnate shines,/Upon the Mountain of the Flood/At the Meeting of the Lines."'

Jon grinned. 'Maybe they snort coke at the PU Club.'

'That's what Burke thinks it means,' said Mary Ann.

Michael demurred. 'They just snort, period, at the PU Club.'

'Wait!' exclaimed Jon. 'What about the cable cars?'

'What about them?' asked Mary Ann.

'The cable car lines. They cross at California and Powell, just a block away from the PU Club!'

Mary Ann and Michael yelped in unison. 'That's brilliant,' blurted Michael. 'That's positively brilliant!' Mary Ann beamed in agreement. 'That *must* be it.'

Jon bowed grandly. 'Now all we have to do is figure out what any of this has to do with a florist from St Sebastian's Hospital, right?'

Mary Ann nodded, deep in thought. '*And* what any of this has to do with transubstantiation.'

Michael did a double take. 'Come again, ma'am?'

'Have you got a dictionary?'

'On the shelf by the door,' said Michael. 'Next to *The Persian Boy*.'

Mary Ann found the dictionary and began to thumb through it. 'I went down to the AP today. Where Burke used to work. A man there told me he ran into

Burke about five months ago, and he said Burke told him he was working on . . . Here it is. Transubstantiation.' She handed the book to Jon.

The doctor read aloud. '"The changing of one substance into another."'

'Read the second definition,' said Mary Ann.

'"In the mass of the Roman Catholic Church, the conversion of the whole substance of the bread and wine into the body and blood of Christ, only the external appearance of bread and wine remaining." So what does that have to do with Burke?'

'This guy at the AP says he was working on a really bizarre story connected with transubstantiation.'

Michael frowned quizzically. 'Have you tried this out on Burke yet?'

Mary Ann shook her head soberly. 'I think he's beginning to resent my curiosity, Mouse. I'm not sure what that means, but I'm trying to be discreet about all this, until I've got something solid to go on.'

'Do you know what I think?' said Jon.

'What?' asked Mary Ann.

'I think you've got *too many* clues.'

Mary Ann sighed. 'I think you're right.'

Betty

The first thing Mona noticed about Betty Ramsey was her clothes. She was decked out in Kelly green and white, the recognizable racing colors of women realtors everywhere.

And Mona's clothing was the first thing Betty noticed.

'Where *did* you get that frock? Goodwill?'

Mona's smile was smug. 'As a matter of fact, yes.'

'Well, it's grossly unflattering.'

'Thank you.'

'The hippie thing is over, Mona. The pendulum is swinging.'

Mona ignored her, heading for the window.

'What are you doing?' asked Betty.

'Checking out your view.' She turned and smiled at her mother. 'The first thing *every* San Franciscan does when visiting somebody else's apartment.' She parted the curtains and gazed down upon the nighttime splendor of the city. 'Mmm. Very nice. Whose place is this, anyway?'

Betty began dropping ice cubes into a glass. 'Susan Patterson's. Someone I knew *years* ago in Carmel. She's in Switzerland for the spring.'

Mona surveyed the room. 'It looks like you've been here since *last* spring.' The floor was cluttered with Gump's boxes and shopping bags from Saks; Betty's yoga mat and an assortment of French body creams were visible through the bedroom door.

Betty held up a gin bottle. 'This or bourbon?'

'Neither, thanks.'

'I don't have any Perrier.'

'That's fine. I took a Quaalude a little while ago.'

'For God's sake!'

Mona sat down on the sofa. 'Would you rather I'd taken one of your Valiums?'

'A *doctor* prescribed those.'

'Don't they always.'

'You shouldn't have to rely on . . . Mona, let's not argue. We haven't seen each other for a long time, darling. The least we can do is—'

'Why are you here, Betty?'

Betty didn't answer immediately. She finished fixing her gin-and-tonic, then joined her daughter on the sofa. 'Why do you think?'

Mona locked eyes with her mother. 'I don't think it has a damned thing to do with me.'

'That's not fair, Mona.'

'It's the truth.'

Betty looked down at her drink. 'You know about Andy, don't you?'

Mona made her face into a mask. 'I know that he left you. That's old news.'

'Don't play games, Mona. I know he's your landlord. I know about the sex change, and I know that you know about it.'

Mona held firm. 'I repeat. Why are you here?'

'Because I have a bloody *right* to be! He deserted me, Mona! He left me with a child to support! He walked out of my life without leaving so much as a note, and now he thinks he can waltz right back and lay claim to the child he never even—'

'I am not a child and nobody's *laid claim* to me, Betty. I didn't even know that he – that she was my father until two weeks ago.'

Betty glared at her in disgust. 'And now you're living with him!'

'Her.'

'Did he tell you – oh, pardon me, *she* – did *she*, by any chance, tell you what she did with the private detective I hired?'

'The *what*?'

'Mona, darling, this is so much more complicated than you could ever—'

'Just tell me what you're talking about.'

Betty held her daughter's hand. 'Last summer, when you sent me that photograph of your landlady, I saw the similarities immediately, so I hired a private detective to help me find out if it was true.'

Mona stared in amazement.

'And', continued Betty, 'he never reported back.'

'What?'

'I never heard another word from him. He was living in your house, Mona. At 28 Barbary Lane.'

'Mr Williams? That guy on the roof?'

Betty nodded, holding tight to Mona's hand. 'We

243

stayed in touch by telephone. He called me at least once a week. He said he thought Andy had become . . . Anna Madrigal, and he told me that Anna Madrigal was an anagram for something. Then he just disappeared.' She let go of Mona's hand and took a sip of her drink. 'Did you *know* him, Mona?'

Stunned, Mona shook her head. 'Not at all. He was . . . weird.'

'I know. He was the best I could round up on short notice. The point is, what *happened* to him?'

Mona took a sip of Betty's gin. 'We wondered that too.'

'We?'

'*Everybody*. Including Mrs Madrigal. She even called the police about it.'

'I want to see her, Mona. Will you arrange it?'

A look of wretched resignation came over Mona's face. 'You'll do it anyway,' she sighed.

'You're right,' said Betty. 'I will.'

The Rose Incarnate

In keeping with her new strategy, Mary Ann said nothing to Burke about the Pacific Union Club. Or about her transubstantiation findings. She kept quiet all through breakfast and all through a leisurely morning walk across Russian Hill.

Finally, at noon, she excused herself.

'Jon's at his office,' she explained. 'I promised him I'd keep Mouse company for a while.'

When she entered Michael's apartment, the invalid was pacing the room in his wheelchair, his eyes flickering with excitement. 'You know what?' he said without preliminaries. 'We didn't even consider the red rose business in our discussion last night.'

'I got the feeling you guys were OD'ing.'

Michael smiled. 'Not me, Babycakes. I'm *hooked*. Look, it all comes back to the man with the transplant, doesn't it?'

'Maybe. Burke only *thinks* that the transplant man recognized him.'

'Assuming he did, then what do we have?'

'He could be a member of the PU Club, I guess.'

Michael shook his head. 'I suggested that to Jon. He says the PU Club would *never* admit a hospital florist. Maybe Burke worked as a waiter or something at the PU Club.'

'It's hard to picture,' said Mary Ann.

'OK, then maybe we're on the wrong track altogether. You know, the Mountain of the Flood could mean just Nob Hill in general.'

'So what else is *there*?'

'Plenty. The Mark, the Huntington, the Fairmont.'

'Great. A hotel cult.'

Michael grinned. 'You're stuck in that cult rut, aren't you?'

'I don't know,' groaned Mary Ann. 'Sometimes I feel like I made the whole thing up.'

Michael laughed. 'It's possible. I was looking through some of my old high school lit books this morning – you know, *Silas Marner* and *The Great Gatsby* and all that – and I just about cracked up because I had written 'symbolism' in the margin on every other page. Christ! In *The Great Gatsby* I had underlined the word 'yellow' every time it appeared.'

'God!' smiled Mary Ann. 'I remember those awful papers, but I don't get it, Mouse. What does that have to do with all this?'

'Well, maybe *we're* looking for too much symbolism. *Everything* doesn't have to mean something.'

'Yeah, but it sure would be nice if *something* did.'

'What about the transub . . . whatchamacallit?'

'What about it?'

'Well, for starters, is Burke Catholic?'

245

Mary Ann shook her head. 'Episcopalian.'

'That's close.'

'It is?'

Michael nodded. 'The High Church ones are more Catholic than the Catholics. Believe me, I know. I used to have a boyfriend who was a High Church Episcopal seminarian. He practically *shaved* in holy water. I'm sure *he* believed that the bread and wine turn into the body and blood of Christ.'

Mary Ann shuddered a little. 'Is that what they believe? Literally?'

'Literally. You saw the definition, Babycakes.'

'I know, but that's kind of creepy, isn't it?'

Michael shrugged. 'Christians are the only people on earth who kneel before an instrument of torture. If Christ had been martyred in this century, I guess we'd all be wearing little electric chairs around our necks.'

Mary Ann was shocked. 'Mouse, that's sacrilegious!'

'No it's not. It's just an observation about the nature of—' Suddenly, Michael's hands clamped onto the arms of his wheelchair, his face screwed into an expression of intense concentration. 'Jesus Christ!' he shouted. *'Jesus Christ!'*

'Mouse, for heaven's sake, what's the matter?'

'The Sacred Rock! The goddamn Sacred Rock! It's Grace Cathedral, it's gotta be Grace Cathedral!'

'Grace Cathedral?'

'What else? Right next door to the PU Club, Mary Ann! On the Mountain of the Flood at the Meeting of the Lines! And guess what the Rose Incarnate is?'

'What?'

'The biggest rose in the whole friggin' city! The rose window at Grace Cathedral!'

Labor of love

D'orothea Wilson paused briefly in the lobby of St Sebastian's Hospital to study an antique portrait of the institution's namesake.

The holy man was tied to a tree, wearing only a loincloth and a beatific smile. His bloodied body was prickly with arrows. Half a dozen of them, at least.

D'orothea made a face that attracted the attention of a passing nurse. 'I know,' winced the nurse. 'Isn't it awful?'

'Why do they even hang it? In a hospital, for God's sake!'

The nurse smiled wearily. 'The board fights over it every year. I think it came with a big endowment or something. Nobody wants to offend the old bat who donated it. They've moved it two or three times. This is the least conspicuous it's ever been.'

'Someone should come in here some night with a can of spray paint,' suggested D'orothea.

'Right on!' said the nurse.

After checking at the desk on the location of DeDe's room, D'orothea made a quick stop at the hospital florist, where she picked up a dozen roses. Then she hurried to the second floor to see her friend.

'You can't stay long,' grinned DeDe. 'They just chased my mother out.'

'I won't.' D'orothea set the roses on the bedside table, then leaned over and kissed DeDe on the cheek. 'You look *fabulous*, hon.'

'Thanks. And thanks for the roses.'

'How's the tum-tum?'

247

DeDe rolled her eyes. 'Thumpety-thump. Thumpety-thump.'

'You mean . . . ?'

'The pains are fifteen minutes apart.'

'Holy shit! When you called, you sounded so casual about it. I thought . . . Oh, hon, aren't you excited?'

DeDe smiled thinly. 'Sure.'

'*Course* you are! Hey, you haven't even told me about names.'

'Names?'

'For the babies. You picked 'em yet?'

DeDe smoothed the bedsheet over her mountainous belly. 'Oh, Edgar, I guess, if one is a boy. After my father. And if one is a girl, I'll name her Anna.'

'That's pretty. Any particular reason?'

'Daddy asked me to. Just before he died.'

'A family name, huh?'

DeDe shook her head. 'Not that I know of. Daddy just said he liked the name.' She fidgeted with the sheet again, looking away. It took D'orothea a moment to realize that she was crying.

'Hon? Hey, hon. What's the trouble?'

'I'm so frightened, D'or.'

D'orothea sat on the edge of the bed and stroked DeDe's hair gently. 'Why?' she asked.

'I feel like I'm going to be punished or something.'

'Punished? What for?'

DeDe's face was shiny with tears. She reached for a Kleenex, blew her nose, then dropped the tissue on the bedside table. Finally, she looked up at D'orothea and sighed. 'The twins are gonna be Chinese, D'or.'

D'orothea stared at her expressionlessly. Then she said, 'Big fucking deal.'

A smile fought its way through the desolation of DeDe's face. 'That's easy for you to say.'

'Fine,' said D'or. 'Then I'll say it again. Biiiiig fucking deal!'

DeDe laughed at last. 'Oh, D'or, thank you!'

'Don't mention it. Eurasians are *always* gorgeous, by the way.'

'They are, aren't they?'

'Does Big Mama know?'

DeDe winced, then shook her head.

'Thought so,' said D'or. '*That's* what you're bawling about, isn't it?'

'In part, I guess.'

'What's the other part?'

'I don't know. D'or . . . none of my friends have even called.'

'Why, your luck is changing, hon.'

'Why?'

' 'Cause I'm the first of your *new* friends, DeDe. And we're not that easy to get rid of.' She leaned over and kissed DeDe again. ' 'Cept when you're dropping babies. Then I get squeamish as hell. I'll be here, though. Right outside the door.'

'You don't have to.'

'I want to.'

'Thanks, D'or.'

'Do you want me to tell your mother about the babies, by the way?'

'No, I'll do it. I love you, D'or.'

'Ditto, Kiddo.'

Back to Nantucket?

Burke, of course, was the hardest one to convince.

'It's just plain goofball, Mary Ann. Why would a *cathedral* make anybody have amnesia? You seem to forget I get violently ill whenever I—'

'You threw up at Beauchamp's funeral, didn't you? That was a church.'

Burke gestured impatiently. 'That was the rose, for God's sake.'

'But don't you see? Maybe it isn't the *image* of the rose that nauseates you. Maybe it's just the word, the association with the rose window.'

Looking bleaker than ever, he sat down on the edge of his bed. 'It isn't a window I see in my dream. It's a red rose. Not a pink one or a yellow one – a *red* one, Mary Ann.' He peered up at her through eyes that had changed from vibrant gray to dull pewter. 'I think it's time for me to go home.'

Her first thought was that they were already *in* his apartment. Then his meaning struck her like a bundle of briars across the face. 'Burke, you don't mean that!'

The kindness of his tone was devastating. 'Yes, I do,' he said softly. 'I have to put this behind me, Mary Ann.'

'But, Burke . . .' She sat next to him and slipped her arm across his hunched shoulders. 'You'll *never* put it behind until you find the cause of your amnesia. You can't go on being terrified forever.'

'I'm not terrified.'

She squeezed his shoulder gently. 'I know, but what about the roses?'

'I can handle that. I just have to . . . I have to start getting on with life.'

'What will you do back East?'

'My father's offered me a position in his publishing firm.'

She looked at him soulfully. 'Couldn't you do something like that here?'

He smiled, stroking her hair. 'I *will* miss you. I should have said that first thing.'

She felt tears welling in her eyes. 'Dammit,' she said quietly. 'I'm so pissed at myself.'

'Why?'

'I shouldn't have pushed it. I shouldn't have freaked you out.'

His face turned the color of an American Beauty. *'You didn't freak me out, Mary Ann!'*

She looked at him in silence, reading the anguish in his face. Then she stood up and walked across the room. If this was it, if they had passed the point of no return, she had nothing to lose by telling the whole truth.

She turned to face him. 'Burke, the man with the transplant sings in the choir at Grace Cathedral.'

'What?'

'I checked on it this morning. And I think you used to sing with him.'

'Wait a minute! How did you find that out?'

She averted her eyes. She didn't want to seem too proud of herself. 'I . . . well, first I asked Jon to call the hospital and find out his name. Then I called Grace Cathedral and talked to some guy they call the verger, and he told me that the transplant man – his name is Tyrone, by the way – he said that Tyrone sings in the choir at Grace.'

Something like hope glimmered in Burke's eyes. 'And you think . . . you think I sang with him?'

'You *could* have,' she said warily. 'You told me you sang in the choir back in Nantucket. You also told me, when we were in Mexico, that you had sent letters to your parents about attending services at Grace Cathedral.'

Mary Ann must have looked like a frightened rabbit, for Burke smiled suddenly and patted the bed next to him. She came to him and sat down, peering at him balefully. 'Am I a pain in the ass?' she asked.

He kissed the tip of her nose. 'So you think that Burke Andrew, boy reporter, stumbled onto some sinister goings-on at Grace Cathedral?'

She smiled sheepishly. 'It's only *today's* theory.'

'An *Episcopal* cult, huh?'

She goosed him. 'Don't rub it in.'

'Actually,' he smiled, 'I kinda like it.'

*   *   *

Scurrying back to her own apartment, Mary Anne encountered Mrs Madrigal, who was vacuuming the hallway. The landlady's hair was up in curlers.

'Trying out a new do?' asked Mary Ann.

'We'll see. I may end up looking like Medusa. Where are *you* off to in such a hurry.'

'Burke's taking me to church.'

'How very sweet,' said Mrs Madrigal earnestly.

'I'm expecting lightning bolts. This is the first time I've been to church since I came to San Francisco ten months ago.'

The landlady smiled. 'Well, say one for me.'

'You don't need it.'

'I do *tonight*.'

'Why?'

Mrs Madrigal leaned forward furtively. 'Tonight, my dear child, I have a heavy date with my ex-wife.'

Questions and answers

'Hello, Betty.'

Mrs Madrigal spoke the words with a warmth and self-assurance that astounded Mona. Furthermore, the landlady had never looked more beautiful. Smooth, glowing skin. Shining eyes. A pale green kimono fluttered about her like butterfly wings.

And tonight she wasn't wearing her usual cloche. Her hair fell about her face in soft, romantic ringlets. Betty was visibly stunned.

'Hello. I hope this isn't . . . How are you?'

Mrs Madrigal smiled like a benign Hindu goddess. 'Call me Andy, if you like. I know Anna must be a little hard to get out.'

'No, that's perfectly . . . This is a *darling* neighborhood. I see why Mona's so mad for it.'

Mrs Madrigal took her guest's coat. 'I understand you're just a few blocks away.'

'Yes. Well, that's a high-rise. This is just . . . precious. Those steps up from the street are straight out of . . . I don't know where.' She stepped into the living room, nervously appraising everything in sight. Except, of course, the person who had once been her husband.

Mrs Madrigal brought sherry from the kitchen. 'There's not one for you, Mona, dear. I think your mother and I should have a little talk.'

Mona rose like a shot. 'OK. Fine. I'll take a walk or something.'

'We won't be long,' said Mrs Madrigal. 'Why don't you go to the Tivoli. Perhaps we can join you later.'

'Fine,' said Mona lamely, heading out the door.

Mrs Madrigal sat sipping her sherry in silence, her eyes glued on Betty Ramsey's rapidly wilting smile. 'My goodness,' she said at last, 'you've certainly held up well. Your figure's as good as it was thirty years ago.'

Betty tugged at her skirt, assuring that her knees were covered. 'Yoga helps,' she said flatly.

'Mmm. And a few snips here and there.'

Betty stiffened. 'I don't see what that—'

'I'm not being bitchy, Betty.' She laughed heartily. 'I'm the *last* person to denigrate the value of surgery!' Her merriment vanished as rapidly as it had come. 'So what can I do for you?'

The realtor looked down at her glass. 'I have a right to see my daughter,' she said quietly, measuring her words, as if on the verge of exploding. 'I have a right to know what you're doing with her.'

A faint smile rippled across the landlady's face. 'It's monstrously perverse. I'm giving her a home. And love.'

'And I didn't. Is that what you're saying?'

'This is silly, Betty. Mona's over thirty.'

A large vein began to pulse in Betty's sinewy neck. 'I know what you're doing. You're deliberately poisoning her against me. You're using her to satisfy some sick maternal urge that will make you feel like a *real* woman! God! That's so bloody twisted I can't even . . .'

'I'm sorry you resent me so much. It may help you to know that I think there's some justification for the way you feel.'

'*Some* justification! Listen to me, Andy! I want more than a bloody glass of sherry and a few weak-kneed apologies. I want some answers, goddammit!'

Mrs Madrigal set down her glass and folded her hands in her lap.

'Fine,' she said quietly. 'I'll do my best.'

Her composure rattled Betty. 'For one thing, I want to know what happened to Norman Williams.'

Mrs Madrigal's Wedgwood eyes turned into saucers. 'You *knew* him?'

'Don't give me that!' snarled Betty.

'Betty, honestly, what *are* you talking about?'

'I hired him, and you know it! What did you do? Buy him off?'

'He disappeared several months ago. He just never came back, Betty. My God, was he a *detective*?'

'How *demurely* you lie.' Betty sprang to her feet. 'I should have known better than to expect the truth from you. And I think it's about time that Mona learned the truth about her *real* father!'

'Betty, please . . .'

'Unless, of course, you've already told her, in all your liberated candor.'

Silence.

Betty smiled savagely. 'I didn't think you had.'

'How can you be so vindictive? You'll only hurt her.'

'You said it yourself. Mona's over thirty. She can take it. She's a big girl now.'

The Sacred Rock

It was dusk when they reached Nob Hill. In front of the Mark and the Fairmont, pastel-colored tourists scrambled in every direction. They reminded Mary Ann of baby chicks that had been dyed for Easter and were looking for their mothers.

But these people, more likely, were looking for their children.

Like Mona's mother. Like Michael's parents and Burke's and her own. And even like Mother Mucca. Stunned and scandalized, yet secretly titillated, they had flocked to this latter-day Sodom to observe firsthand the fate of their long-flown offspring.

There was fear in their eyes. And confusion. And a kind of mute despair that made Mary Ann want to reach out and hug them. Some of them were nearing the end of their lives, yet, in many ways, they *were* the chicks. They were the children of their children.

The traffic light changed. Burke and Mary Ann pressed through the mob at the crosswalk and strode west up California Street. To their right, the mud-brown fortress called the Pacific Union Club squatted disapprovingly in the midst of this middle-American chaos. Silent, foreboding, impenetrable.

Mary Ann ran her fingers along the massive bronze fence that protected the building, examining its ornamentation for some sort of rose motif. Nothing. Only Nancy Drew found clues that easily.

When they reached Huntington Park, they sat on a bench near the fountain, their backs to the PU Club, their eyes fixed on the mammoth rose window of Grace Cathedral.

'Did you call them?' asked Burke.

Mary Ann nodded. 'A woman in the cathedral office says there's a Holy Communion service tonight.'

'What time?'

She looked at her watch. 'Forty-five minutes.'

'We should go in now, then. I don't want to be there with a lot of people around.'

'Why?'

He smiled and pointed to his mouth. 'I've had enough scenes for one week.'

'You don't think you'll . . . ?'

'How do *I* know?' he shrugged. 'I think we should stay long enough to see if it triggers anything, then get the hell out.' He smiled at his own phraseology, apologizing to the huge window. 'Sorry about that.'

'Burke, before we go in . . .'

'Yeah?'

'I was just wondering. Back in Nantucket, when you went to church there, did you believe that the wine turned into blood and the bread turned into flesh?'

He smiled. 'Didn't everybody?'

She shook her head. 'We were Presbyterian. It was all grape juice to me.'

'I guess we were pretty High Church,' he grinned.

'Don't you find that a little grotesque?'

'Maybe. If you stop to think about it long enough. But not grotesque enough to make a hot news story, if that's what you're thinking. Look, Mary Ann, for most Episcopalians, it's just a bunch of words. If you actually backed a High Churcher into the corner, he might *say* he believed he was drinking the blood of Christ, or eating His flesh, but I think most people regard it in a kind of mundane, symbolic way.'

'Have you thought about why you might have been writing a story on it then?'

He chuckled. 'You're more literal than the High Churchers. Look, you said Jack Lederer told you I had *mentioned* the word "transubstantiation" in connection with the story I was writing. In a broad sense, that word can simply mean transformation. Hell, maybe I was talking about my career . . . or *anything*. The only reason Lederer wrote the word down was because he himself didn't know what it meant.'

A chill evening wind whipped through the little park. Mary Ann turned up her coat collar and gazed again at the great cathedral. She slipped her arm through Burke's.

'It's beautiful,' she said reverently. 'It's almost blue in this light.'

He nodded, pulling her closer.

'Why do I feel so creepy, Burke?'

He turned and smiled at her. 'Because *your* heritage is the Little Brown Church in the Dell.' He rose suddenly, taking her with him. 'C'mon, you heathen. Let's go get religion.'

The irony of the turnabout did not escape her.

Now she was the one who wanted to back out.

Showdown

Mrs Madrigal sat down on the edge of her red velvet sofa, momentarily stunned. The horrid part, the part that made her knees weak and her throat dry, was that Betty was clearly enjoying herself.

'She wouldn't even *be* here', snarled the realtor, 'if she didn't think your blood was flowing in her veins.'

'That's not true,' said Mrs Madrigal ineffectually. 'Anybody can tell you that's not true.'

Betty's eyes narrowed. 'Why don't we ask Mona? Hmmm?'

'What point is there in doing that? What would you gain, Betty?'

Betty's lip curled. 'Not as much as you'd lose, I suppose.'

'No. You're wrong. Mona would be the loser, Betty. She needs a family now. She needs to feel kinship. The *last* thing she needs is to hear about your long-dead little escapade with an oversexed plumber.'

'He was a *contractor*. And I find it *very* odd, Andy, that you don't think the identity of Mona's *real* father might be of some interest to her.'

'It was of no interest to *him*. Then or now. It was a one-night stand, for heaven's sake!'

'And *you* have more claim on her, I suppose? You who left her *completely* fatherless!'

Mrs Madrigal's eyes grew moist. 'I've tried to make good on that, Betty. Can't you *see*?' She gestured feebly around the room, as if 28 Barbary Lane might somehow testify to the purity of her intentions. 'Can't you see what I've tried to do for her?'

'It's too late for that, Andy. Thirty years is too late.'

'Do you want me to beg you, is that it?'

'I'm telling you, Andy. You're not going to stop me.'

'She won't come back to Minneapolis. I can promise you that.'

'I don't care.'

'Then what can you *gain*, other than hurting Mona? In the long run, it won't make any difference to her. She'll love you less, Betty, not more.'

The realtor's features were rigid. 'We'll see.'

'No,' said Mrs Madrigal firmly. 'No, we won't.'

'*What?*' The landlady's tone had jolted her.

'You will leave town, Betty. You will leave town tomorrow or I will tell all parties concerned about what you've been doing in that building at Leavenworth and Green.'

Betty sensed the shift in power. It hung in the air like ozone after a thunderstorm. 'What', she said testily, 'are you talking about?'

'I mean', said Mrs Madrigal, sipping her sherry, 'that you've been in town a lot longer than you told Mona.'

'And what if I have?'

'More like a month than a few days,' smiled the landlady.

'Look, Andy. I *knew* something was wrong. Norman Williams had disappeared, for God's sake!' She paced the room frantically, casting angry sideways glances at her ex-husband. 'I had to do *something*.'

'Mmm. So you thought you'd do a little poking around on your own.'

'What else could I do?'

'Indeed,' said Mrs Madrigal calmly. 'So how's the view from the eleventh floor?'

Silence.

'I did get the floor right, didn't I? I believe Mona said it was the eleventh.'

'Andy, I haven't the slightest idea what—'

'There must be a *lovely* view of this place from the eleventh floor.'

Mrs Madrigal's eyes locked on her prey. '*Particularly* at midnight.'

Betty stopped pacing. Her determinedly pursed mouth went slack. 'Did Mona tell you that?'

The landlady smiled. 'I have many more children than Mona.'

Betty stood there staring. Finally, she said, 'Jesus.' It came out like the hiss of a snake.

'So', said Mrs Madrigal cheerily, 'I think you will agree with me that there are *lots* of things that Mona would be better off not knowing. Besides, Betty, she *needs* that boy, almost as much as he needs her.'

'She . . . doesn't know about . . . me?'

Mrs Madrigal shook her head. 'Nor does he. He thinks you're a veritable Salome, a siren on the rocks!' She winked at the realtor. 'I won't tell him, if you won't.'

Betty glared at her in silence.

'I won't tell *anyone*, Betty. Not if you leave. Tomorrow.'

'I can't trust you.'

'Yes, you can. I was a weasel of a man, but I'm one helluva nice woman.'

'You're a *bastard* is what you are!'

'Please,' smiled Mrs Madrigal. 'Call me a bitch.'

The man who wasn't there

As Burke and Mary Ann entered the cathedral, their shoes clattered angrily on the floor, betraying their presence to the handful of worshipers scattered throughout the great room.

'I feel such a tourist,' Mary Ann whispered.

Burke smiled, squeezing her hand. 'It's all right. No one would ever take you for a Presbyterian.'

'Shouldn't we sit down or something?'

He shrugged. 'If you want.'

They ducked into a pew next to an awesome stone pillar. Above them to the left, the Technicolor grandeur of a stained-glass window was fading into black. Mary Ann sat down and fumbled in her purse for a Dynamint.

'Want one?' she asked.

Burke shook his head. 'Let's just sit quiet for a while.'

Complying, Mary Ann scanned the room, wondering uneasily if she and Burke were registering the same impressions. Two pews in front of them, an old woman was saying her prayers, a pink floral hanky pinned to the back of her gray bun. Across the aisle, a man wearing a T-shirt that said 'the pines 75' was crossing himself with great aplomb.

These people weren't Catholics, Mary Ann reminded herself. They were Episcopalians, High Church presumably, but ordinary Protestants who had come to this echoing chamber so that wine could turn to blood in their mouths.

She shuddered and popped another Dynamint. Then she caught Burke's eye.

'Anything?' she asked.

He shook his head.

'Do you even remember this space?'

'Not really. It's a lot like St John the Divine's in New York.'

'It's so huge,' Mary Ann observed vacantly.

Burke peered around the pillar. 'I guess the choir sits up by the altar. Maybe we should go up there.'

'Uh . . . why?'

He smiled at her. 'Are you scared, Mary Ann?'

'No. I just . . . Well, we'll be so . . . obtrusive, won't we?'

He took her hand. 'C'mon. Just for a minute. Maybe I'll recognize the choir loft or something.'

So they walked down the aisle together. Mary Ann forgot her anxiety for a moment, secretly amused at the symbolism of this action. Was this how a wedding rehearsal felt?

As they passed the communion rail, he slowed down to read the message inscribed in needlepoint on the kneeling pads: IF ANY MAY EAT OF THIS BREAD YE SHALL LIVE FOREVER. She tugged at Burke's elbow. 'Look,' she whispered. 'Transubstantiation.'

He couldn't hide his amusement. 'You act like you're visiting an Incan ruin or something.'

The organist was positioned just beyond the communion rail near the enclosure for the choir. He was the only person in that part of the cathedral. He adjusted his sheet music gravely, without looking up. Then he began to play.

Mary Ann flinched as the music rolled thunderously through the cathedral. 'Burke, maybe they're starting.'

'He's just practicing,' explained Burke. 'Let's go. I don't need to see the choir loft.'

'If you'd *really* like to—'

He shook his head. 'None of this is familiar. I'd know by now if it was.'

They turned in their tracks and made a dignified exit down the aisle. The old lady in the pink hanky looked up as they passed her pew. Mary Ann smiled at her apologetically, then gazed heavenward at the great rose window. Its brilliance was gone now; it was black as the night outside.

'Burke?'

'Mmm?'

'Let's do something mindless and cheerful tonight. Like a Burt Reynolds movie, or maybe that country-western sing-along place in the – Oh, God, stop! Don't look, Burke!' She grabbed his hand and jerked him unceremoniously into a pew, pulling him down to the prayer bench. 'Don't move,' she whispered. 'Don't turn around.'

'What in the hell are . . . ?'

She kept her head bowed in pseudo piety. 'Shhh! Mr Tyrone is here.'

'*Who?*'

'*The man with the transplant.*'

'Where?'

'By the door. *He was standing by the door, Burke.*'

Burke's tone accused her of overdramatizing. 'If he sings in the choir, Mary Ann, he has every reason in the world to—'

'Burke, he had something with him.'

Burke peered over his shoulder.

'*Don't*, he'll see you.'

'He's doing better than I am, then.'

'What?'

'There's no one there, Mary Ann.'

She turned slowly and looked toward the door again.

Burke was right. *There was no one there.*

Mona was beginning her second half liter of red wine when Mrs Madrigal arrived at the Savoy-Tivoli.

Alone.

'Are you all right, Mrs Madrigal?'

The landlady nodded. 'It could have been nastier, I suppose.' She slipped into a chair and grasped Mona's hand across the table. 'I did my best, dear.'

'Did she make a scene?'

'She tried to.'

Mona hesitated, then blurted out the question that had been plaguing her all evening. 'Did she talk to you about Mr Williams?'

'Yes.'

'Well?'

'I was flabbergasted. I had no idea he was a detective, much less *hers*. And of course, I can't imagine what happened to him.'

Mona was gazing down at her wineglass.

'Look at me, dear. That's the truth.'

'I believe you.'

'You must, Mona. You *must*.'

'I do,' smiled her daughter. 'Where is she, anyway? Was she bent out of shape?'

'Totally. May I have a sip of your wine, dear?'

Mona pushed her glass across the table. 'I'm sorry you had to go through all this.'

'She's leaving tomorrow. You should give her a call.'

'All right.'

'Don't forget, she loves you, Mona. She made a lot of sacrifices for you in her time.'

'I know.' Mona retrieved the wineglass and took a sip. 'Do you mind if I ask you about one more thing?'

'Go ahead.'

'Betty said that Mr Williams told her your name was an anagram.'

'How interesting.'

'Well?'

'Well what?'

'Is it true?'

Mrs Madrigal smiled enigmatically. 'Haven't you tried to work it out yet?'

'Then it is?'

The landlady picked up a bread stick and nibbled on it. 'I'll make a very shady deal with you, young lady. I'll tell you the anagram, if you'll invite a friend of mine to dinner.'

'Who?'

'Brian Hawkins.'

'Forget it.'

Mrs Madrigal set the bread stick down demurely. 'Very well.'

'I'm your daughter,' countered Mona. 'I have a right to know that anagram.'

'Indeed. And as your parent, I have a right to discuss grandchildren.'

'Bullshit.'

Mrs Madrigal wagged her finger. 'Mother Mucca will wash your mouth out with soap.'

'Brian Hawkins is not even *vaguely* interested in me.'

'I think he *will* be.'

'Huh?'

'Trust me, Mona.'

Mona looked away. 'He made me feel such a damned fool.'

'Oh, Mona, we're all damned fools! Some of us just have more fun with it than others. Loosen up, dear! Don't be so afraid to cry . . . or laugh, for that matter. Laugh all you want and cry all you want and whistle at pretty men in the street and to *hell* with anybody who thinks you're a damned fool!' She lifted the wineglass in a toast to the younger woman. 'I love you, dear. And that makes you free to do anything.'

Mona didn't answer. There were tears streaming down her face. Mrs Madrigal reached across the table and dabbed her eyes with a napkin.

'Wet enough for you?' asked Mona.

Suddenly, the waiter loomed over them.

'Oh, Luciano,' exclaimed Mrs Madrigal. 'Have you met my daughter?'

The waiter made a courtly bow. Mona flushed and extended her hand. The waiter kissed it, saying, '*Bella.*'

Mrs Madrigal smiled proudly. 'Of course she's *bella*! She takes after her . . . whatever.'

Mona smiled at her through bleary eyes. 'You're so weird.'

'*Grazie,*' said her landlady.

Descent into nowhere

Mary Ann's eyes grew as big as communion wafers as she stared at the spot where the man with the transplant had been. 'I swear, Burke. He was right there next to the door.'

'Maybe,' shrugged Burke. 'But he ain't there now.'

'I guess he went back outside.'

'Do you want to look?'

She hesitated. 'I think we should. But we can't look like we are.'

'Right. And what did you mean, he had something with him?'

She shifted from a kneeling to a sitting position, following Burke's cue. 'I'm not sure,' she said uneasily. 'It looked like a Styrofoam cooler.'

He blinked at her. 'Am I supposed to know what that means?'

She shook her head. 'I never mentioned it. Jon saw him leaving the hospital with a Styrofoam cooler last week.'

'So?'

'So nothing. That's just what he saw. Out in the parking lot.'

Burke raised his eyebrows. 'Do you think', he asked dramatically, 'that he prefers beer to wine at communion?'

'I'm not making a big deal out of it, Burke.' She knew his flippancy was a defense, but it still irritated her.

He stood up and led her out of the pew. As they headed toward the doorway, three or four more worshippers entered the building. 'How much time have we got?' asked Burke.

'Fifteen minutes,' came the reply.

They reached the doorway. 'I'll go first,' said Mary Ann. 'We'll just stroll out naturally, like we're getting some fresh air or something.'

Burke winked and gave her a thumbs-up sign.

Mary Ann tugged at the heavy door and led the way into the dark. As casually as possible, she checked out the people chatting in the courtyard in front of the cathedral. The man with the transplant was not there.

She took Burke's arm and reentered the cathedral. 'It doesn't make sense,' she whispered. 'There's nowhere else he could've gone.'

'Unless . . .' Burke turned and pointed to the elevator just to the right of the entrance. Set back in the shadows, it had totally escaped their notice. 'It must go up to the bell tower or something.'

'To *what*?'

'Beats me. Quasimodo, maybe?' He reached out and pushed the button.

'Burke! *What are you doing?*'

'We can't stop now, can we?'

The elevator door slid open suddenly, spilling profane fluoresent light into that inky corner of the cathedral. Burke gripped Mary Ann's arm and pulled her into the elevator. The door closed immediately.

'Burke, we could get in trouble.'

He didn't answer. He was examining the control buttons. 'There's 2 and 3 and LL,' he said. 'LL must be Lower Level. Let's try 2 for starters. It's more celestial to go up, don't you think?' He pushed the 2 button. Nothing happened.

'C'mon, Burke. Open the door.'

'Wait a minute.' He tried the 3 button. The elevator didn't budge.

'Burke!'

'One more.' This time the LL button got them moving. Down. The ride took less than ten seconds. The door opened onto a lighted hallway. Burke stepped out, taking Mary Ann with him. The elevator abandoned them.

'It's just the gift shop,' whispered Mary Ann. A series of windows along the hallway offered a glimpse of the religious emporium. Mostly St Francis statuary and felt wall hangings with hippie peace-and-love mottoes.

The shop was in semi-darkness, but Burke tried the door. It was locked. So were the other two doors in the hallway. The elevator was the only way out. Burke grinned sheepishly at Mary Ann, then pushed the Up button. Nothing happened.

'Aha!' said Burke. 'Mr Tyrone Transplant must be on the way down.'

Mary Ann's blood froze. 'Down *here*?'

Burke smiled. 'Down from 2 or 3. Obviously, he went up instead of down. He's probably getting off on the ground floor right now. That is, unless someone else is using it.'

'But how could he have gone up, when we could only go down?'

The answer came to her in a single dizzying flash, just as the door of the elevator opened.

They boarded the elevator in silence and rode to the main floor. When the door opened, Mary Ann moved to the control panel and pushed the Close Door button. Burke stared at her in bewilderment.

'Push the 2 button again,' she said.

He did. Nothing happened.

Her hands moved to the nape of her neck and unfastened the latch on the gold chain he had given her in Mexico. She handed him the key, then pointed to a slot on the control panel.

'See if it fits,' she said.

The way out

'Edgar and Anna, huh?'

D'orothea's smile seemed almost maternal as she sat by DeDe's bed and held the new mother's hand.

DeDe beamed. 'You saw them, huh?'

'You betcha. They're magnificent, hon. And one of each. How perfect can you get?'

'Would you tell my mother that?'

D'orothea frowned. 'She couldn't handle it, huh?'

'You might say that. She told me I should have had an abortion.'

'I thought she was Catholic.'

'She is,' muttered DeDe. 'She's also from Hillsborough and a member of the Francisca Club. Those things have a dogma all their own. One of their most well-known tenets is that you don't have a baby with slant eyes.'

D'orothea squeezed her hand. 'Don't even think about it, hon.'

'I have to. I have to live with it.'

'Do you?' D'orothea's eyes challenged her.

'I can't run away, D'or.'

'Maybe not. But you could run *toward* something.'

'Like what?'

D'orothea shrugged. 'A new life. A life where you don't have to deal with the kind of people you're dealing with.'

'I think it's a little late for me.'

D'orothea shook her head. 'Wrong, hon. It wasn't too late for me.'

'I don't get it.'

D'orothea smiled understandingly. 'We're not that far apart, you know. I may be from the wrong part of Oakland, but I got very grand *very* early. I was worshiping false idols before I was out of a training bra. Hell, I was *worse* than you, hon. With me, it was a conscious choice. With you, it's just a question of family tradition.'

'Never underestimate the power of family tradition,' said DeDe ruefully.

'*Or* the power of the Almighty Dollar. Listen, I wanted money so bad I dyed my skin black to get it.'

'*What?*'

'It's a long and sordid story. I'll tell it to you someday when you . . . DeDe, look: do you remember that night we went to the fashion show at the Legion of Honor, when you said it was tough living at the end of the rainbow?'

'Sure.'

'Well, maybe your premise was wrong.'

'How's that?'

'Maybe this isn't it, hon. Maybe San Francisco isn't the end of the rainbow.'

DeDe absorbed this radical suggestion slowly. 'D'or, do you mean *leave*?'

'Why not?'

'I *can't*, D'or. My family is here. My mother, at least. And all my friends are here.'

269

'What good have they done you so far?'

DeDe studied her friend's face for a moment. 'Why do I get the feeling you're trying to convert a sinner.'

D'orothea laughed. 'I *have* been going to church a lot lately. And that's part of it, I guess. We don't get that much time on this planet, DeDe, and unless a few of us make an effort to change ourselves and the corruption around us . . . well, it just won't happen, that's all.'

'I see that, D'or. I *agree* with it, but I don't see how running away can—'

'Not *away*, hon. To. *To* something.'

'What are you driving at?'

D'orothea smiled. 'I guess I should come right out and say it, huh?'

It took her fifteen minutes to outline her proposal. When she had finished, DeDe stared at her with a mixture of doubt and fascination.

'You mean I could take the babies?' she asked.

'Of course! That's the really wonderful part of it. A brand-new life for them, free from the bigotry and small-mindedness of your mother's friends! A brand-new life for all of us, DeDe!'

DeDe flushed excitedly. 'In a crazy way, it makes a lot of sense.'

'Damn straight!'

'Mother will have a fit.'

'No she won't. Well, maybe at first. But in the long run, this saves her from all that embarrassment. You can get the hell out of town before the Hillsborough crowd has a chance to prey on your children. Your mother will be *grateful* for that, DeDe.'

'I have to think about it,' said DeDe.

'I know. Of course. There's time.'

'It *is* exciting!'

'You betcha!' said D'orothea.

The cooler

Burke's hands were trembling when he slipped the key into the slot on the control panel of the elevator. Mary Ann hovered over him. 'Burke, jiggle it or something.'

'I did. That's it.' The key was only halfway in.

'Try it the other way, then.'

Burke removed the key and inserted it again. This time, it slid in effortlessly. Mary Ann let out a little yelp. Burke turned and beamed at her admiringly. 'We can turn it to 2 or 3 now. What'll it be?'

Without knowing why, Mary Ann chose 3.

Burke pushed the 3 button and the elevator began its slow ascent.

Mary Ann's exhilaration gave way to gnawing fear again. 'What if he's up here, Burke? The transplant man.'

'We'll play dumb,' shrugged Burke.

'Yeah. And we don't know for sure that he even *took* the elevator.'

'He took it.' His grim certainty terrified Mary Ann.

'But why would someone who just sings in the choir have a key to this elevator?'

'Obviously', said Burke flatly, 'the same reason I had one.'

The elevator shook them when it stopped. The door opened. They stepped out into a space about the size of Mary Ann's living room. There were no windows. A flickering fluorescent tube mounted on the wall next to the elevator cast a greenish light on the stacks of hymnals and prayerbooks lining the room.

The only way out was a cast-iron spiral staircase.

Going up.

Mary Ann shuddered and stepped back into the elevator. 'Burke . . . let's try 2.'

Burke shook his head. 'This is it.'

'This is *what*?'

'I don't know. It just feels right somehow.'

'This room?'

'No.' He nodded toward the spiral staircase. 'Up there.'

'Oh, God, Burke! Are you sure we ought to?'

His jaw was set, but his voice sounded thin and unsure. 'I have to.'

'Maybe we could come back later or something.'

'No. I might lose my nerve.'

'But what if the transplant man is up there?'

Burke looked away from her. 'He had time to come back down.'

'But what if . . . ?'

'I'm going up, Mary Ann. You can do what you want. You've helped me enough already.'

She took his hand, silencing him. 'I'll come,' she said softly.

Burke went first. Mary Ann followed so closely that the back of his corduroy jacket kept grazing her face. They passed through the ceiling into a darker place. A much darker place. Mary Ann tugged on Burke's coattail.

'We can't even *see*, Burke.'

'It's OK,' he whispered. 'Our eyes'll get used to it.'

The staircase continued to wind upwards. Some fifteen feet above the room with the prayerbooks they arrived at a kind of landing.

'We can't go any higher,' said Burke.

'Burke, for God's sake, let's—'

'Wait.' She heard him fumbling with something. 'I think there's a door here.'

Suddenly, there was a door. It swung outward, blinding them momentarily with light. Both of them shrank from the sight that confronted them: A metal

272

catwalk, stretching towards the altar. *At least a hundred feet above the floor of the cathedral.*

'I *can't*,' said Mary Ann, without being asked.

'If I can, you can. Look, there's a railing. There's no way you can fall.'

'It isn't a matter of—' The word 'railing' was what silenced her. 'Burke! *"A walkway with a railing!"* This is the place in your dream!'

'I repeat,' he said somberly. 'If I can, you can.'

He took her hand and led her onto the catwalk. Mary Ann checked her watch. The mass would begin in twelve minutes. Eight stories beneath them, the congregation materialized in splotches of red and blue and yellow, reduced at this height to their primary colors. A human rose window.

They walked at least fifty yards, until they were directly above the transept of the cathedral. There, conforming to the cross-shaped structure of the building itself, another catwalk intersected the one they were on.

And there sat a Styrofoam cooler.

Mary Ann looked behind her, then left and right on the other catwalk. The man with the transplant was nowhere in sight. Burke stood stone still, eyes locked on the cooler. The sickly, grayish caste to his face compelled Mary Ann to be strong.

'Burke, is this the Meeting of the Lines?'

He nodded.

She reached for the cooler. 'Do you want me to open it?'

'Please,' he said feebly.

She lifted the lid. A thick cloud of white smoke billowed over the edges of the cooler. No. Not smoke; dry ice. She knelt by the cooler and blew on the surface of the cloud. It parted.

What she saw was pale purple, mauve almost. A thin ridge of hair ran along the top of it. It was black on one

273

end, where it had been severed, and the toenails were a horrid shade of yellow.

But it was undeniably a human foot.

Dropping the lid, Mary Ann lurched to her feet and fell into Burke's arms. She tried to scream, but gagged instead, pulling away from him just in time to lean over the railing.

The people below hardly knew what hit them.

The cult

When Mary Ann straightened up again, Burke's distorted features filled her with fresh terror.

'Burke . . . God, did you see it?'

He nodded mechanically, his eyes fixed on the lid of the cooler.

'It was a foot, Burke. *It was somebody's foot.*'

He blinked dumbly, never shifting his gaze.

'We have to get out of here, Burke!'

He gripped her wrist. 'No . . . wait . . .'

'Burke, for God's sake! We have to tell someone. We can't just—'

'It wasn't a foot.'

'What?'

'It wasn't a foot.' His eyes widened as he spoke the words, as if some rare spiritual revelation were sweeping over him. 'It was . . . something else.'

Mary Ann's voice grew shrill. 'I *saw* it, Burke. There's nothing else it *could* be.' She tried to break free from his hold, but his hand was like a vise. 'Burke, what are you doing? *Let go of me, Burke!*'

His hand went slack. Huge beads of sweat erupted like blisters along his hairline. He turned and looked at her. 'It wasn't a foot,' he said pathetically. 'It was an arm.'

'Burke, for God's . . . !'

'It *was*, Mary Ann. When I was here before . . . it was an arm.'

'You were . . . ? Burke, you *remember*?'

'They wanted me to . . . They told me I had to . . .'

'*Who*, Burke?'

'Them. *Him*.'

'The man with the transplant?'

Burke nodded.

'What did he want you to do?'

Silence.

'Burke?'

'We have to get out of here.'

'Wait, Burke. *What did they want you to do?*'

Now Burke was moving down the catwalk, away from the cooler, back to the spiral staircase. Reaching out to take Mary Ann's hand, he quickened his pace until they were almost running.

'Burke, what if the man with the transplant . . . ?'

'What time is it?' He pulled her wrist into view and looked at her watch. 'Christ! We have three minutes!'

'*For what?*'

'They'll be here in three minutes! The mass starts in three minutes!'

They were back at the door now, plunging once more into darkness. Burke led the way down the staircase, holding tight to Mary Ann's hand. When they reached the room with the prayerbooks, he lunged at the button by the elevator, then leaped back as if it had shocked him.

'Shit!'

'What's the matter?' whispered Mary Ann.

'Listen . . . the elevator! They're coming!'

'Dear God.'

Burke looked about him frantically, pulled Mary Ann into the darkest corner of the room, behind the towering pillar of prayerbooks. They were crouching in the shadows when the elevator door clattered open.

There seemed to be five or six of them, at least two of whom were women. Their voices were jovial and matter-of-fact until the man with the transplant began the incantation that Mary Ann now knew by heart.

High upon the Sacred Rock
The Rose Incarnate shines,
Upon the Mountain of the Flood
At the Meeting of the Lines.

The coppery taste of her own vomit made Mary Ann nauseous again. She tried to think of daisy-strewn fields, of raindrops on roses and whiskers on kittens, but the image of that grisly purple foot flashed in her brain like a strobe light.

Instinctively, Burke reached for her hand and gave it a reassuring squeeze. In doing so, he grazed the pillar of prayerbooks, causing it to wobble menacingly. Mary Ann sucked in her breath and did her best to steady the trembling monolith.

They waited for an eternity.

Finally, the faceless celebrants began to ascend the staircase to the catwalk. When their footsteps had died out, Burke dashed to the elevator and leaned on the button.

The door opened immediately.

'Where's the key?' asked Burke.

Mary Ann clutched at her neck. 'I must've left it—'

'Christ!'

'Check the floor, Burke! Maybe it—'

'Hold it! We might not need it!' He pushed the button for the first floor. The elevator made an eerie sighing noise and the door rumbled shut again. They began their descent.

When they were back on the main floor of the cathedral, a growl from the great organ signaled the start of the mass. Never stopping to look back, they fled through the mammoth doors and ran all the way to Huntington Park.

*   *   *

Now they were huddled together on a bench, catching their breath.

'It's come back, hasn't it?'

'Yeah.'

'All of it?'

'Most of it.'

'Why are you crying?'

'I'm . . . relieved, that's all.'

'Did you know those people?'

'Yeah.'

'Should we talk about it now?'

'I guess. That is, if you don't mind.'

'I don't mind.'

'That foot, Mary Ann . . . Those people.'

'Uh huh?'

'They're eating it. They're up there now eating it.'

Walking alone

One week later.

Leaning on Jon, Michael took faltering steps to the bathroom.

'Look at you!' Jon beamed. 'You're fabulous!'

'I am, aren't I?'

'I think you can do it on your own.'

'Oh, no.'

'C'mon, turkey. Try.'

'Don't be so goddamn B-movie! I'm not ready yet!'

'I'm gonna let go.'

'You do and I'll tell your father you sleep with boys!'

'Get ready!'

'Jon!'

'You've been copping feels long enough. You're on you own now.'

The doctor slipped out from under Michael's arm and withdrew several feet. Michael's arm flailed as he fought to maintain his balance. His knees were jelly, but he managed to remain in a static, upright position.

'Now, walk,' said Jon calmly.

'This is really corny. I hope you know that.'

'Go ahead.'

'You could have picked a better room for this touching human drama. I'll fall and hit the toilet. I'll die with a Johnny Mop in my hand.'

'Shut up and walk.'

Michael sighed and lifted his left foot, placing it about six inches in front of him. Then he dragged his right foot forward. 'Godzilla approaching Tokyo,' he groaned.

He repeated the process until he was in front of the toilet. Using a towel rack for support, he turned himself around. He made a face and let go.

He landed on target.

Jon was leaning cavalierly against the doorway, smiling at him. 'You see?'

'Can't a lady have a little privacy?' said Michael.

'Just a sec.' Jon dashed into the living room and came back with the *Chronicle*. He dropped it in Michael's lap. 'A little light reading for you.'

The front page was dominated by a picture of Burke and Mary Ann, looking flustered at a press conference.

The banner headline read:

EPISCOPAL CANNIBAL CULT EXPOSED.

Later, Jon and Michael discussed the week's events over coffee and raisin toast in the kitchen. Michael held up the newspaper.

'What's with this, anyway? I thought Burke was gonna break the story in *New West*.'

'He was, but the police jumped the gun on him. The chief apparently called a press conference yesterday and scarfed up on a little publicity of his own. Burke

278

was livid, because the chief had promised to keep quiet about it until the *New West* piece broke. Anyway, the end result was roughly the same. Pandemonium. Burke called his own press conference at *New West* late yesterday afternoon.'

Michael smiled. 'Mary Ann must be wrecked.'

'She's holding up OK, actually. She says she's coming by to see you this afternoon.'

'Good.'

'But *no* wisecracks, Michael. She's still a little shaken over the whole thing.'

'OK. I promise not to put my foot in my mouth.' Michael grinned. 'So to speak.'

'That's *exactly* the sort of thing I'm talking about.'

'OK. OK. Look, in one way, I'm just as involved as Mary Ann was.'

'How's that?'

'Well, what if I had died at St Sebastian's? Those cultists would have been munching on *me* up there on the catwalk.'

Jon shook his head and smiled. 'They didn't eat whole people, my love. Just parts. Amputated parts.'

'Well, they *could* have.'

'Nope. The parts were easier to hide. And to transport. They had no problem at all moving them from surgery to the refrigerated room in Tyrone's flower shop. And they could also fit nicely into the cooler for the trip to the cathedral.'

Michael made a face. 'How many times did they *do* that, anyway?'

'Who knows?' shrugged the doctor. 'Maybe as often as twice a week for four or five months. Burke apparently stumbled onto the cult in its early stages, when he was still singing in the choir.'

Michael rolled his eyes. 'That's when I would have moved back to Nantucket.'

'No way. Burke's a journalist, remember? He wanted the story badly. Bad enough to sweet-talk his way into the cult and sneak a peek at the goings-on up on the catwalk at Grace. He expected something freaky, of course, but not *that* freaky. He couldn't handle it.'

'Then he never went to the flower shop at St Sebastian's?'

'Apparently not. He says he knew nothing at all about the contacts at the hospital until Mary Ann pointed it out to him.'

Michael frowned. 'That doesn't make any sense.'

'Why?'

'Because of the rose phobia. What about the god-damn red rose?'

'Good question,' said the doctor.

A rose is a rose

Michael was using his walker when he greeted Mary Ann at the door. 'Hi,' he said breezily. 'Welcome to the Barbary Lane Home for the Disabled.'

She kissed him on the cheek. 'You look pretty fabulous to me.'

'Guess what I did this morning?'

'What?'

'I *walked*, Babycakes. Without *this* damn thing.'

'Mouse!'

'Ain't that the cat's ass?'

'Do it now, Mouse. Do it for me.'

He grinned at her. 'Sorry, I never perform without my organ grinder. What about *you*, anyway? How does it feel to be a Media Star?'

She moaned and sat down on the sofa. 'I'm exhausted. I've talked to all three networks, *People* magazine, *Time*, *Newsweek*, the *New York Times*, the *National Enquirer* and my parents. My parents were the toughest of all.'

'Of course.'

'They are totally *hysterical*, Mouse. You'd think the town was *teeming* with Episcopal cannibals. I tried to explain that the press was blowing it all out of proportion, but they won't even listen to me. They want me on the next flight back to Cleveland.'

'Are you going?'

She shook her head, smiling. 'Sit down, Mouse. I need a hug.'

He abandoned the walker and dropped to the sofa. They held on to each other for a long time.

'How's my girl?' asked Michael.

'All right.'

'It'll get better. I promise.'

'I shouldn't gripe, I guess. I've got it easy compared to Burke. He's been with the police all morning, trying to remember stuff.'

'Naming names?'

Mary Ann nodded. 'He's come up with fourteen so far, including three members of the cathedral choir, two surgeons at St Sebastian's, and even a couple of businessmen.'

'His memory must be completely back, then?'

'Just about. He regained most of it the night we found the . . . that night. Though he still can't remember how he ended up in Golden Gate Park. My guess is they drugged him after they realized he had amnesia.'

'It seems funny that they wouldn't have been a little more thorough about getting rid of him.'

'Not really. For one thing, they weren't really committing a crime. That part's driving the police crazy right now. The doctors can be nailed on some sort of ethical-practices violation, of course, but the law isn't very clear about the rest of it. Those body parts were just medical garbage, really. There's no law against eating garbage.'

Michael frowned. 'Is that *actually* what they were doing?'

She nodded. 'Apparently, they sort of . . . tasted it. It was supposed to be symbolic or something. One step beyond transubstantiation. Burke says they did it at the very moment the people below were eating the bread and wine. The transplant man's job was to see that the stuff was delivered to the catwalk at each of the designated masses.'

'What's gonna happen to that guy, anyway?'

'Who knows? Burke says he'll probably make a fortune. He's already hired a literary agent.'

'You're kidding!'

'Nope. It's disgusting, isn't it?' She shivered a little, turning away. 'I just want it to be over with as soon as possible.'

Michael looked at her a moment, hesitating. 'Do you mind if I ask you one more thing?'

'Sure. Go ahead.'

'What was all this red rose business? Was that just the rose window – the Rose Incarnate they chanted about?'

Mary Ann smiled faintly. 'That's what I thought at first. Or that it had something to do with the flower shop at St Sebastian's. It turned out to be neither. It was a tattoo.'

'A *tattoo*?'

She nodded. 'The night Burke lost his memory was the first night the cult trusted him enough to let him join them on the catwalk. The thing he hadn't counted on was that they expected him to participate in the ceremony. He knew they were High Church, of course—'

Michael chuckled, interrupting her. 'You can't get much higher than that,' he said.

She managed a laugh. 'Anyway, he didn't *really* know what was going to happen until they started chanting and Tyrone opened the Styrofoam cooler and pulled out an arm.'

'Arrggh!'

'I know,' winced Mary Ann. 'Who *wouldn't* try to block that one out?'

'My God! Then the red rose was . . .'

Mary Ann nodded. 'Tattooed on the arm.'

'Did Burke . . . I mean, did he . . . ?'

Mary Ann shrugged. 'I guess he must've *tried*, poor baby.'

The anagram

'Well?' said Mrs Madrigal, smiling.

'Well what?' asked Mona.

'How did your date go?'

'None of your business. That wasn't part of the deal.'

The landlady arched an eyebrow mischievously and looked down at the tray of dope she was cleaning. 'It was that good, was it?'

Mona flushed. 'You're avoiding the subject.'

'Which is?'

'The anagram. *The anagram.*'

'Ah.'

Mrs Madrigal looked up. 'Goodness gracious! Does love make you testy?'

'You're not gonna tell me, are you?'

'I didn't say that.'

'Do I have to *guess*, then?'

Mrs Madrigal craned her neck to examine the piece of paper in her daughter's hands. 'We have a list, do we? What fun! I feel like Rumpelstiltskin.'

Mona groaned and slumped down onto the sofa next to her. 'You are *truly* perverse!'

Mrs Madrigal directed her attention to the dope tray again. 'What's your first guess?'

Sighing noisily, Mona read from the paper: 'DARLING AMANA.'

'DARLING AMANA? What does *that* mean?'

Mona frowned peevishly, 'It means you're a cute refrigerator.'

'Indeed. Next.'

'A GRANDMA IN LA.'

'A GRANDMA IN LA,' repeated the landlady. 'My, my. Now *that's* a dark secret!' She looked up briefly at Mona, who was scowling exactly like a certain madam from Winnemucca. 'Go on, dear. This is wonderful!'

'A GRAND ANIMAL.'

Mrs Madrigal roared, nearly spilling the dope. 'I *adore* that one! A GRAND ANIMAL! I am indeed!'

'That's it?'

'Nope.'

Mona rolled her eyes. 'I hate this game.'

'Go on. What's next?'

'That's it, goddammit.'

'What about LAD IN ANAGRAM?'

Mona dropped the paper and stared at her father. 'LAD IN ANAGRAM? You're kidding!'

Mrs Madrigal smiled faintly. 'Yes. But I rather like it just the same.'

'You're sick,' said Mona.

'Give me that pencil,' said the landlady.

Mona obeyed her. The landlady scrawled five words at the bottom of her daughter's list: A MAN AND A GIRL.

Mona blinked at it in disbelief. 'This . . . this is it?'

Mrs Madrigal nodded.

'God . . . it's so . . . sexist.'

'I beg your pardon, young lady.'

'Girl?' gasped Mona. 'You're a woman!'

Mrs Madrigal shook her head. '*You're* a woman, dear. I'm a *girl*. And proud of it.'

Mona smiled. 'My own goddamn father . . . a sexist!'

'My darling daughter,' said Mrs Madrigal, 'transsexuals can *never* be sexists!'

'Then . . . you're a transsexist!'

The landlady leaned over and kissed Mona on the cheek. 'Forgive me, won't you? I'm terribly old-fashioned.'

Happy ending

Mother's Day, 1977.

The mistress of Halcyon Hill sat in her late husband's study, listening to a Bobby Short album and sipping a Mai Tai. Her maid, Emma, entered the room, carrying a stack of mail.

'There's a card from Miss DeDe, Miss Frances.'

The matriarch set down her drink. 'Thank heavens!'

'I knew she'd write her mama,' said Emma. 'She's a good child.' She handed the mail to Frannie and remained standing by the side of the wingback chair. Emma's lonely too, thought Frannie. She wants to talk about DeDe.

Making a face, Frannie set aside the latest issue of *New West.* The cover story was 'Inside the Cannibal Cult' by Burke Andrew. 'I won't even *look* at that,' said the matriarch. 'I simply can't believe what's happening to this city.'

Emma grunted her agreement. 'Some folks get mighty serious about religion.' The remark, Frannie knew, was more an indictment of Episcopalians than anything else. She declined to defend the church, however. She had too many crosses to bear already.

'Where's the card, Emma?'

'There, next to the phone bill, Miss Frances.'

To Frannie's disappointment, it wasn't a picture postcard; it was one of DeDe's own Florentine gilt-and-green things, and the message was thoughtlessly terse:

Mother,
Happily settled in now. Babies are
just fine, and I feel all tan and
healthy. I've met so many nice
people here. This is my first
job ever, and I love it.
Miss you much, but think this is
for the best. D'or sends hugs.

All my love,
DeDe

Frannie sighed noisily and laid the card down. Emma reached out and touched her shoulder consolingly. 'Don't you fret, Miss Frances. She'll grow out o'that. She's a smart child. She'll come to her senses.'

The matriarch shook her head, then dabbed her eyes with a cocktail napkin. 'It's too much, Emma.'

'What do you mean?'

'It's *Mother's Day*, Emma. Edgar usually brought me some Godiva chocolates or something, sometimes I just forget that he's gone and it's like losing him all over again. And now Beauchamp's gone . . . and DeDe . . . and my only grandchildren.'

Emma squeezed her mistress' shoulder. 'You gotta be strong, Miss Frances.'

Frannie was silent for a moment, then smiled wanly at her maid.

'You're so *wise*, Emma.'

'Just don't you fret.'

Frannie nodded decisively and picked up the postcard again. Squinting slightly, she examined the stamp and postmark. 'I don't even know where Guyana *is*,' she said.

Back in the courtyard of 28 Barbary Lane, Michael Tolliver was testing his legs like a newborn colt. Mary Ann emerged from the house. 'I just talked to Mildred,' she yelled.

'Yeah?'

'It's OK, Mouse. They can start you as mailboy in two weeks, if you're up to it.'

He let out a cheer. 'A working girl at last!'

'You'll like the new boss, I think. He used to be the creative director.'

'Uh oh,' mugged Michael

Mary Ann nodded. 'Gay as a goose.'

'Oh, happy ending! Happy ending!'

'In part, at least.'

'*In part?* The world has never been so good! Mona and Brian have been shacked up for almost a week. Mrs Madrigal is grinning like the Cheshire Cat. You may get rich selling your confessions . . . and Burke even *richer*. I'm a healthy, strapping boy again, and Jon and I can . . . well, never mind that part. *Plus* – oh, miracle of miracles! – my mother sent me a pound cake yesterday.'

Mary Ann smiled. 'I know. Jon gave me some. I'm glad she's coming around, Mouse.'

'We don't know that yet. There wasn't a message. Just the pound cake.'

'She's *trying*, Mouse.'

He smiled. 'A fruit cake would've made me a little nervous.'

Mary laughed half-heartedly.

'What is it?' asked Michael. 'Something's the matter.'

Silence.

'Oh, God! Not Mr Williams? His body hasn't shown up, has it?'

'No! For God's sake, Mouse, don't bring that up again! It's Burke, Mouse. He's moving to New York. He's been offered a job with *New York* magazine.'

'Oh, no!'

'I *should* be happy for him, Mouse. It's a fabulous opportunity. Most journalists would kill to have a chance to work there.'

'Has he asked you to go with him?'

She nodded. 'It was the *first* thing he asked.'

'And . . . ?'

'I *can't*, Mouse.' She looked despairingly around the courtyard. 'It's too pretty here.'

'Good girl.'

'No. Dumb girl. *Dumb* girl.'

He shook his head.

'What's the matter with me, Mouse?'

'*Nothing*, Babycakes. You're just tired of running away from home.' He took her arm and steered her slowly toward the house.

'Where are we going?' asked Mary Ann.

'Back to Tara,' he grinned. 'We'll figure out a way to get him back. After all, my dear, tomorrow *is* another day!'

THE END